THE PERINEUM TECHNIQUE

Ruppert & Mulot

FANTAGRAPHICS BOOKS

Florent Ruppert dedicates this book to Yasmine Dubois.

Thanks to Salvatore Lista for his generosity and wise advice.

Thanks to Isabelle Merlet for her magical powers as a colorist.

Thanks to Bastien Vivès for drawing the characters on JH's dream truck.

Thanks to Lisa Mandel, Astrid De La Chapelle, Leo Maret, Jeremy Piningre, Aude Picault, Jeremy Pradier, Anaïs Vaugelade, Gala Vanson, Charles Berberian, Romain Flizot, Julie and Emmanuel Bellegarde, Nine Antico, Alize De Pin, Dimitri Lecoussis, Vincent Pianina, Claire Braud, Sunita Prasad, Laetitia Bech, Raphaël Barban, Serge Stephan, Gabriela Jauregui, Julie Coutureau, Raphael Rabeau, Diane Chery, Haily, and Guillaume Laugé for their help, their advice, and their love.

Thanks to José-Louis Bocquet, Mathieu Poulhalec, and the whole team at Dupuis for their trust and kindness.

And thanks to sex therapist Brigitte Muller for confirming that the perineum technique is good for one's health unless told otherwise by a doctor.

FANTAGRAPHICS BOOKS INC.
7563 Lake City Way NE
Seattle, Washington, 98115
www.fantagraphics.com

Editor and Associate Publisher: Eric Reynolds
Translation: Jessie Aufiery
Coloring: Isabelle Merlet
Lettering: Cromatik Ltd
Book Design: Keeli McCarthy
Production: Paul Baresh
Publisher: Gary Groth

ISBN 978-1-68396-183-3
Library of Congress Control Number: 2018949689
First printing: March 2019
Printed in China

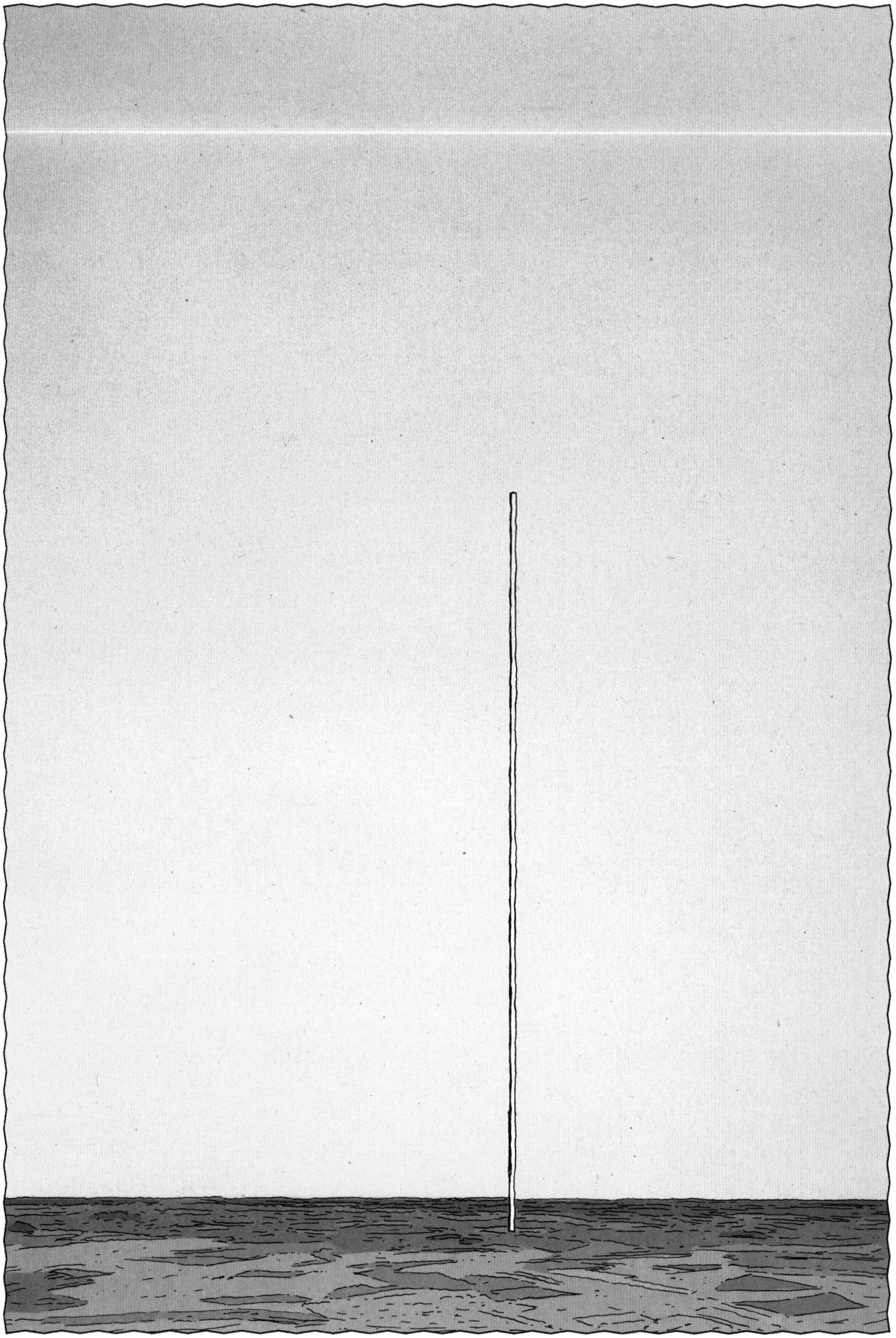

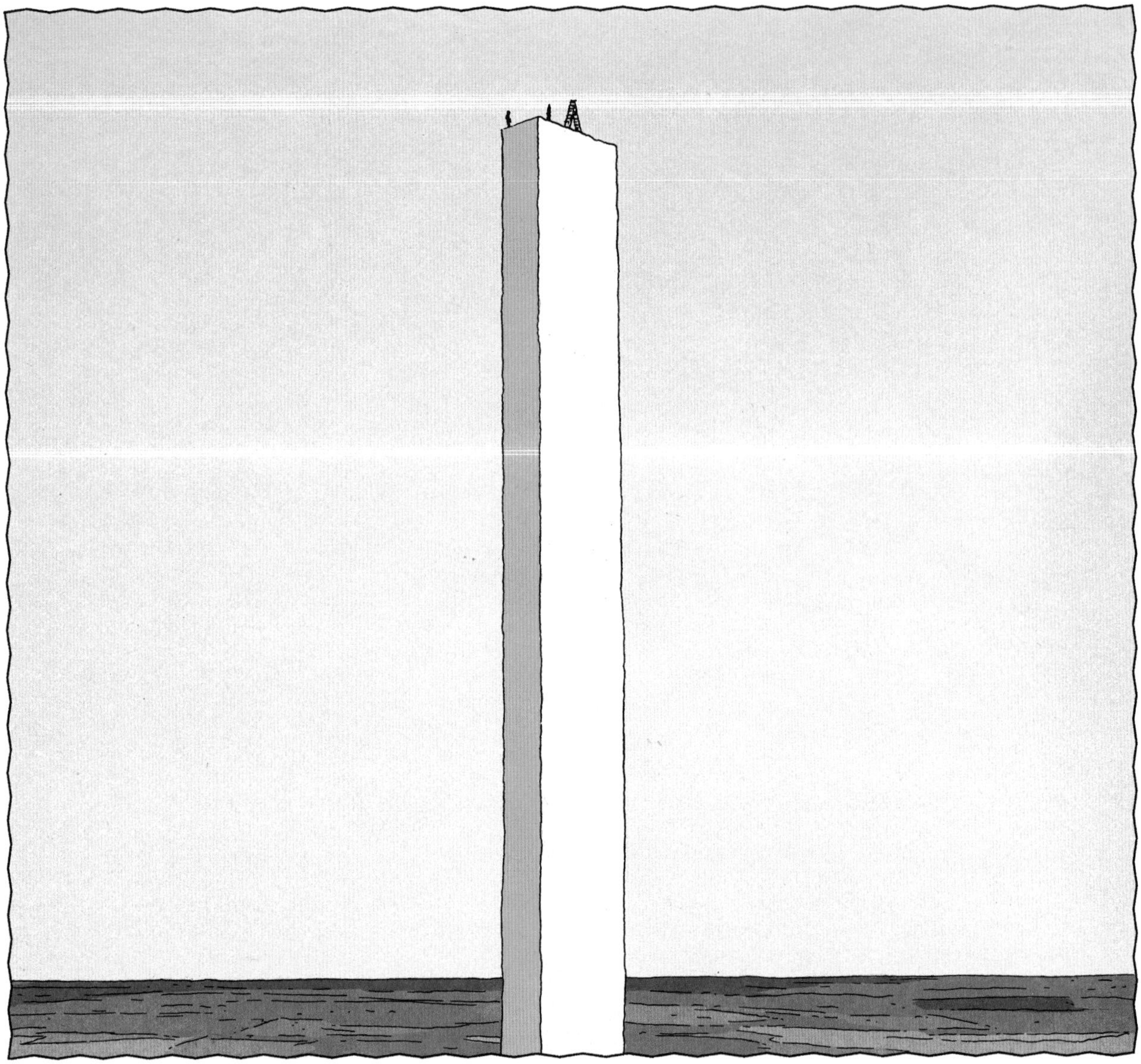
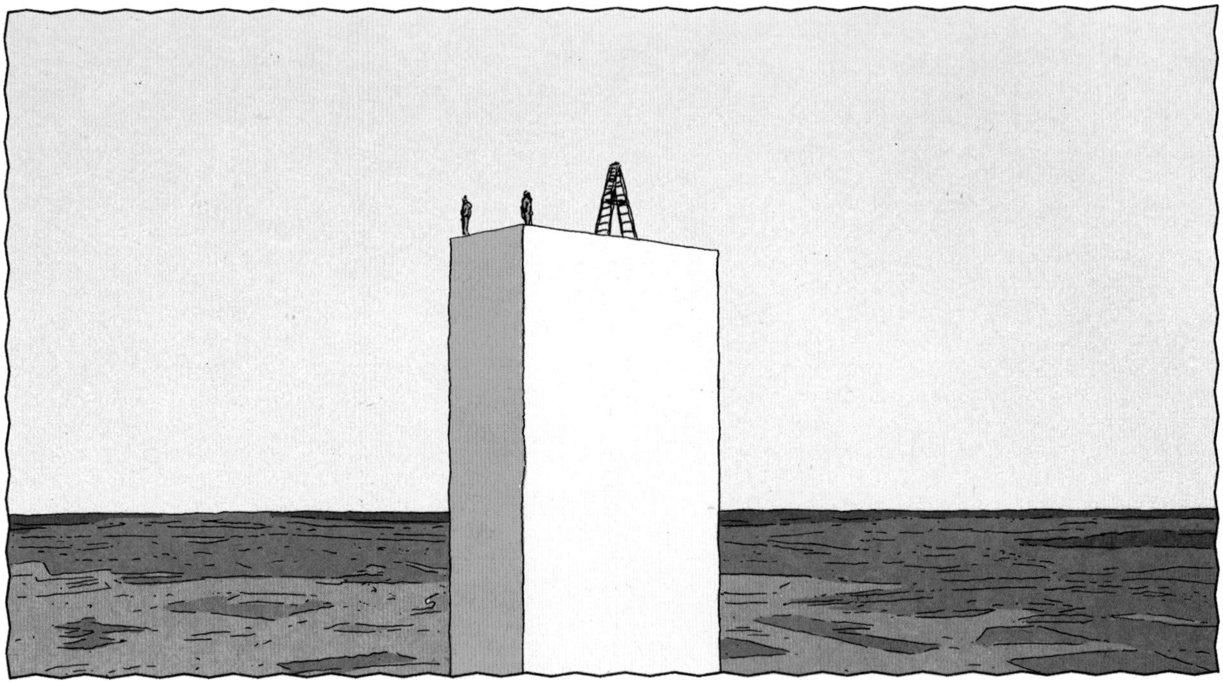

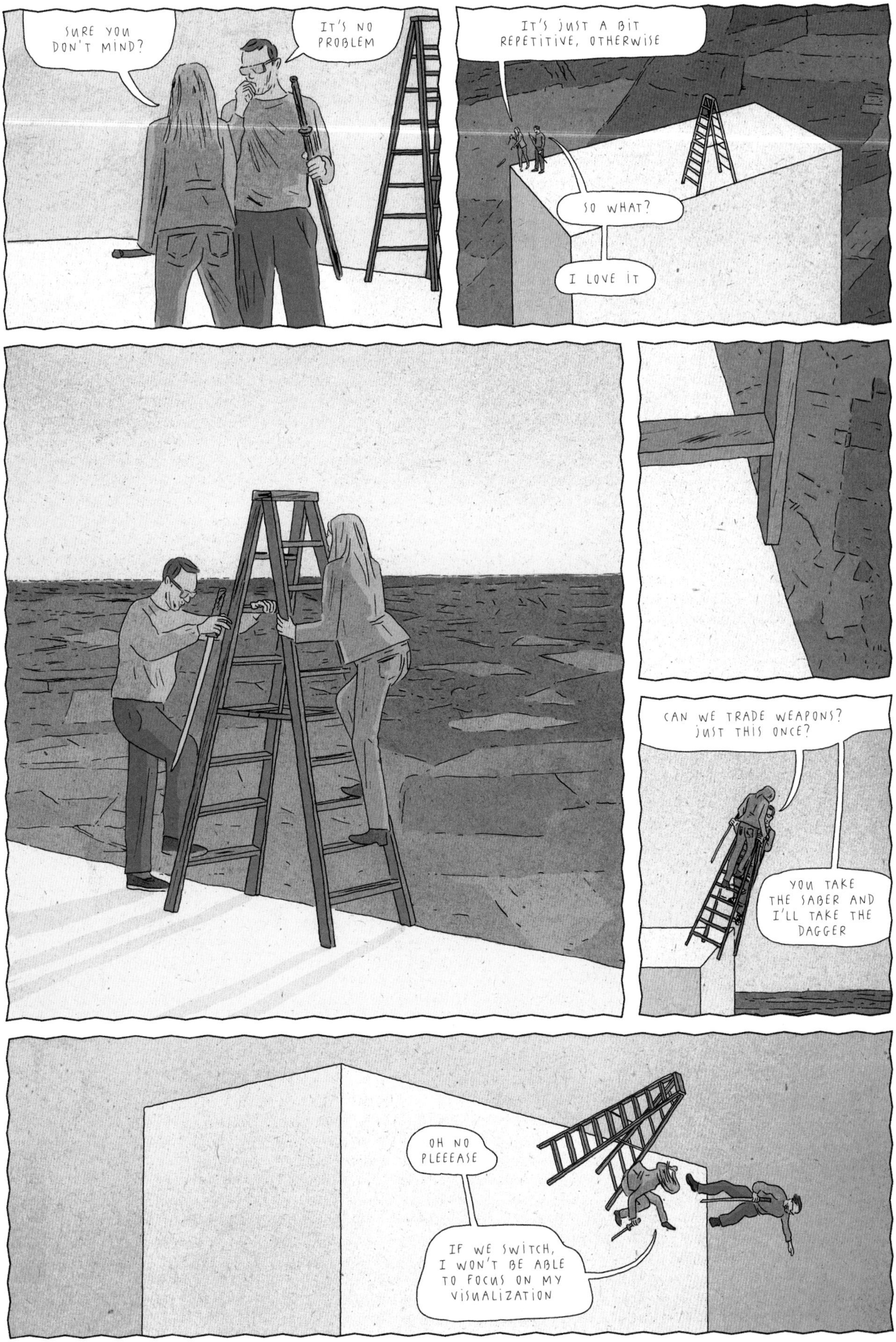
SURE YOU DON'T MIND?
IT'S NO PROBLEM
IT'S JUST A BIT REPETITIVE, OTHERWISE
SO WHAT?
I LOVE IT
CAN WE TRADE WEAPONS? JUST THIS ONCE?
YOU TAKE THE SABER AND I'LL TAKE THE DAGGER
OH NO PLEEEASE
IF WE SWITCH, I WON'T BE ABLE TO FOCUS ON MY VISUALIZATION

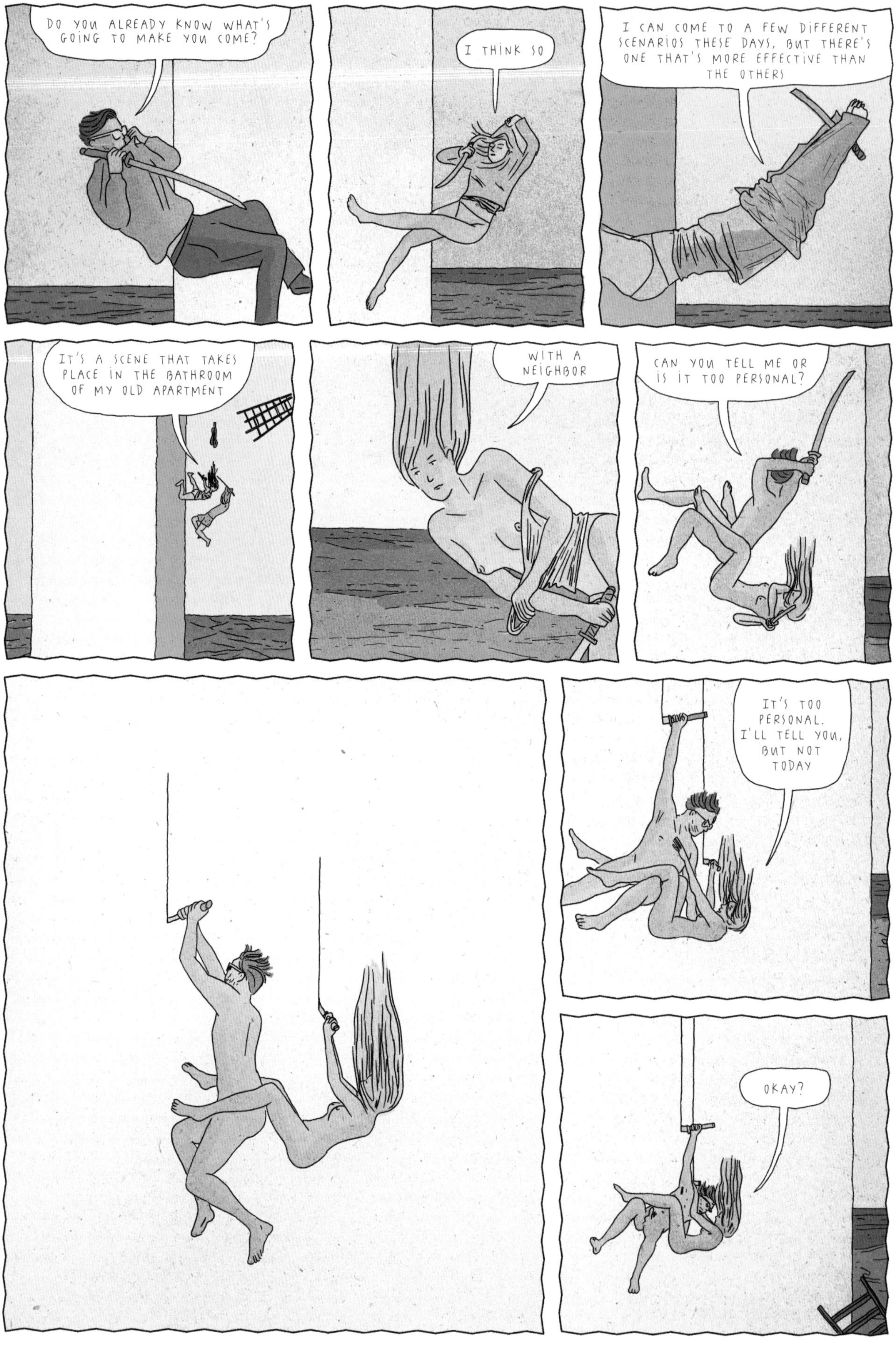
DO YOU ALREADY KNOW WHAT'S GOING TO MAKE YOU COME?
I THINK SO
I CAN COME TO A FEW DIFFERENT SCENARIOS THESE DAYS, BUT THERE'S ONE THAT'S MORE EFFECTIVE THAN THE OTHERS
IT'S A SCENE THAT TAKES PLACE IN THE BATHROOM OF MY OLD APARTMENT
WITH A NEIGHBOR
CAN YOU TELL ME OR IS IT TOO PERSONAL?
IT'S TOO PERSONAL. I'LL TELL YOU, BUT NOT TODAY
OKAY?

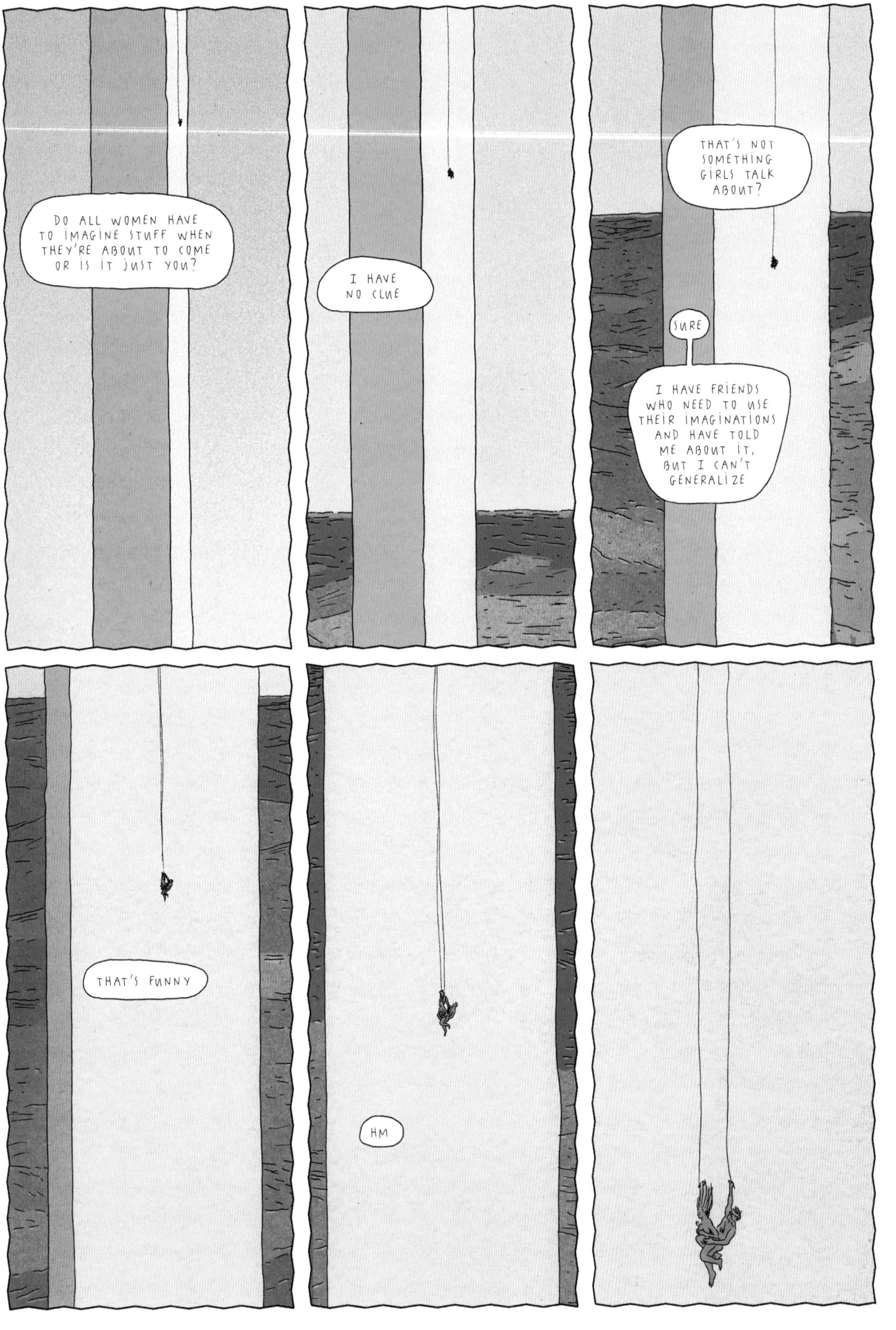
DO ALL WOMEN HAVE TO IMAGINE STUFF WHEN THEY'RE ABOUT TO COME OR IS IT JUST YOU?
I HAVE NO CLUE
THAT'S NOT SOMETHING GIRLS TALK ABOUT?
SURE
I HAVE FRIENDS WHO NEED TO USE THEIR IMAGINATIONS AND HAVE TOLD ME ABOUT IT, BUT I CAN'T GENERALIZE
THAT'S FUNNY
HM

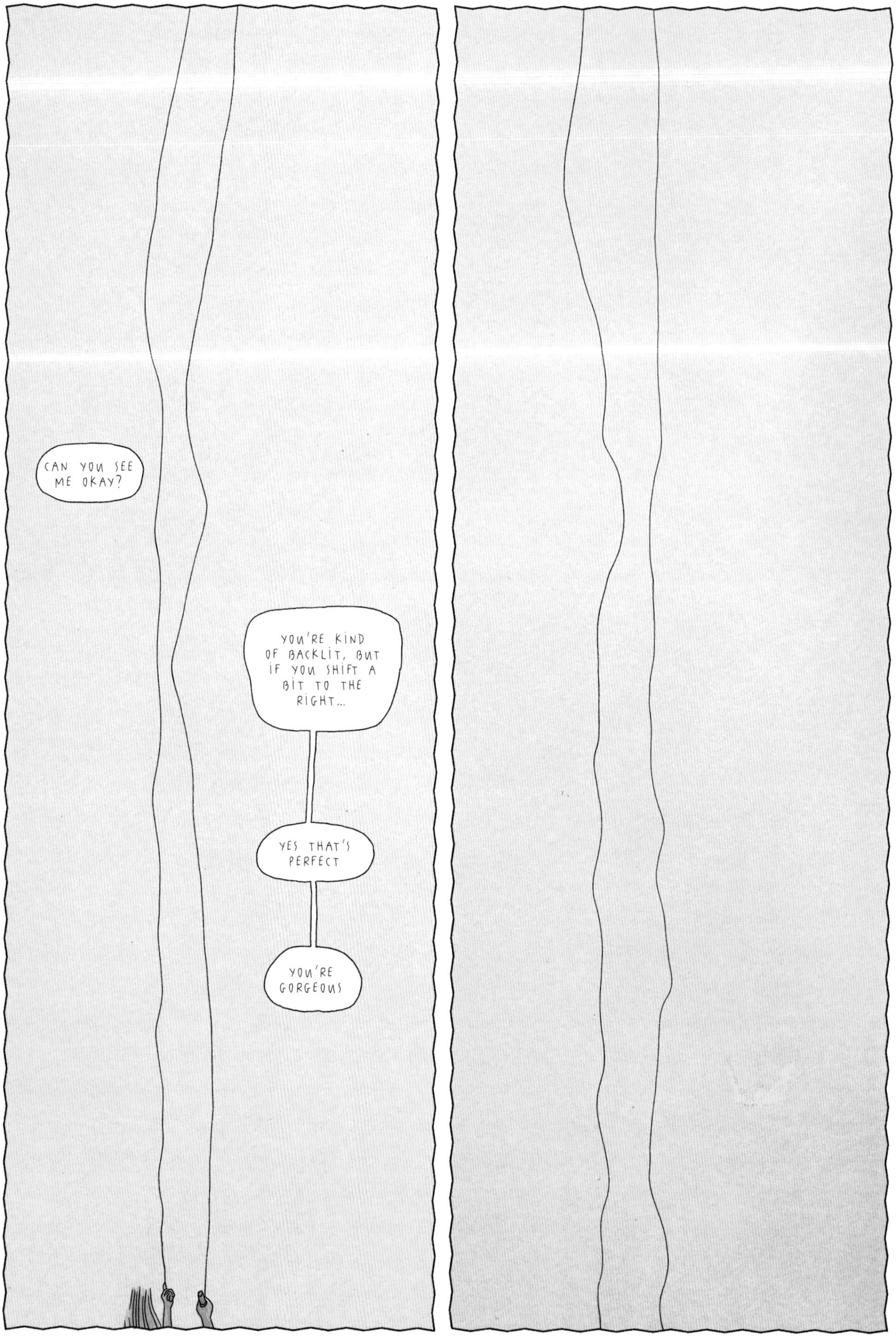
CAN YOU SEE ME OKAY?
YOU'RE KIND OF BACKLIT, BUT IF YOU SHIFT A BIT TO THE RIGHT...
YES THAT'S PERFECT
YOU'RE GORGEOUS

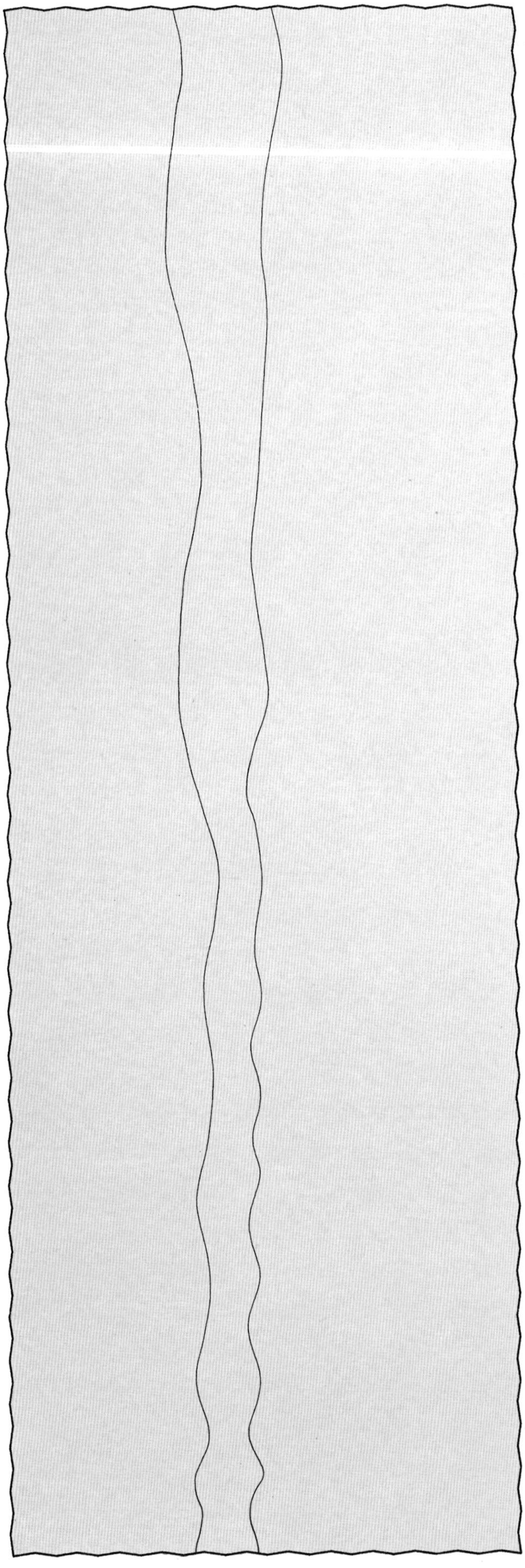

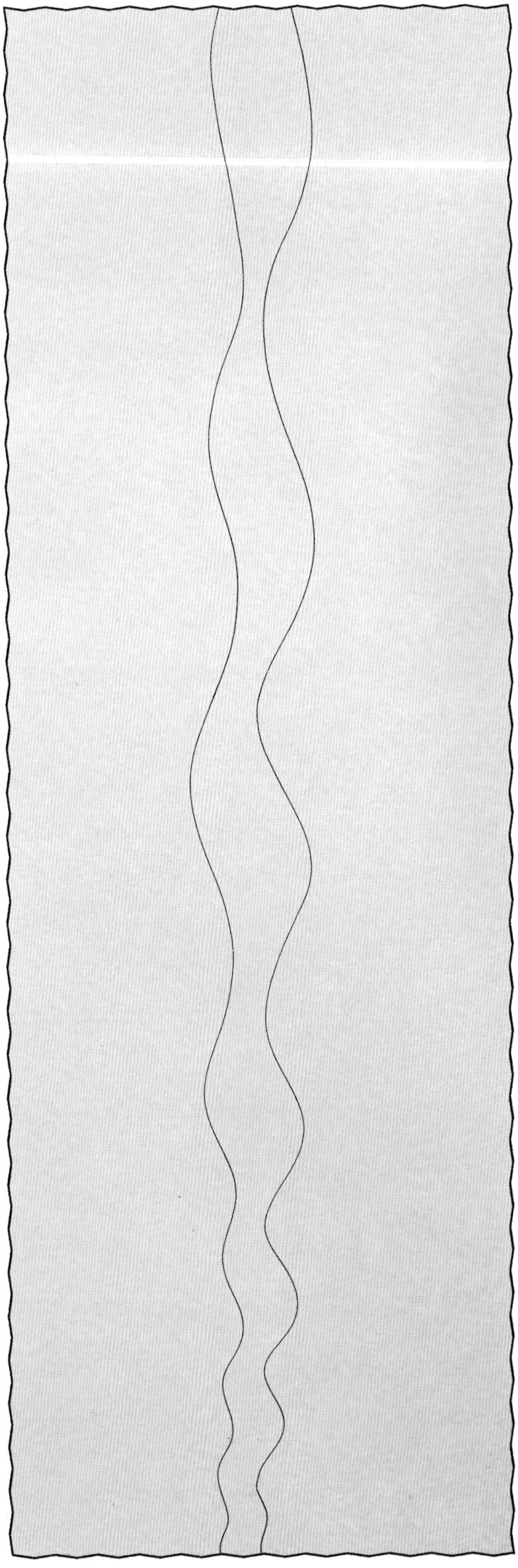

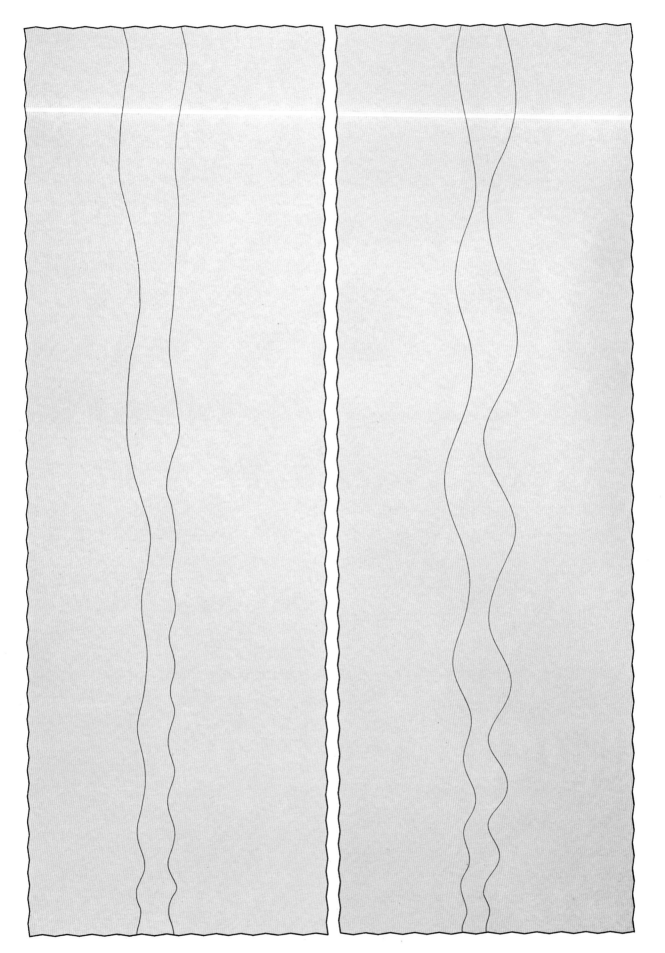

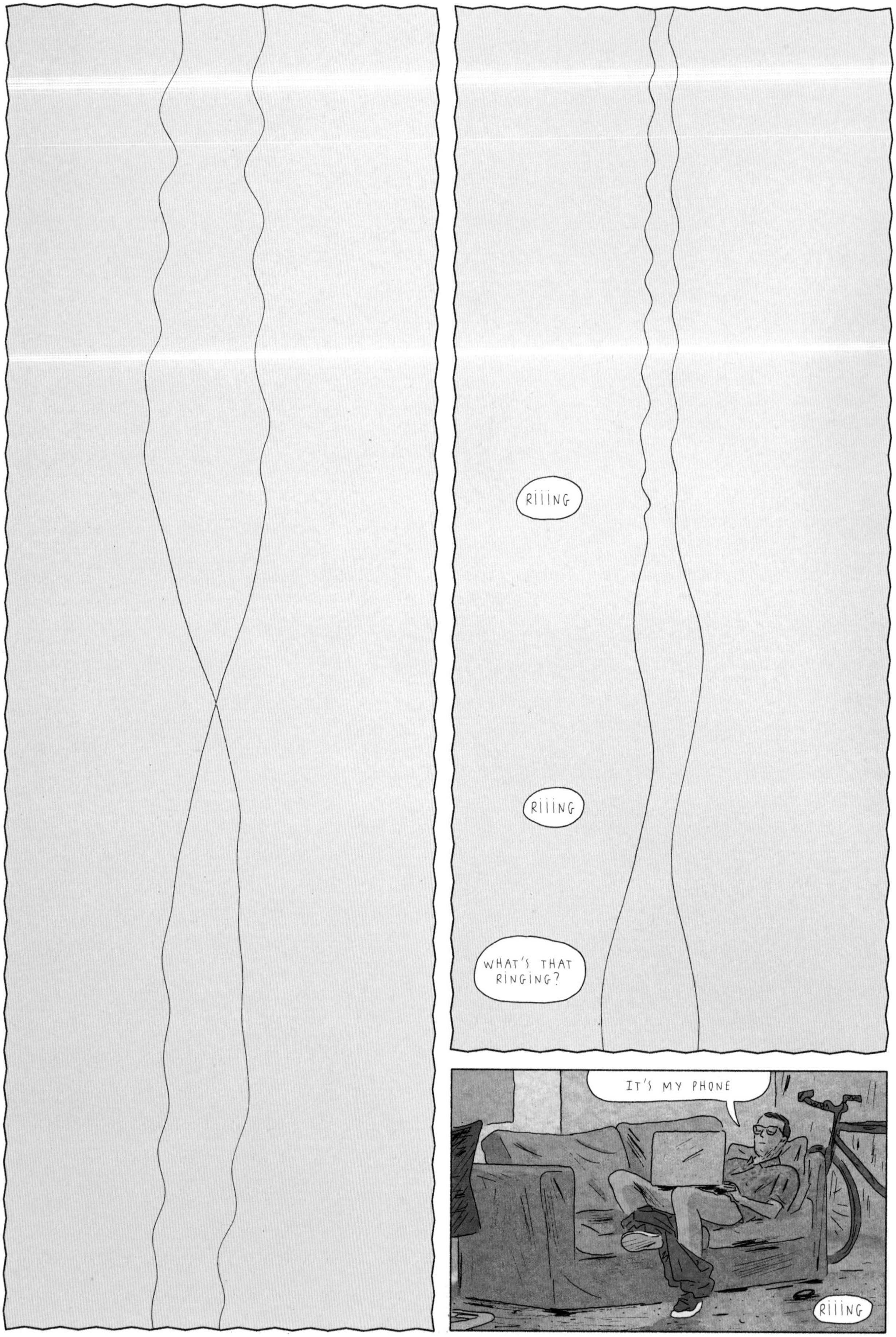
RIIING
RIIING
WHAT'S THAT RINGING?
IT'S MY PHONE
RIIING

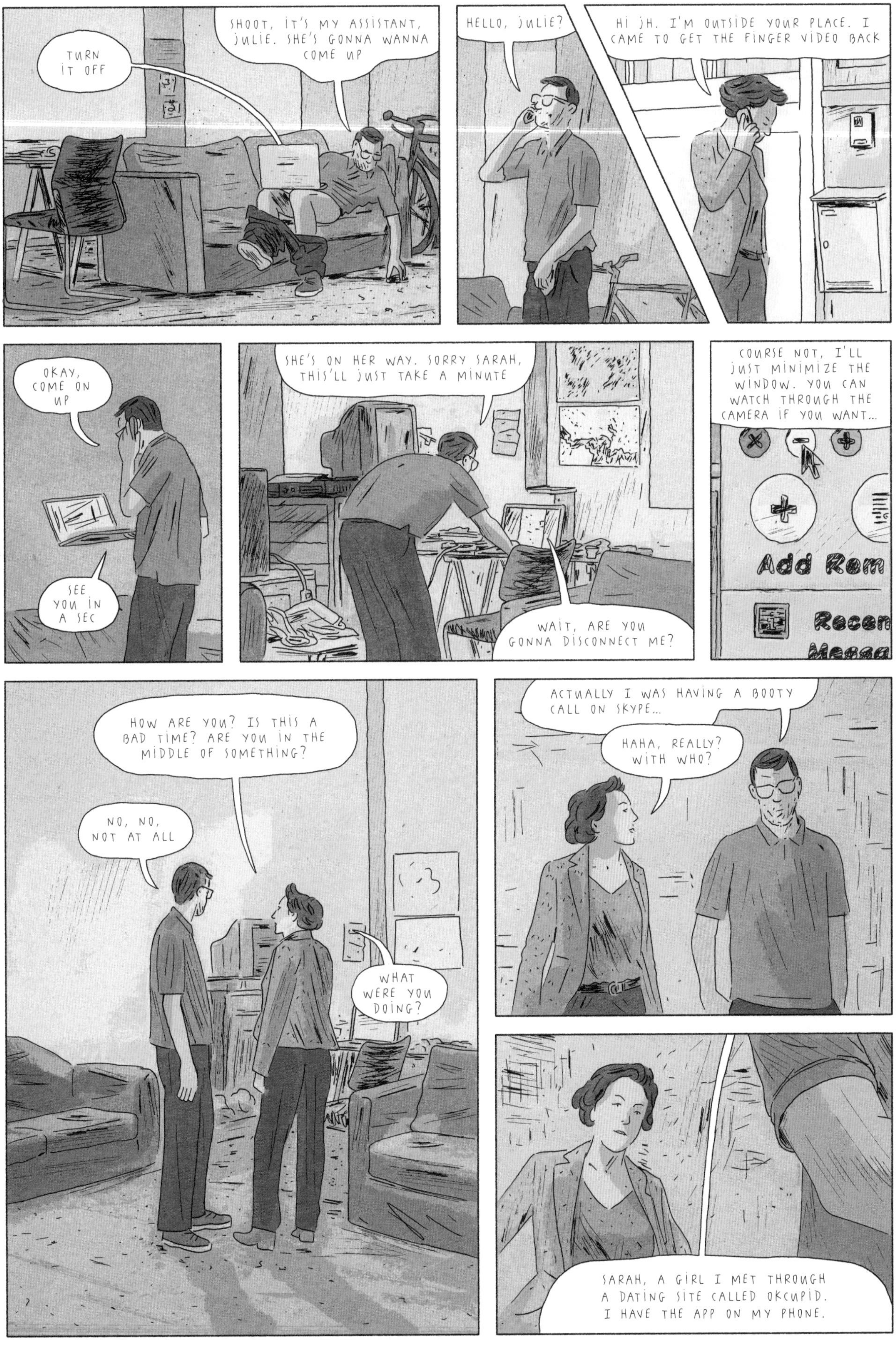
SHOOT, IT'S MY ASSISTANT, JULIE. SHE'S GONNA WANNA COME UP
TURN IT OFF
HELLO, JULIE?
HI JH. I'M OUTSIDE YOUR PLACE. I CAME TO GET THE FINGER VIDEO BACK
OKAY, COME ON UP
SEE YOU IN A SEC
SHE'S ON HER WAY. SORRY SARAH, THIS'LL JUST TAKE A MINUTE
WAIT, ARE YOU GONNA DISCONNECT ME?
COURSE NOT, I'LL JUST MINIMIZE THE WINDOW. YOU CAN WATCH THROUGH THE CAMERA IF YOU WANT...
Add Rem
Recen
HOW ARE YOU? IS THIS A BAD TIME? ARE YOU IN THE MIDDLE OF SOMETHING?
NO, NO, NOT AT ALL
WHAT WERE YOU DOING?
ACTUALLY I WAS HAVING A BOOTY CALL ON SKYPE...
HAHA, REALLY? WITH WHO?
SARAH, A GIRL I MET THROUGH A DATING SITE CALLED OKCUPID. I HAVE THE APP ON MY PHONE.

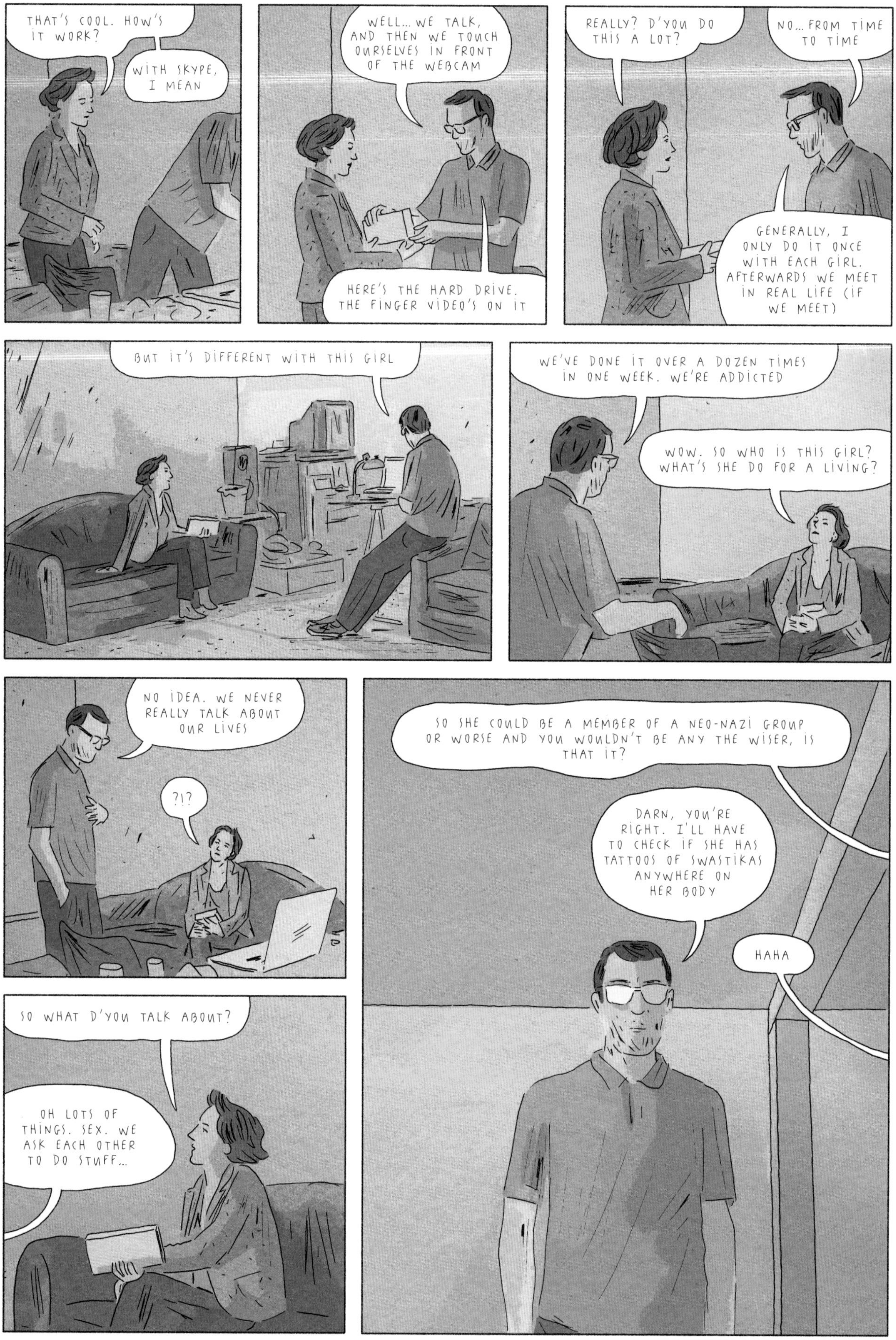
THAT'S COOL. HOW'S IT WORK?
WITH SKYPE, I MEAN
WELL... WE TALK, AND THEN WE TOUCH OURSELVES IN FRONT OF THE WEBCAM
HERE'S THE HARD DRIVE. THE FINGER VIDEO'S ON IT
REALLY? D'YOU DO THIS A LOT?
NO... FROM TIME TO TIME
GENERALLY, I ONLY DO IT ONCE WITH EACH GIRL. AFTERWARDS WE MEET IN REAL LIFE (IF WE MEET)
BUT IT'S DIFFERENT WITH THIS GIRL
WE'VE DONE IT OVER A DOZEN TIMES IN ONE WEEK. WE'RE ADDICTED
WOW. SO WHO IS THIS GIRL? WHAT'S SHE DO FOR A LIVING?
NO IDEA. WE NEVER REALLY TALK ABOUT OUR LIVES
?!?
SO WHAT D'YOU TALK ABOUT?
OH LOTS OF THINGS. SEX. WE ASK EACH OTHER TO DO STUFF...
SO SHE COULD BE A MEMBER OF A NEO-NAZI GROUP OR WORSE AND YOU WOULDN'T BE ANY THE WISER, IS THAT IT?
DARN, YOU'RE RIGHT. I'LL HAVE TO CHECK IF SHE HAS TATTOOS OF SWASTIKAS ANYWHERE ON HER BODY
HAHA

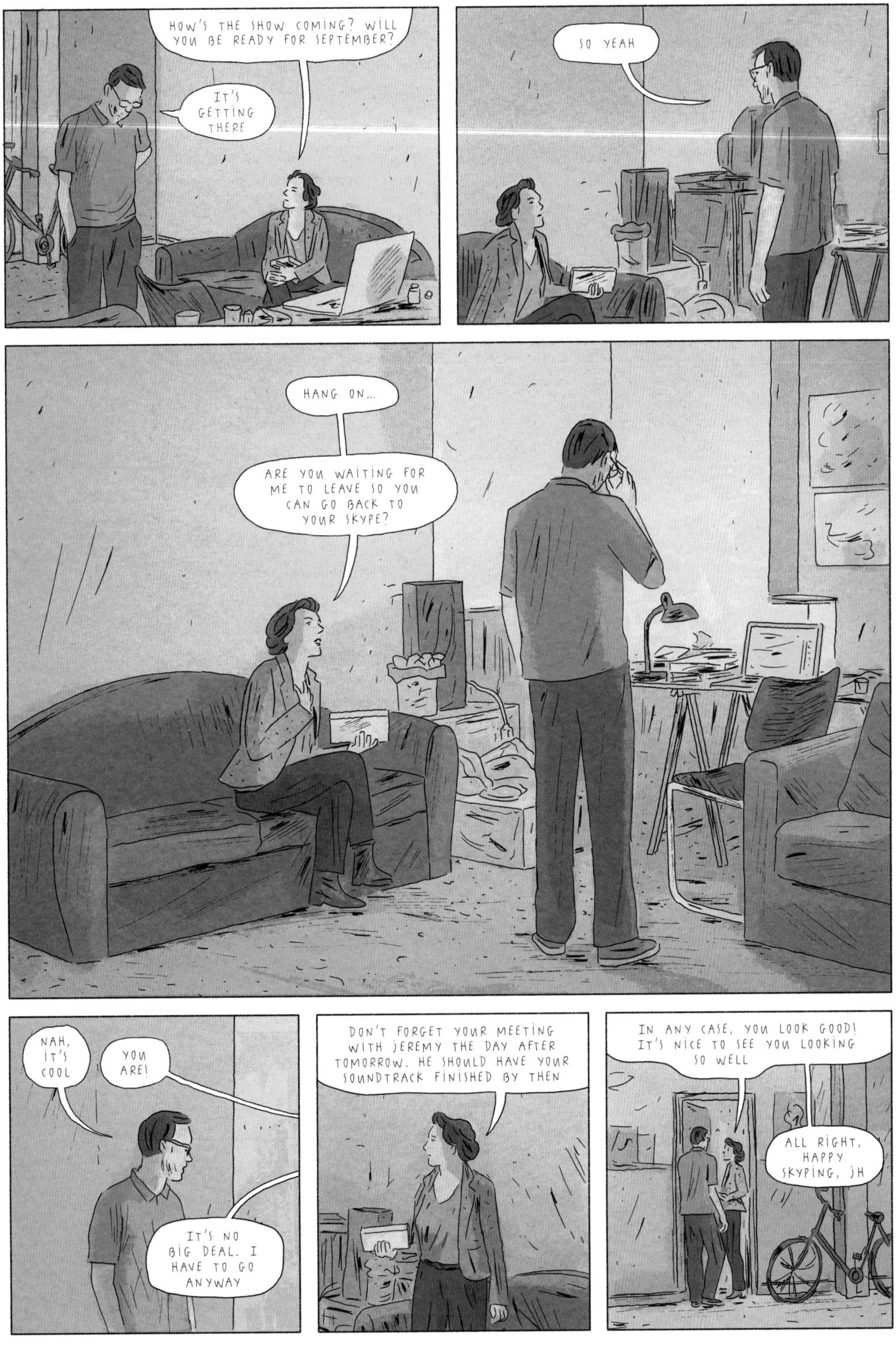
HOW'S THE SHOW COMING? WILL YOU BE READY FOR SEPTEMBER?
IT'S GETTING THERE
SO YEAH
HANG ON...
ARE YOU WAITING FOR ME TO LEAVE SO YOU CAN GO BACK TO YOUR SKYPE?
NAH, IT'S COOL
YOU ARE!
IT'S NO BIG DEAL. I HAVE TO GO ANYWAY
DON'T FORGET YOUR MEETING WITH JEREMY THE DAY AFTER TOMORROW. HE SHOULD HAVE YOUR SOUNDTRACK FINISHED BY THEN
IN ANY CASE, YOU LOOK GOOD! IT'S NICE TO SEE YOU LOOKING SO WELL
ALL RIGHT, HAPPY SKYPING, JH

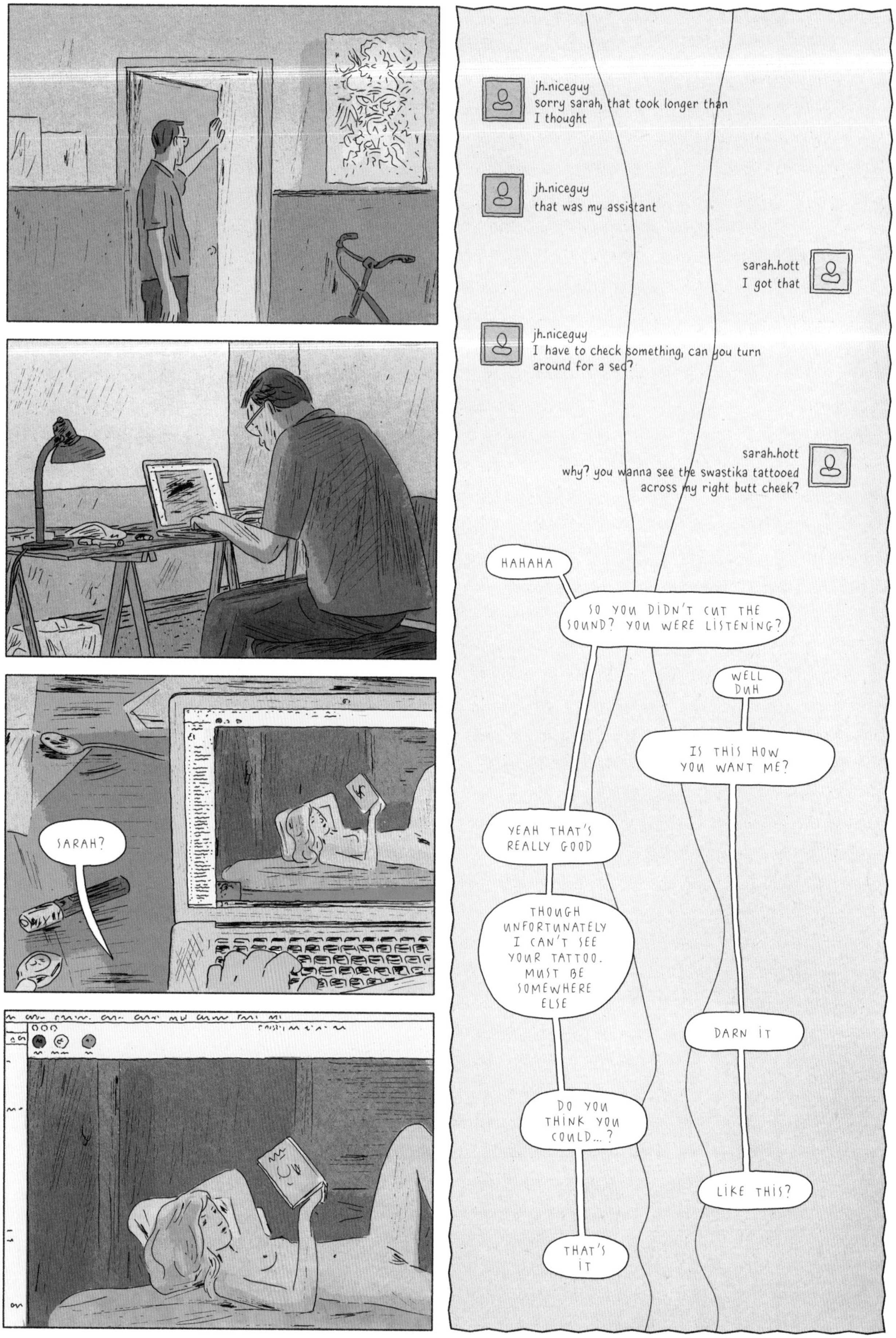
SARAH?
jh.niceguy
sorry sarah, that took longer than I thought
jh.niceguy
that was my assistant
sarah.hott
I got that
jh.niceguy
I have to check something, can you turn around for a sec?
sarah.hott
why? you wanna see the swastika tattooed across my right butt cheek?
HAHAHA
SO YOU DIDN'T CUT THE SOUND? YOU WERE LISTENING?
WELL DUH
IS THIS HOW YOU WANT ME?
YEAH THAT'S REALLY GOOD
THOUGH UNFORTUNATELY I CAN'T SEE YOUR TATTOO. MUST BE SOMEWHERE ELSE
DARN IT
DO YOU THINK YOU COULD...?
LIKE THIS?
THAT'S IT

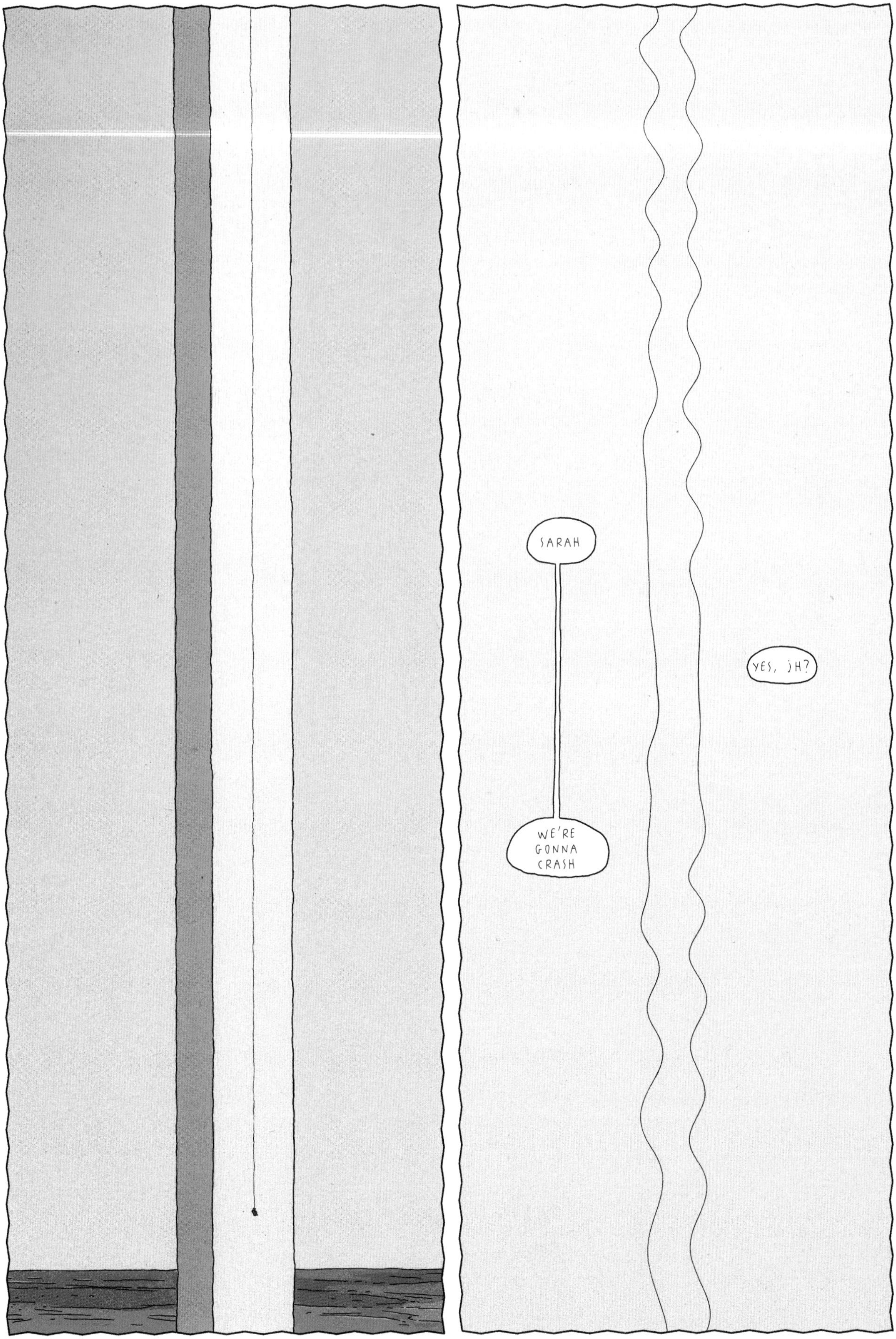
SARAH
WE'RE GONNA CRASH
YES, JH?

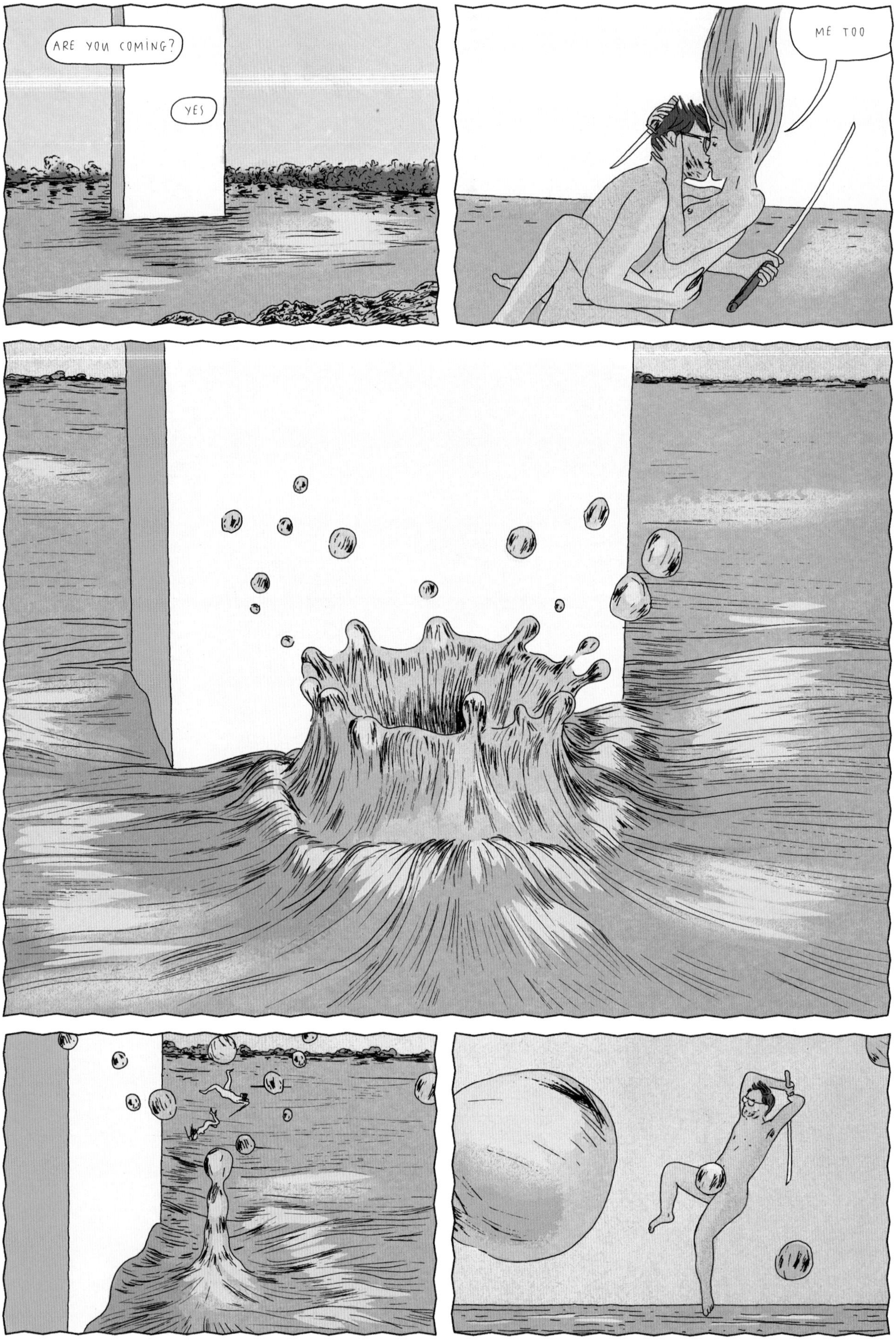
ARE YOU COMING?
YES
ME TOO

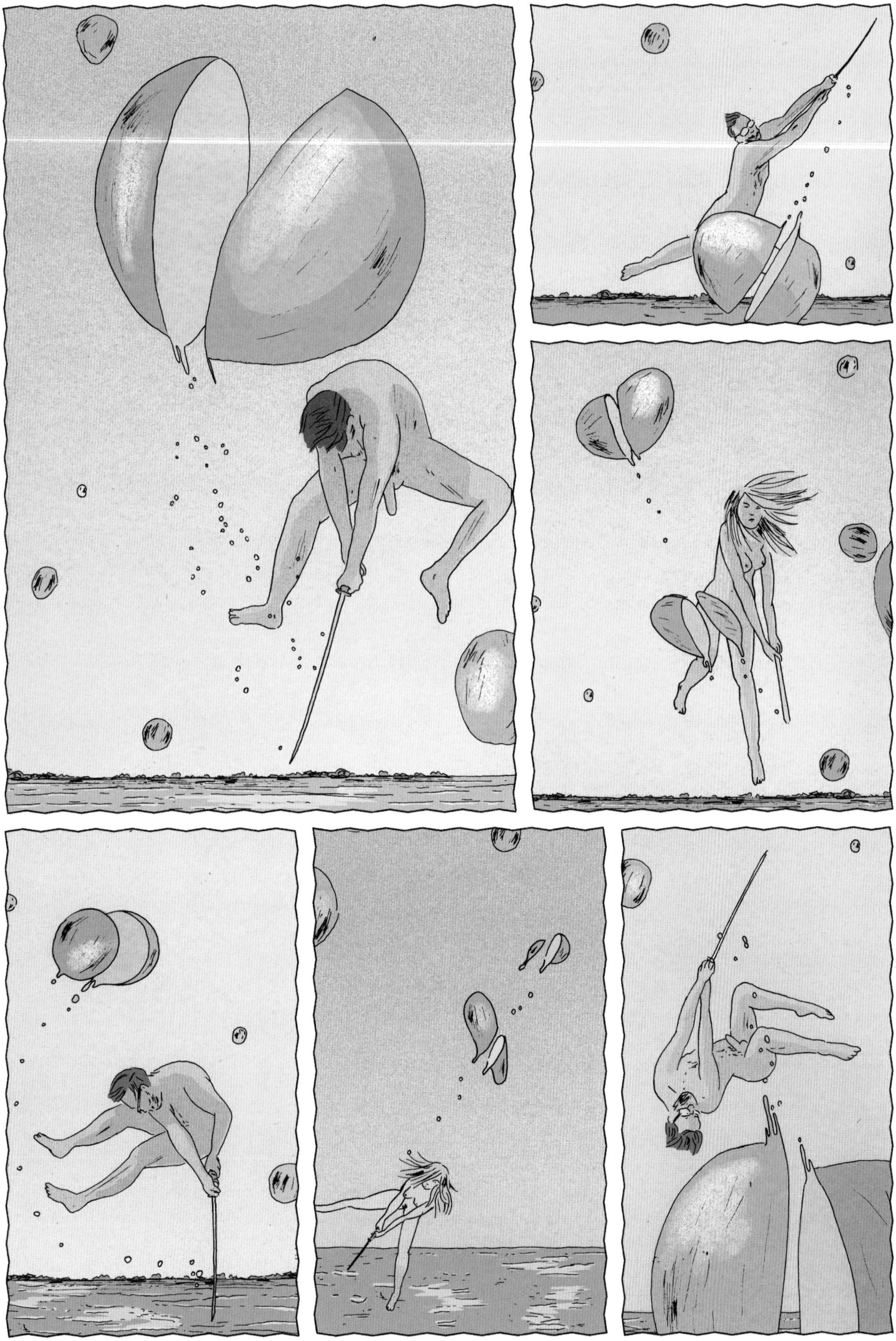

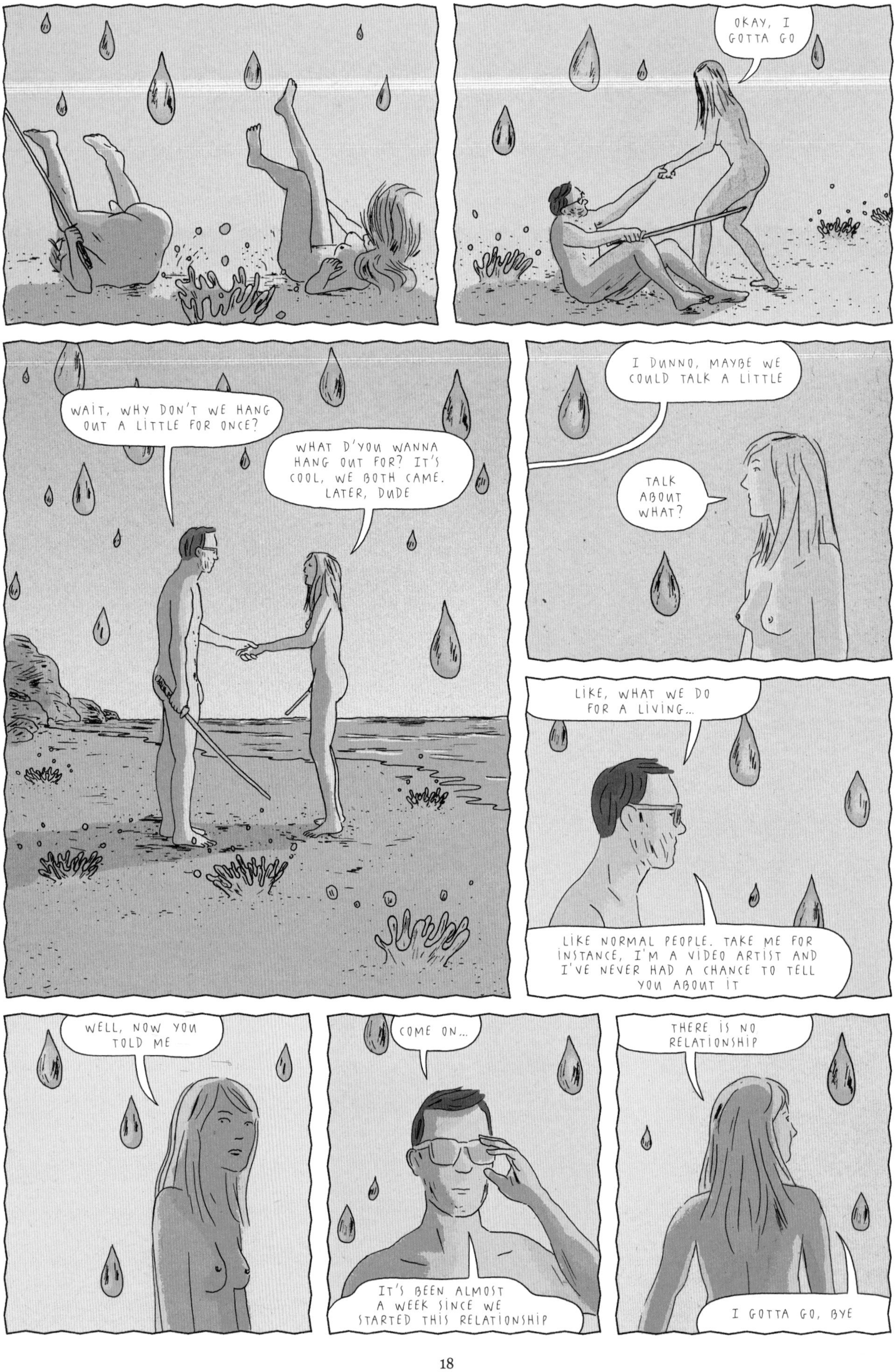
OKAY, I GOTTA GO
WAIT, WHY DON'T WE HANG OUT A LITTLE FOR ONCE?
WHAT D'YOU WANNA HANG OUT FOR? IT'S COOL, WE BOTH CAME. LATER, DUDE
I DUNNO, MAYBE WE COULD TALK A LITTLE
TALK ABOUT WHAT?
LIKE, WHAT WE DO FOR A LIVING...
LIKE NORMAL PEOPLE. TAKE ME FOR INSTANCE, I'M A VIDEO ARTIST AND I'VE NEVER HAD A CHANCE TO TELL YOU ABOUT IT
WELL, NOW YOU TOLD ME
COME ON...
IT'S BEEN ALMOST A WEEK SINCE WE STARTED THIS RELATIONSHIP
THERE IS NO RELATIONSHIP
I GOTTA GO, BYE

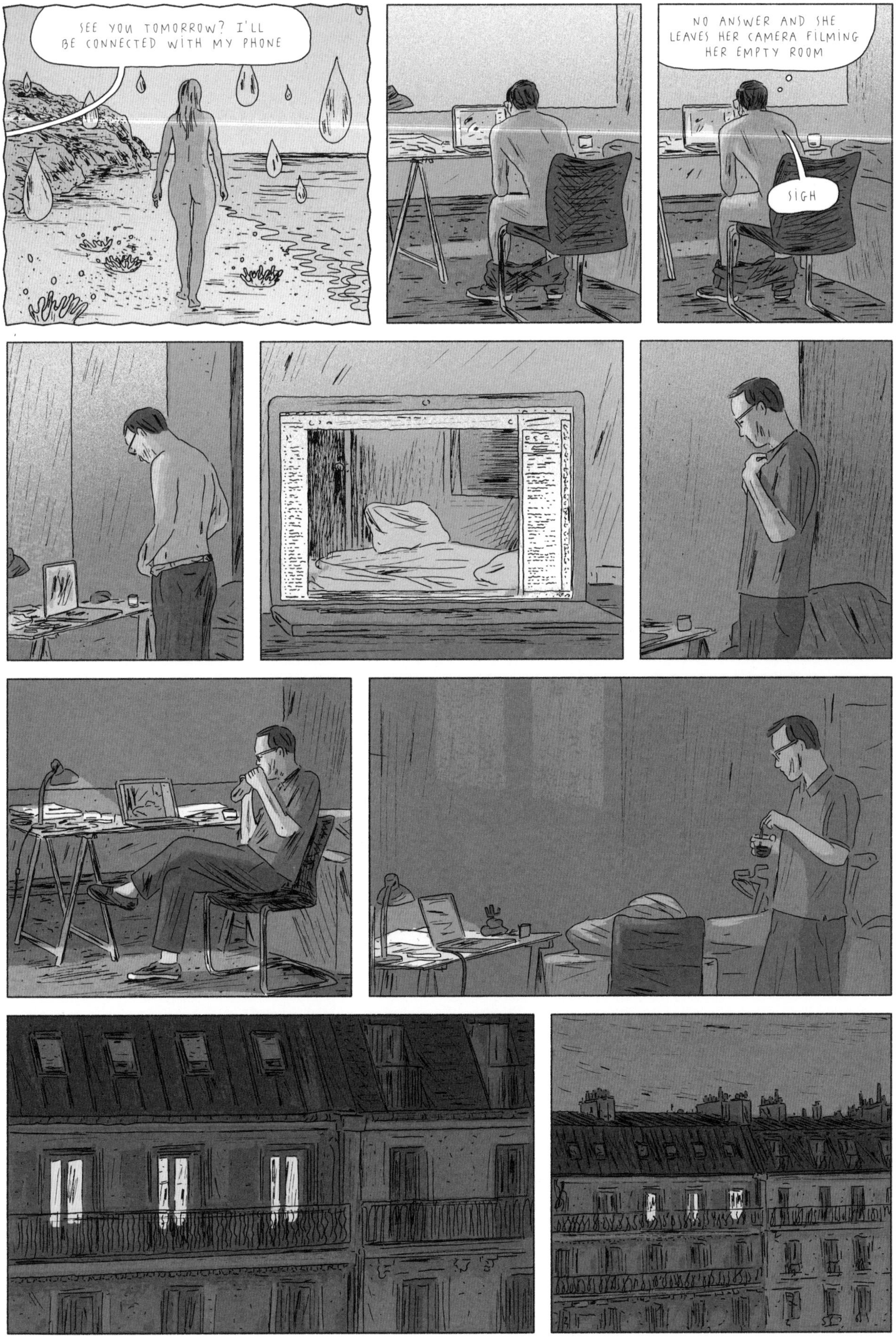

SEE YOU TOMORROW? I'LL BE CONNECTED WITH MY PHONE
NO ANSWER AND SHE LEAVES HER CAMERA FILMING HER EMPTY ROOM
SIGH

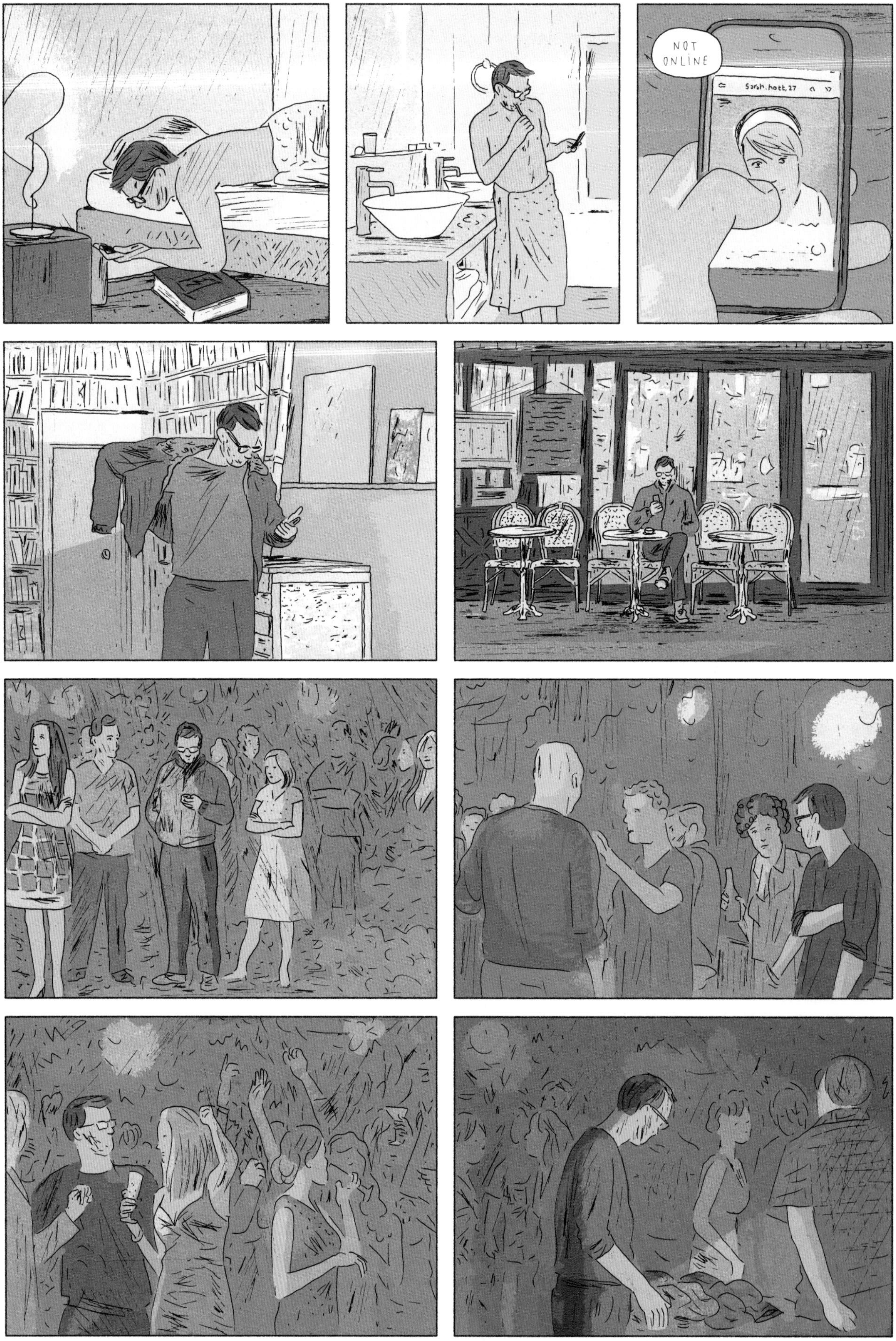
NOT ONLINE
Sarah.hott, 27

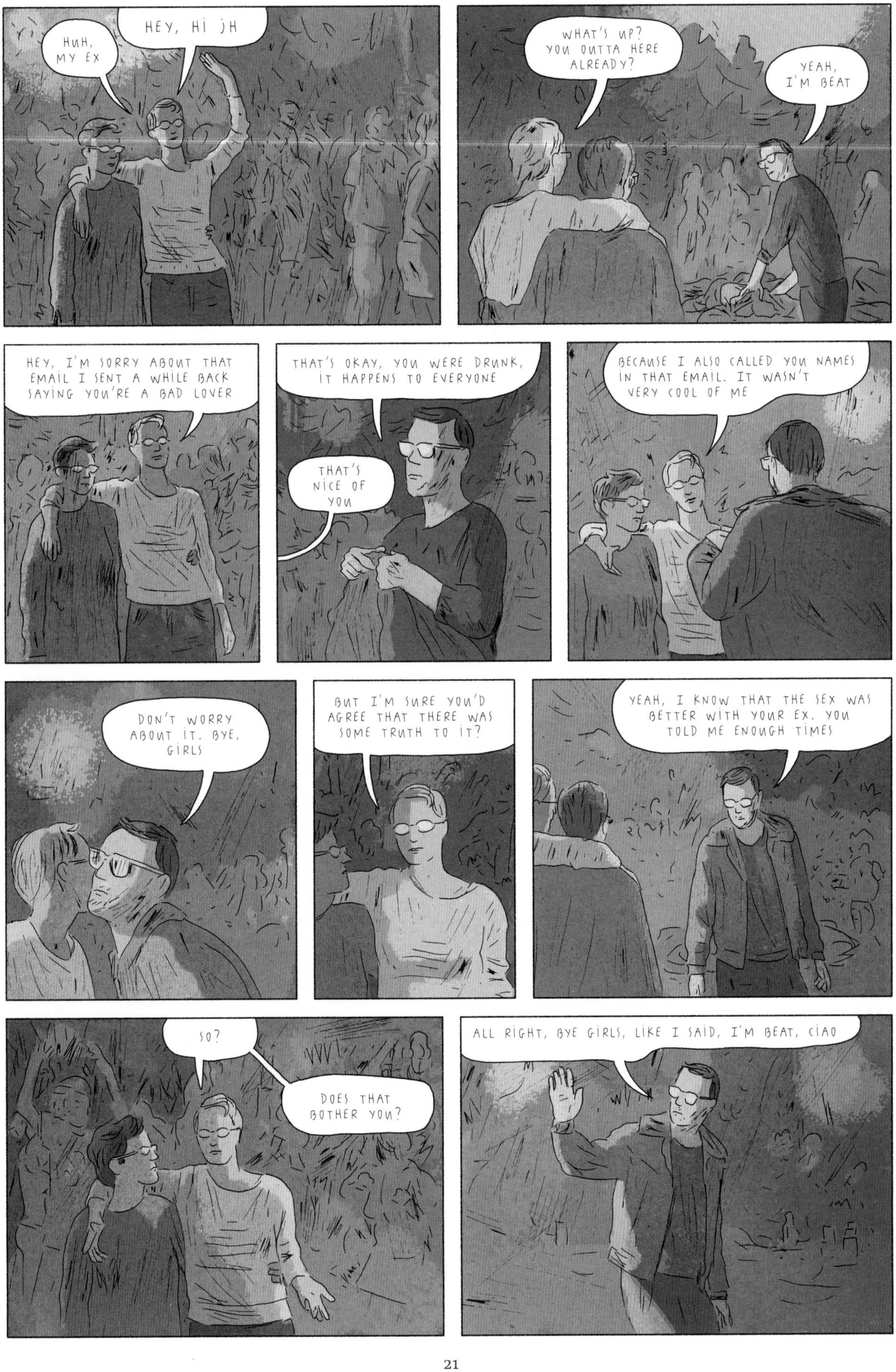
HEY, HI JH
HUH, MY EX
WHAT'S UP? YOU OUTTA HERE ALREADY?
YEAH, I'M BEAT
HEY, I'M SORRY ABOUT THAT EMAIL I SENT A WHILE BACK SAYING YOU'RE A BAD LOVER
THAT'S OKAY, YOU WERE DRUNK, IT HAPPENS TO EVERYONE
THAT'S NICE OF YOU
BECAUSE I ALSO CALLED YOU NAMES IN THAT EMAIL. IT WASN'T VERY COOL OF ME
DON'T WORRY ABOUT IT. BYE, GIRLS
BUT I'M SURE YOU'D AGREE THAT THERE WAS SOME TRUTH TO IT?
YEAH, I KNOW THAT THE SEX WAS BETTER WITH YOUR EX. YOU TOLD ME ENOUGH TIMES
SO?
DOES THAT BOTHER YOU?
ALL RIGHT, BYE GIRLS, LIKE I SAID, I'M BEAT, CIAO

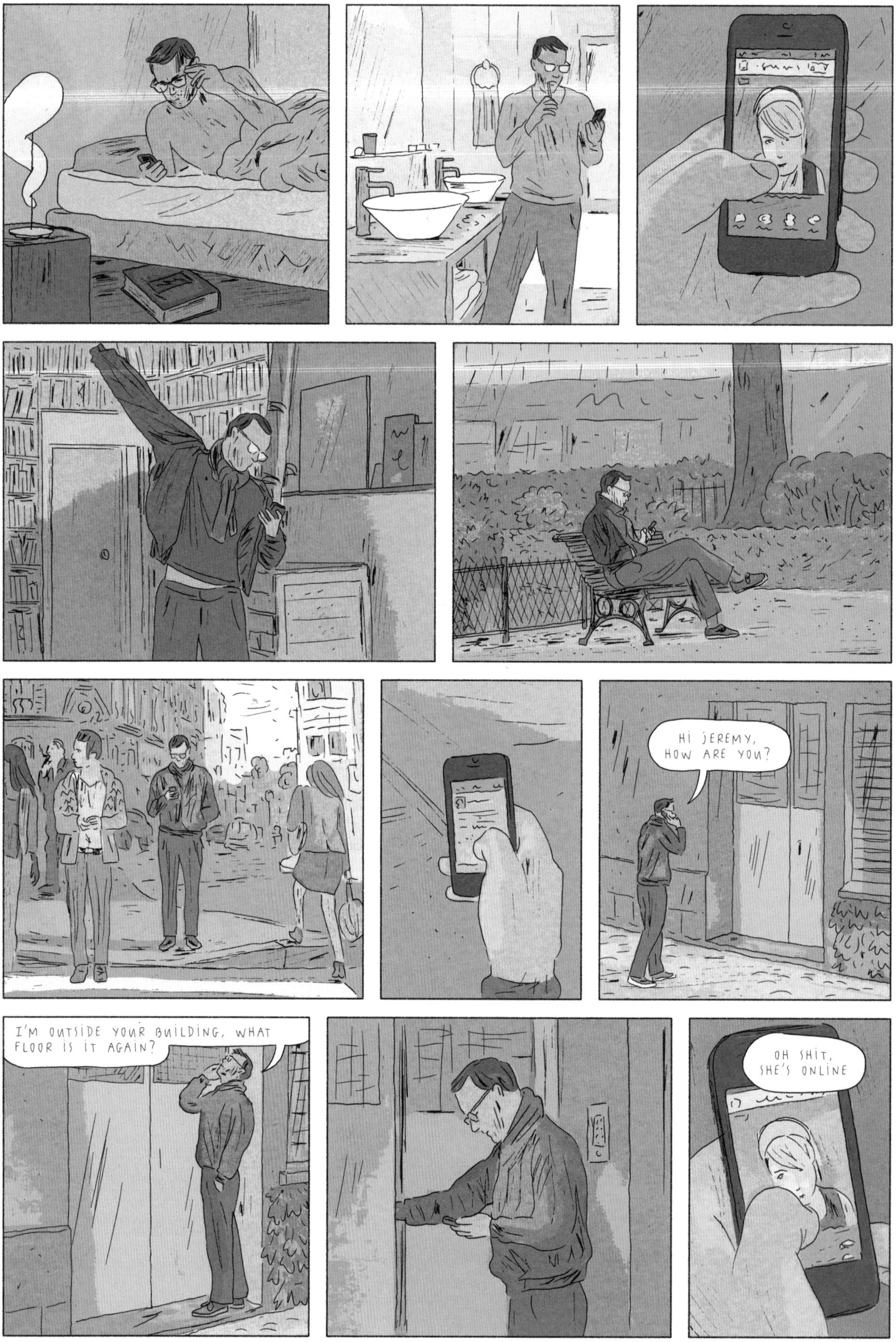
HI JEREMY, HOW ARE YOU?
I'M OUTSIDE YOUR BUILDING, WHAT FLOOR IS IT AGAIN?
OH SHIT, SHE'S ONLINE

with a

Chat

Hi Sarah

Hi jh

Hey Sarah, could you give me access to your private album pls

What for? You've already seen me naked on Skype

Just because. I'm curious

I'm still looking for that swastika

You're only hurting yourself, but ok ;)

sarah.hott, 27

Paris
Looking for someone to hang with, 21-37 years old

Profile   11 Photos   Like   Chat

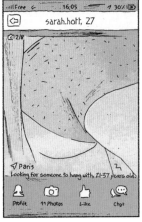

sarah.hott, 27

Paris
Looking for someone to hang with, 21-37 years old

Profile   11 Photos   Like   Chat

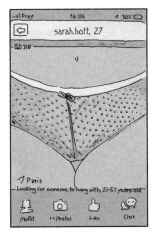

Free   16:06   30%

sarah.hott, 27

Paris
Looking for someone to hang with, 21-37 years old

Profile   11 Photos   Like   Chat

Exquisite. Sarah? Why don't we meet for a drink tonight?

No thanks

Come on, why not?

Because I'm afraid of getting chopped into pieces and ending up in garbage bags

I'm setting a trap for you and you're going to accept my invitation. Wanna bet? Ready? Check out my technique.

Hi Sarah, I'm in the process of making a video using fingers. Can I share it with you to get your opinion?

Maybe over a drink?

Haha nice try, but no thank you

But you can send your video over the Internet if you want ;?

Sorry :)

23

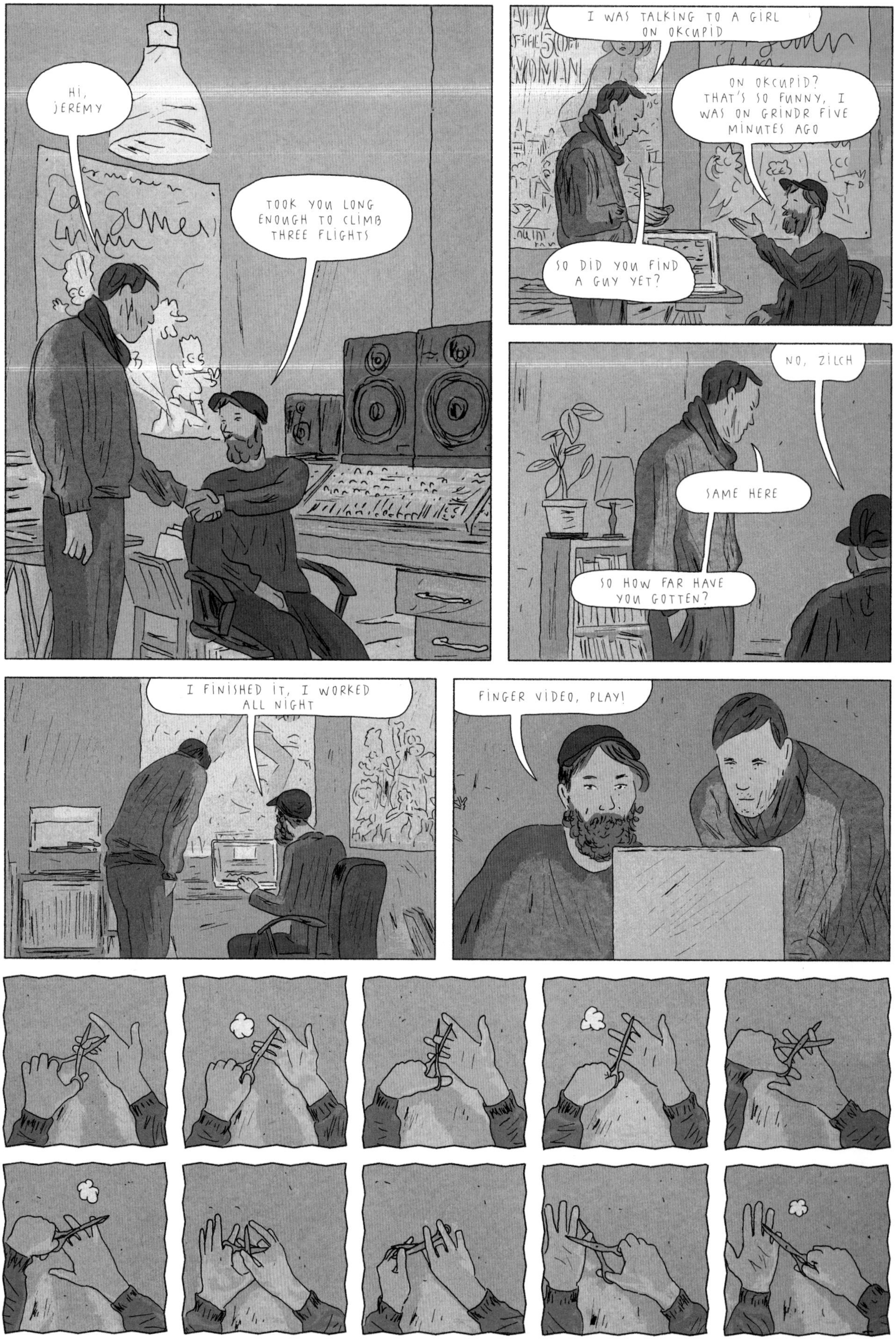
Hi, Jeremy
Took you long enough to climb three flights
I was talking to a girl on Okcupid
On Okcupid? That's so funny, I was on Grindr five minutes ago
So did you find a guy yet?
No, zilch
Same here
So how far have you gotten?
I finished it, I worked all night
Finger video, play!

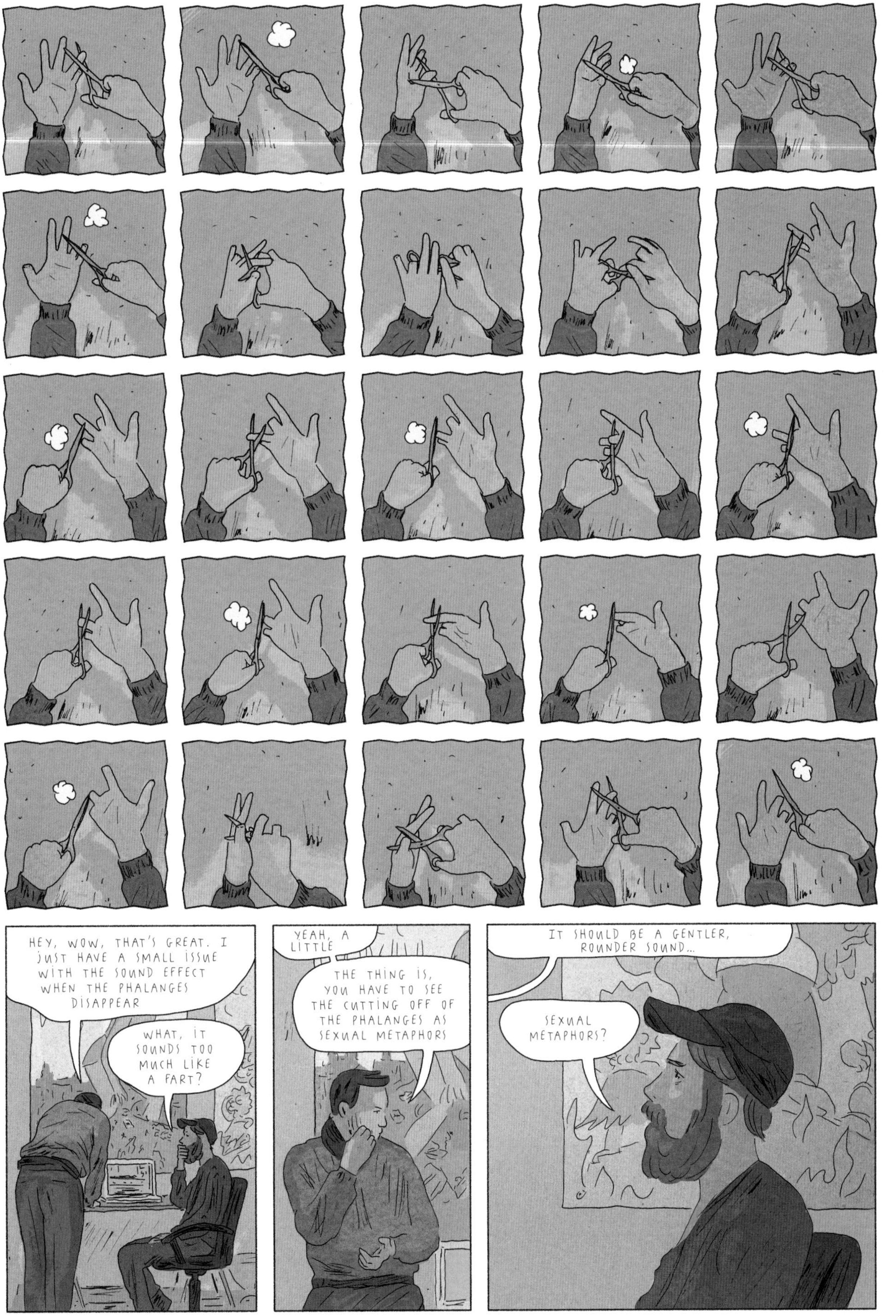
HEY, WOW, THAT'S GREAT. I JUST HAVE A SMALL ISSUE WITH THE SOUND EFFECT WHEN THE PHALANGES DISAPPEAR
WHAT, IT SOUNDS TOO MUCH LIKE A FART?
YEAH, A LITTLE
THE THING IS, YOU HAVE TO SEE THE CUTTING OFF OF THE PHALANGES AS SEXUAL METAPHORS
IT SHOULD BE A GENTLER, ROUNDER SOUND...
SEXUAL METAPHORS?

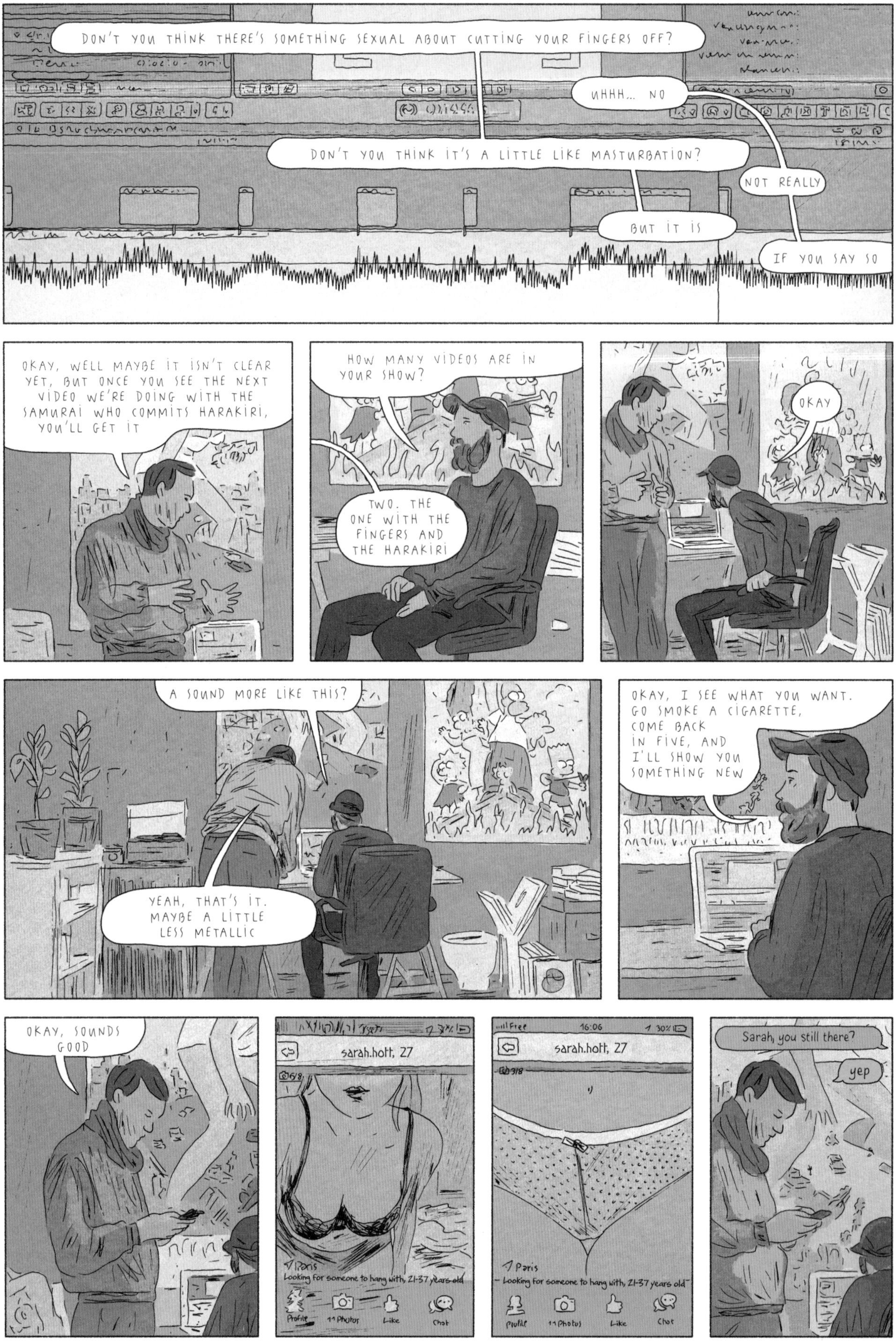
DON'T YOU THINK THERE'S SOMETHING SEXUAL ABOUT CUTTING YOUR FINGERS OFF?
UHHH... NO
DON'T YOU THINK IT'S A LITTLE LIKE MASTURBATION?
NOT REALLY
BUT IT IS
IF YOU SAY SO
OKAY, WELL MAYBE IT ISN'T CLEAR YET, BUT ONCE YOU SEE THE NEXT VIDEO WE'RE DOING WITH THE SAMURAI WHO COMMITS HARAKIRI, YOU'LL GET IT
HOW MANY VIDEOS ARE IN YOUR SHOW?
TWO. THE ONE WITH THE FINGERS AND THE HARAKIRI
OKAY
A SOUND MORE LIKE THIS?
YEAH, THAT'S IT. MAYBE A LITTLE LESS METALLIC
OKAY, I SEE WHAT YOU WANT. GO SMOKE A CIGARETTE, COME BACK IN FIVE, AND I'LL SHOW YOU SOMETHING NEW
OKAY, SOUNDS GOOD
sarah.hott, 27
Paris
Looking for someone to hang with, 21-37 years old
Profile
11 Photos
Like
Chat
Free
16:06
30%
sarah.hott, 27
Paris
Looking for someone to hang with, 21-37 years old
Profile
11 Photos
Like
Chat
Sarah, you still there?
yep

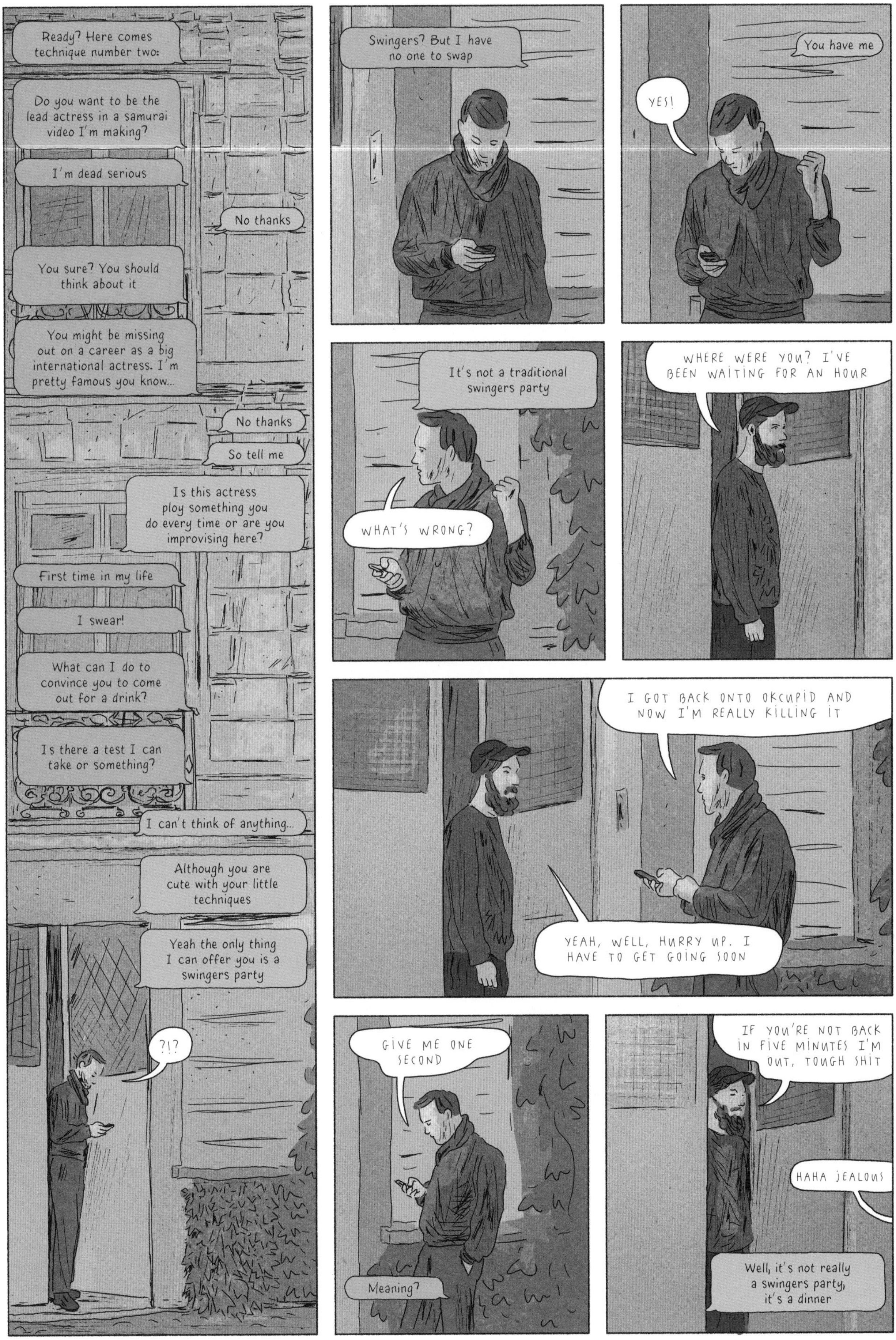
Ready? Here comes technique number two:
Do you want to be the lead actress in a samurai video I'm making?
I'm dead serious
No thanks
You sure? You should think about it
You might be missing out on a career as a big international actress. I'm pretty famous you know...
No thanks
So tell me
Is this actress ploy something you do every time or are you improvising here?
First time in my life
I swear!
What can I do to convince you to come out for a drink?
Is there a test I can take or something?
I can't think of anything...
Although you are cute with your little techniques
Yeah the only thing I can offer you is a swingers party
?!?
Swingers? But I have no one to swap
You have me
YES!
It's not a traditional swingers party
WHAT'S WRONG?
WHERE WERE YOU? I'VE BEEN WAITING FOR AN HOUR
I GOT BACK ONTO OKCUPID AND NOW I'M REALLY KILLING IT
YEAH, WELL, HURRY UP. I HAVE TO GET GOING SOON
GIVE ME ONE SECOND
Meaning?
IF YOU'RE NOT BACK IN FIVE MINUTES I'M OUT, TOUGH SHIT
HAHA JEALOUS
Well, it's not really a swingers party, it's a dinner

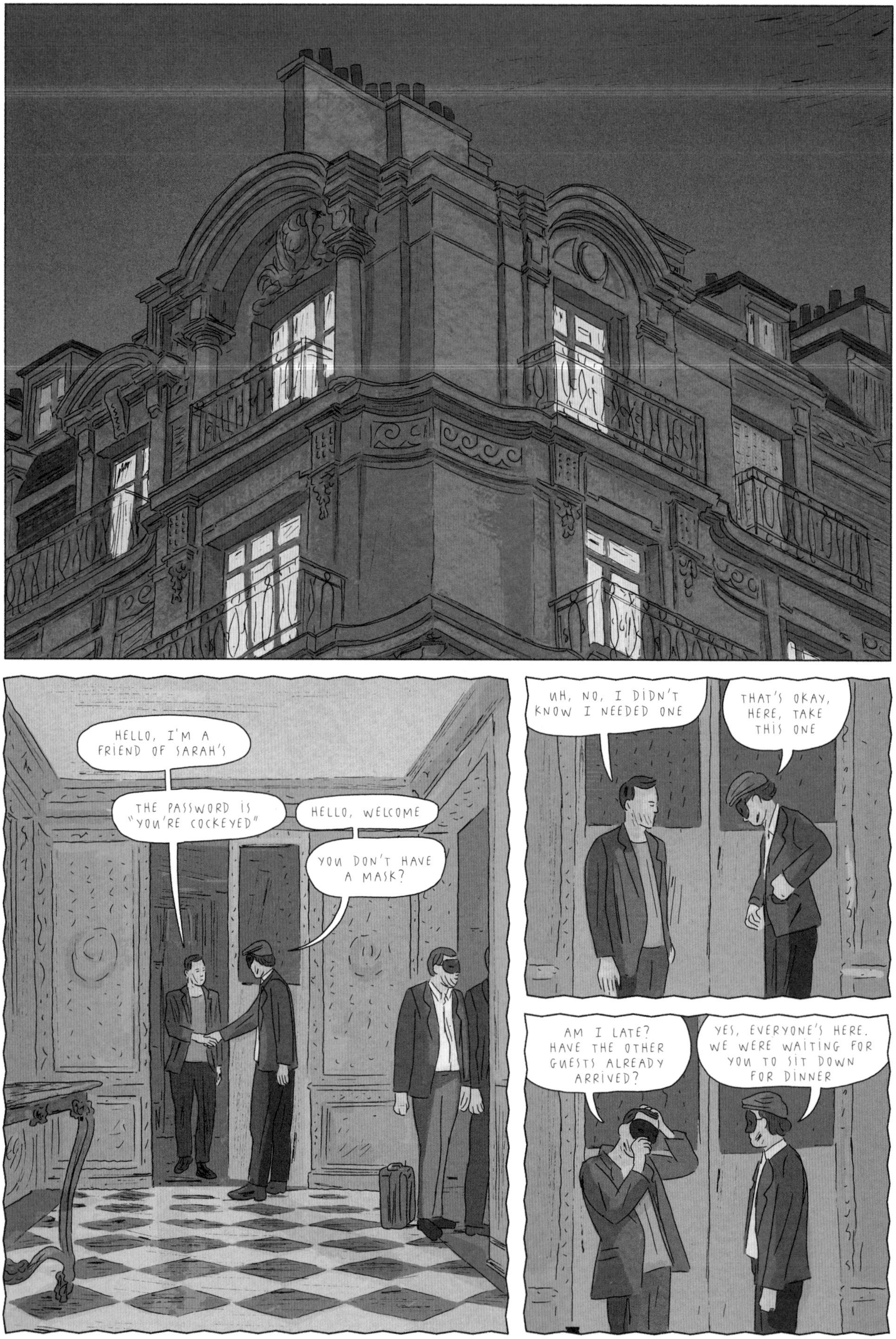
HELLO, I'M A FRIEND OF SARAH'S
THE PASSWORD IS "YOU'RE COCKEYED"
HELLO, WELCOME
YOU DON'T HAVE A MASK?
UH, NO, I DIDN'T KNOW I NEEDED ONE
THAT'S OKAY, HERE, TAKE THIS ONE
AM I LATE? HAVE THE OTHER GUESTS ALREADY ARRIVED?
YES, EVERYONE'S HERE. WE WERE WAITING FOR YOU TO SIT DOWN FOR DINNER

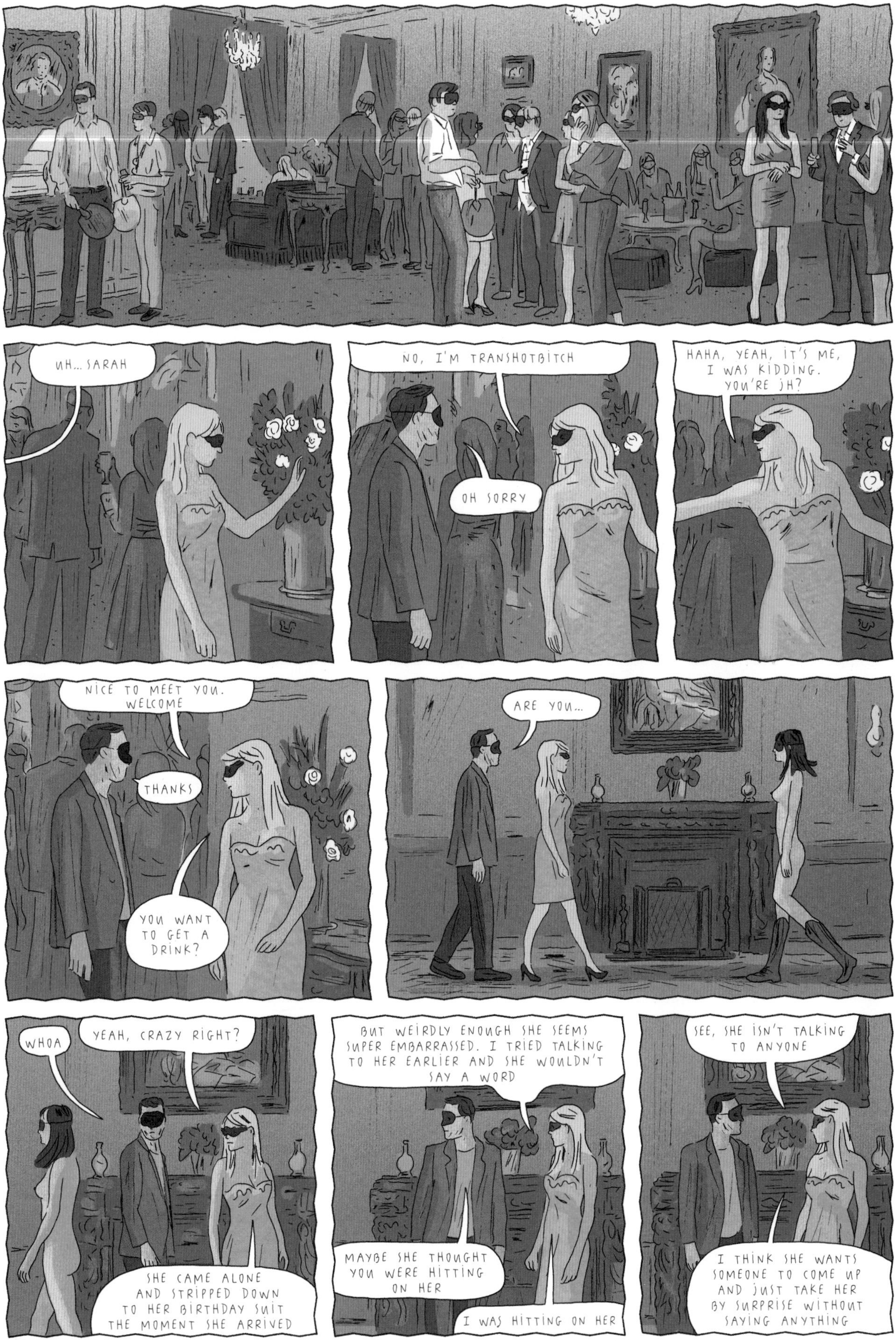
UH... SARAH
NO, I'M TRANSHOTBITCH
OH SORRY
HAHA, YEAH, IT'S ME, I WAS KIDDING. YOU'RE JH?
NICE TO MEET YOU. WELCOME
THANKS
YOU WANT TO GET A DRINK?
ARE YOU...
WHOA
YEAH, CRAZY RIGHT?
SHE CAME ALONE AND STRIPPED DOWN TO HER BIRTHDAY SUIT THE MOMENT SHE ARRIVED
BUT WEIRDLY ENOUGH SHE SEEMS SUPER EMBARRASSED. I TRIED TALKING TO HER EARLIER AND SHE WOULDN'T SAY A WORD
MAYBE SHE THOUGHT YOU WERE HITTING ON HER
I WAS HITTING ON HER
SEE, SHE ISN'T TALKING TO ANYONE
I THINK SHE WANTS SOMEONE TO COME UP AND JUST TAKE HER BY SURPRISE WITHOUT SAYING ANYTHING

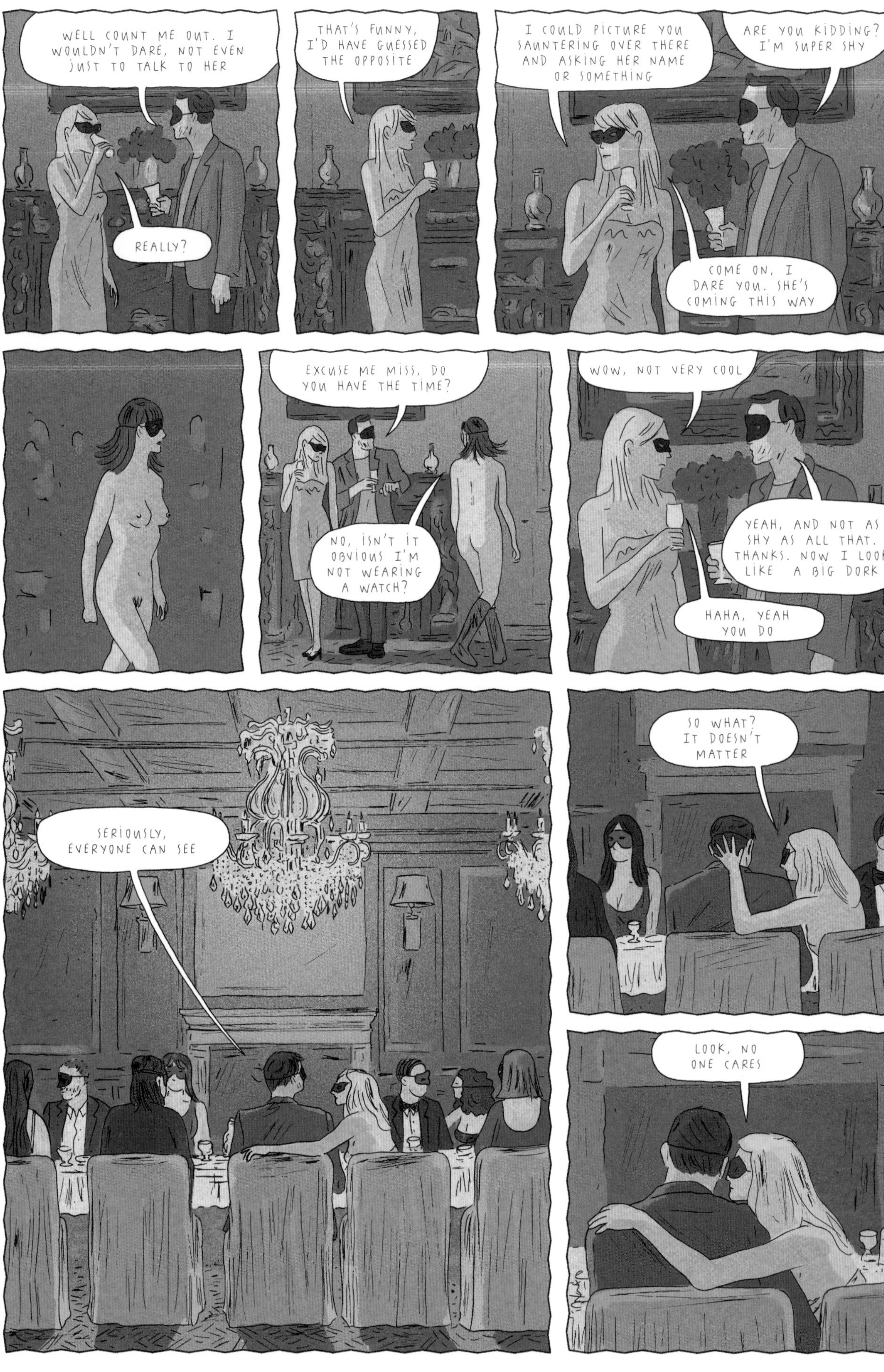

WELL COUNT ME OUT. I WOULDN'T DARE, NOT EVEN JUST TO TALK TO HER
REALLY?
THAT'S FUNNY, I'D HAVE GUESSED THE OPPOSITE
I COULD PICTURE YOU SAUNTERING OVER THERE AND ASKING HER NAME OR SOMETHING
ARE YOU KIDDING? I'M SUPER SHY
COME ON, I DARE YOU. SHE'S COMING THIS WAY
EXCUSE ME MISS, DO YOU HAVE THE TIME?
NO, ISN'T IT OBVIOUS I'M NOT WEARING A WATCH?
WOW, NOT VERY COOL
YEAH, AND NOT AS SHY AS ALL THAT. THANKS. NOW I LOOK LIKE A BIG DORK
HAHA, YEAH YOU DO
SERIOUSLY, EVERYONE CAN SEE
SO WHAT? IT DOESN'T MATTER
LOOK, NO ONE CARES

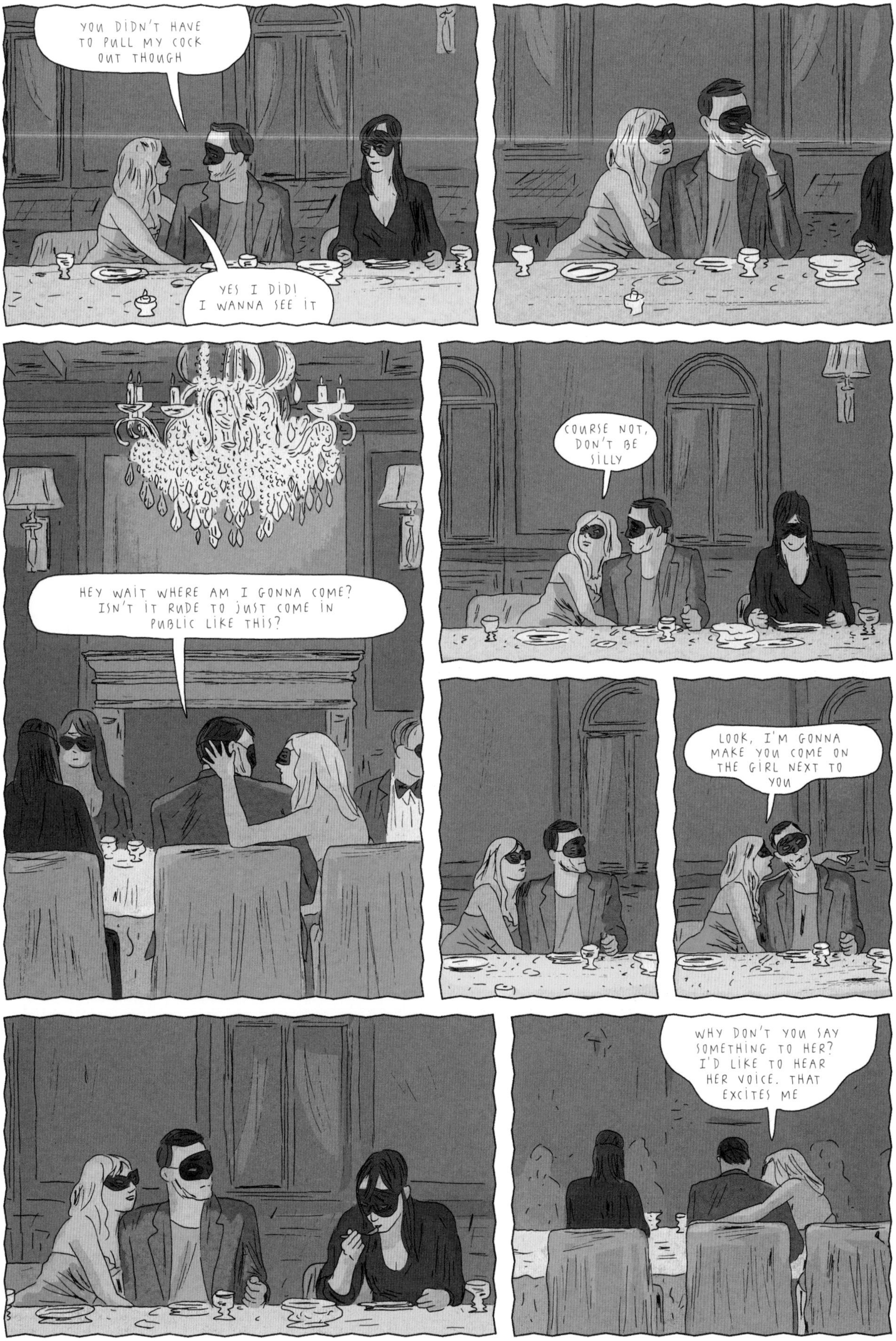
YOU DIDN'T HAVE TO PULL MY COCK OUT THOUGH
YES I DID! I WANNA SEE IT
HEY WAIT WHERE AM I GONNA COME? ISN'T IT RUDE TO JUST COME IN PUBLIC LIKE THIS?
COURSE NOT, DON'T BE SILLY
LOOK, I'M GONNA MAKE YOU COME ON THE GIRL NEXT TO YOU
WHY DON'T YOU SAY SOMETHING TO HER? I'D LIKE TO HEAR HER VOICE. THAT EXCITES ME

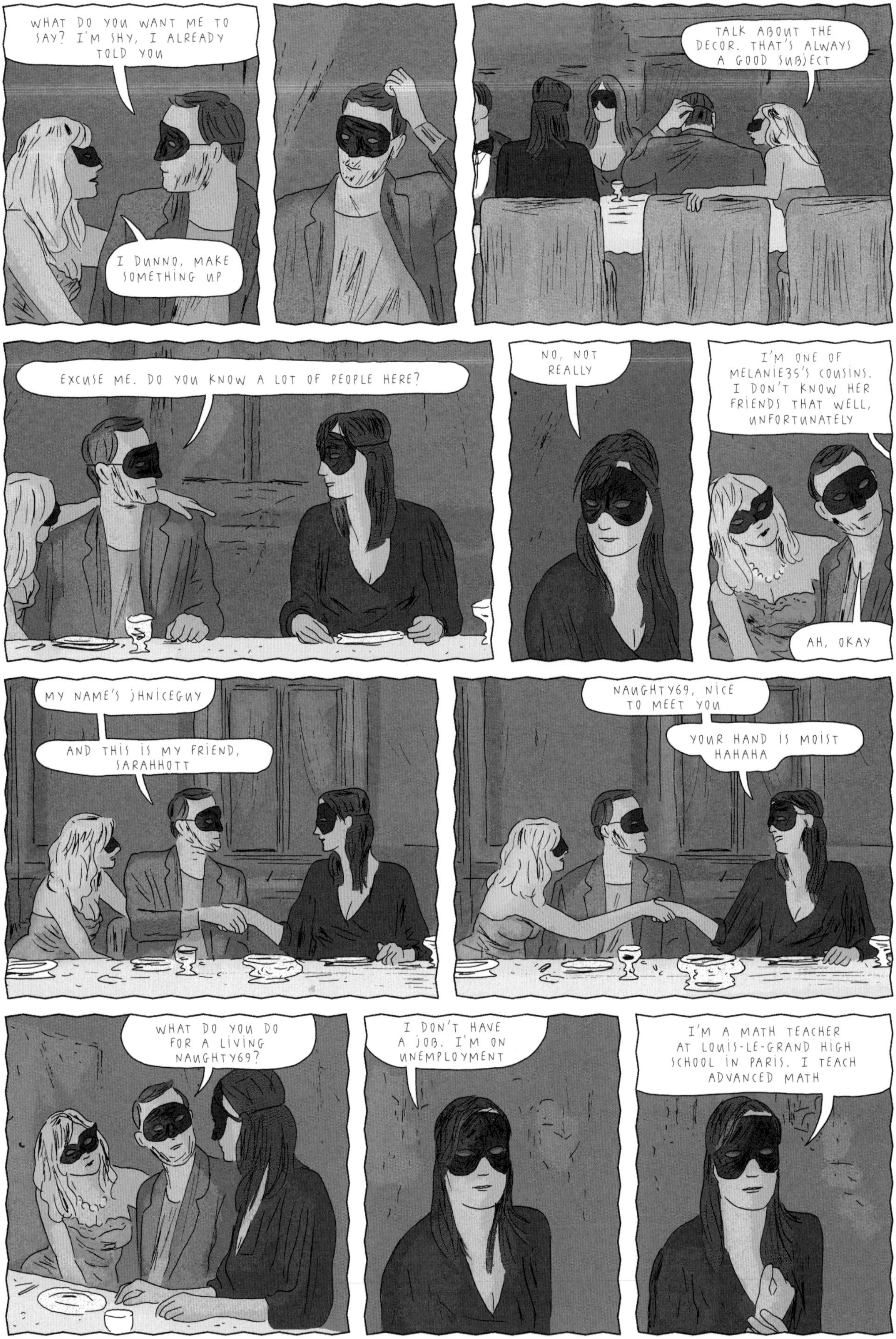
WHAT DO YOU WANT ME TO SAY? I'M SHY, I ALREADY TOLD YOU
I DUNNO, MAKE SOMETHING UP
TALK ABOUT THE DECOR. THAT'S ALWAYS A GOOD SUBJECT
EXCUSE ME. DO YOU KNOW A LOT OF PEOPLE HERE?
NO, NOT REALLY
I'M ONE OF MELANIE35'S COUSINS. I DON'T KNOW HER FRIENDS THAT WELL, UNFORTUNATELY
AH, OKAY
MY NAME'S JHNICEGUY
AND THIS IS MY FRIEND, SARAHHOTT
NAUGHTY69, NICE TO MEET YOU
YOUR HAND IS MOIST HAHAHA
WHAT DO YOU DO FOR A LIVING NAUGHTY69?
I DON'T HAVE A JOB. I'M ON UNEMPLOYMENT
I'M A MATH TEACHER AT LOUIS-LE-GRAND HIGH SCHOOL IN PARIS. I TEACH ADVANCED MATH

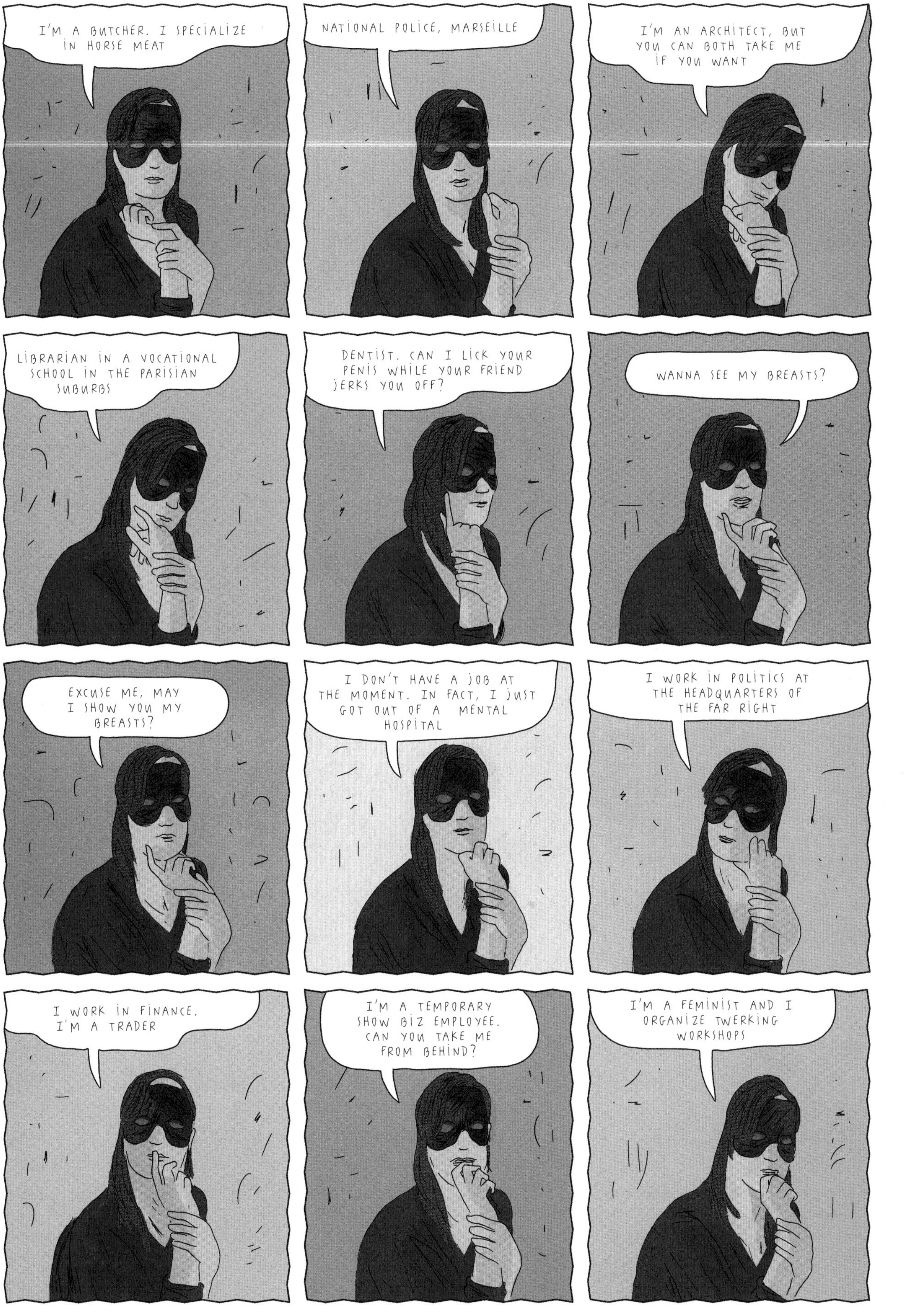
I'M A BUTCHER. I SPECIALIZE IN HORSE MEAT
NATIONAL POLICE, MARSEILLE
I'M AN ARCHITECT, BUT YOU CAN BOTH TAKE ME IF YOU WANT
LIBRARIAN IN A VOCATIONAL SCHOOL IN THE PARISIAN SUBURBS
DENTIST. CAN I LICK YOUR PENIS WHILE YOUR FRIEND JERKS YOU OFF?
WANNA SEE MY BREASTS?
EXCUSE ME, MAY I SHOW YOU MY BREASTS?
I DON'T HAVE A JOB AT THE MOMENT. IN FACT, I JUST GOT OUT OF A MENTAL HOSPITAL
I WORK IN POLITICS AT THE HEADQUARTERS OF THE FAR RIGHT
I WORK IN FINANCE. I'M A TRADER
I'M A TEMPORARY SHOW BIZ EMPLOYEE. CAN YOU TAKE ME FROM BEHIND?
I'M A FEMINIST AND I ORGANIZE TWERKING WORKSHOPS

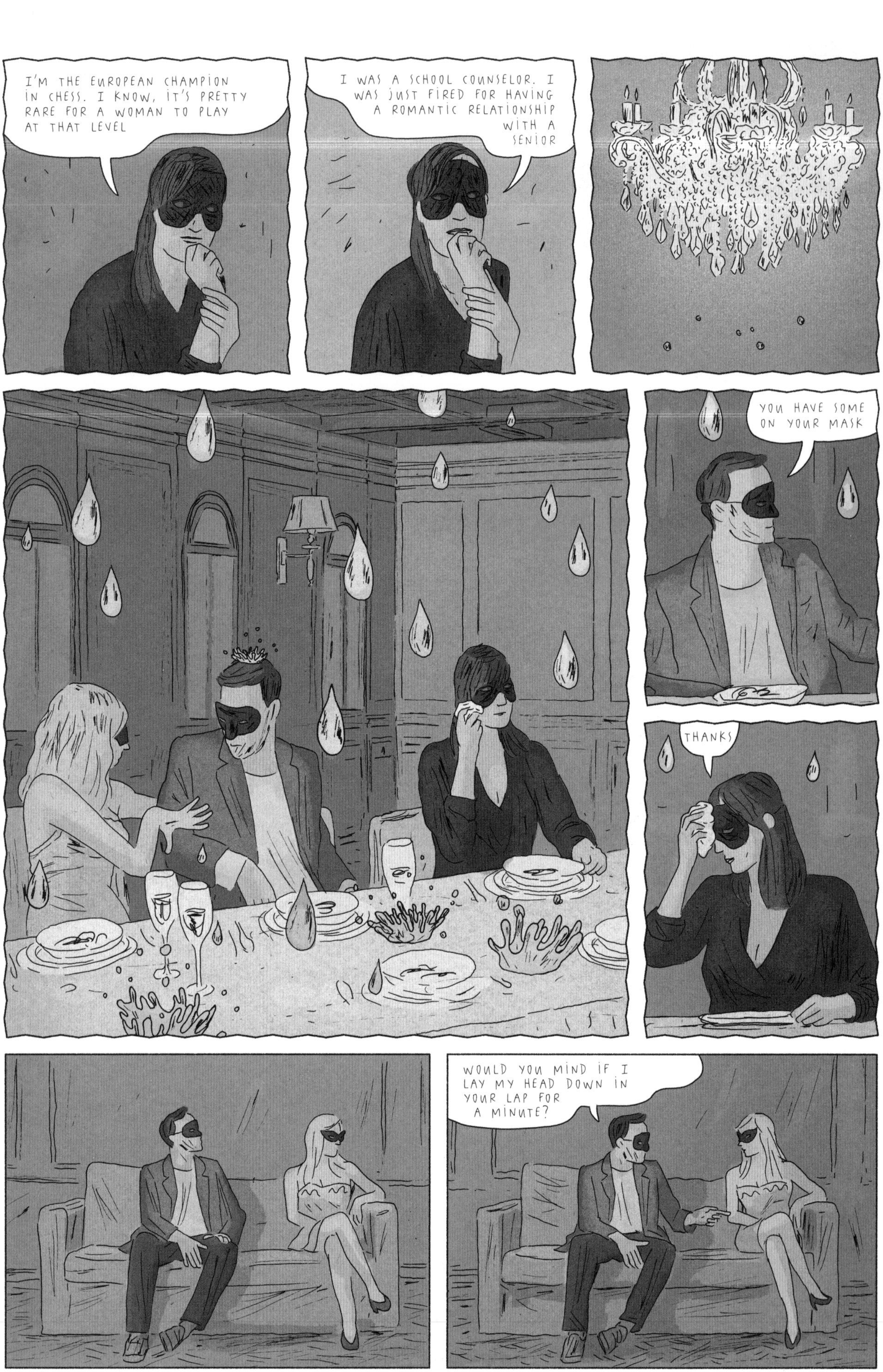
I'M THE EUROPEAN CHAMPION IN CHESS. I KNOW, IT'S PRETTY RARE FOR A WOMAN TO PLAY AT THAT LEVEL
I WAS A SCHOOL COUNSELOR. I WAS JUST FIRED FOR HAVING A ROMANTIC RELATIONSHIP WITH A SENIOR
YOU HAVE SOME ON YOUR MASK
THANKS
WOULD YOU MIND IF I LAY MY HEAD DOWN IN YOUR LAP FOR A MINUTE?

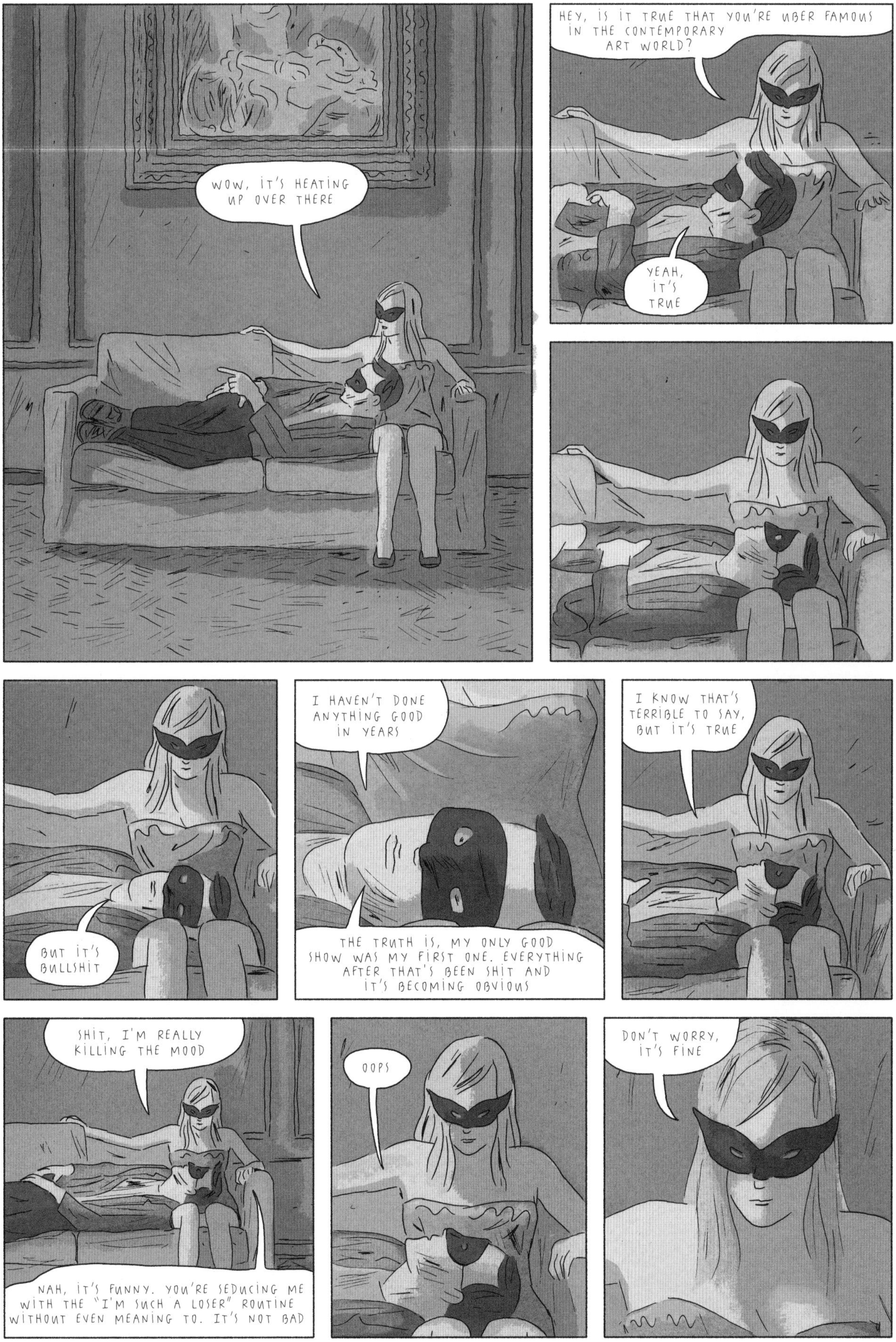
WOW, IT'S HEATING UP OVER THERE
HEY, IS IT TRUE THAT YOU'RE UBER FAMOUS IN THE CONTEMPORARY ART WORLD?
YEAH, IT'S TRUE
BUT IT'S BULLSHIT
I HAVEN'T DONE ANYTHING GOOD IN YEARS
THE TRUTH IS, MY ONLY GOOD SHOW WAS MY FIRST ONE. EVERYTHING AFTER THAT'S BEEN SHIT AND IT'S BECOMING OBVIOUS
I KNOW THAT'S TERRIBLE TO SAY, BUT IT'S TRUE
SHIT, I'M REALLY KILLING THE MOOD
NAH, IT'S FUNNY. YOU'RE SEDUCING ME WITH THE "I'M SUCH A LOSER" ROUTINE WITHOUT EVEN MEANING TO. IT'S NOT BAD
OOPS
DON'T WORRY, IT'S FINE

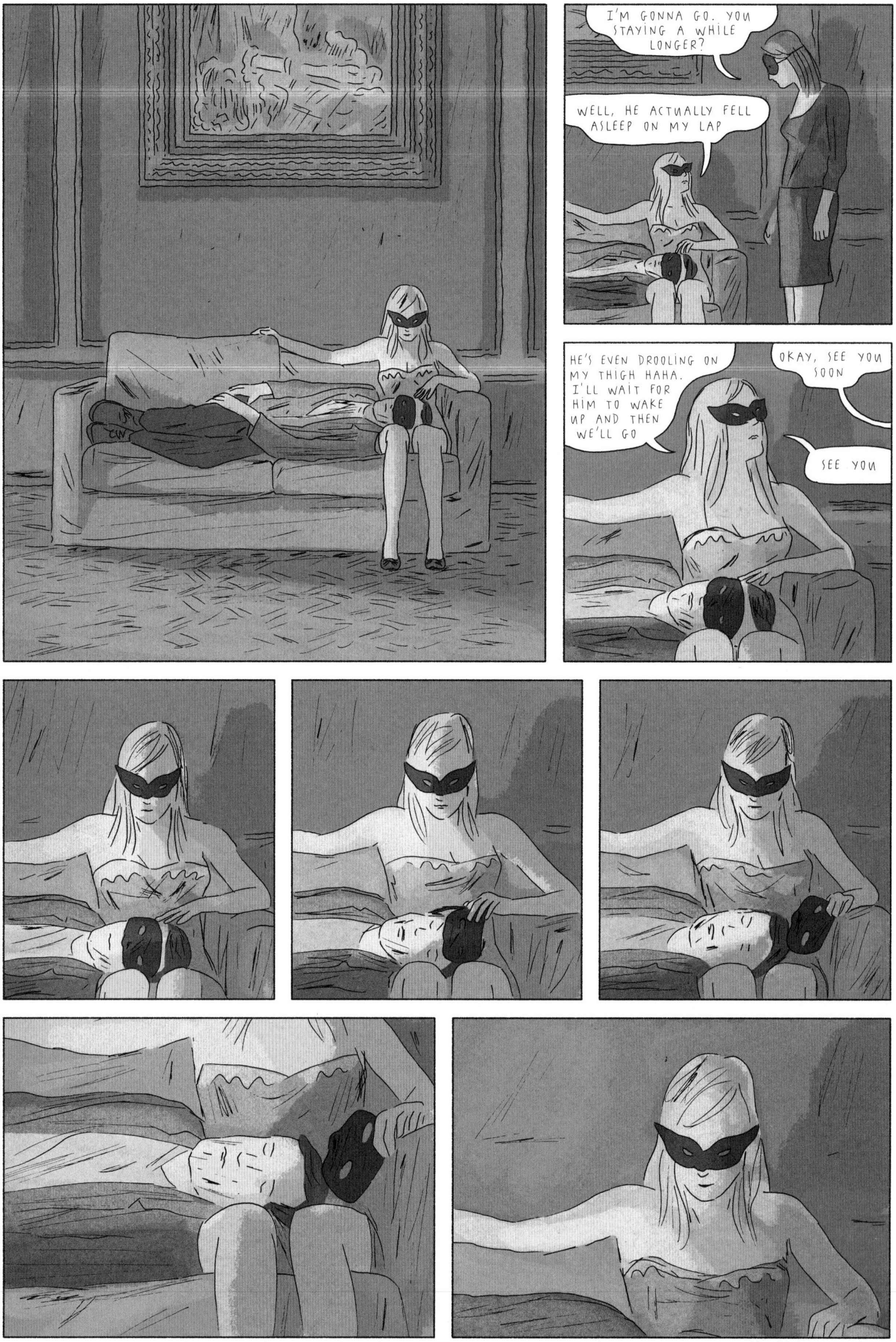
I'M GONNA GO. YOU STAYING A WHILE LONGER?
WELL, HE ACTUALLY FELL ASLEEP ON MY LAP
HE'S EVEN DROOLING ON MY THIGH HAHA. I'LL WAIT FOR HIM TO WAKE UP AND THEN WE'LL GO
OKAY, SEE YOU SOON
SEE YOU

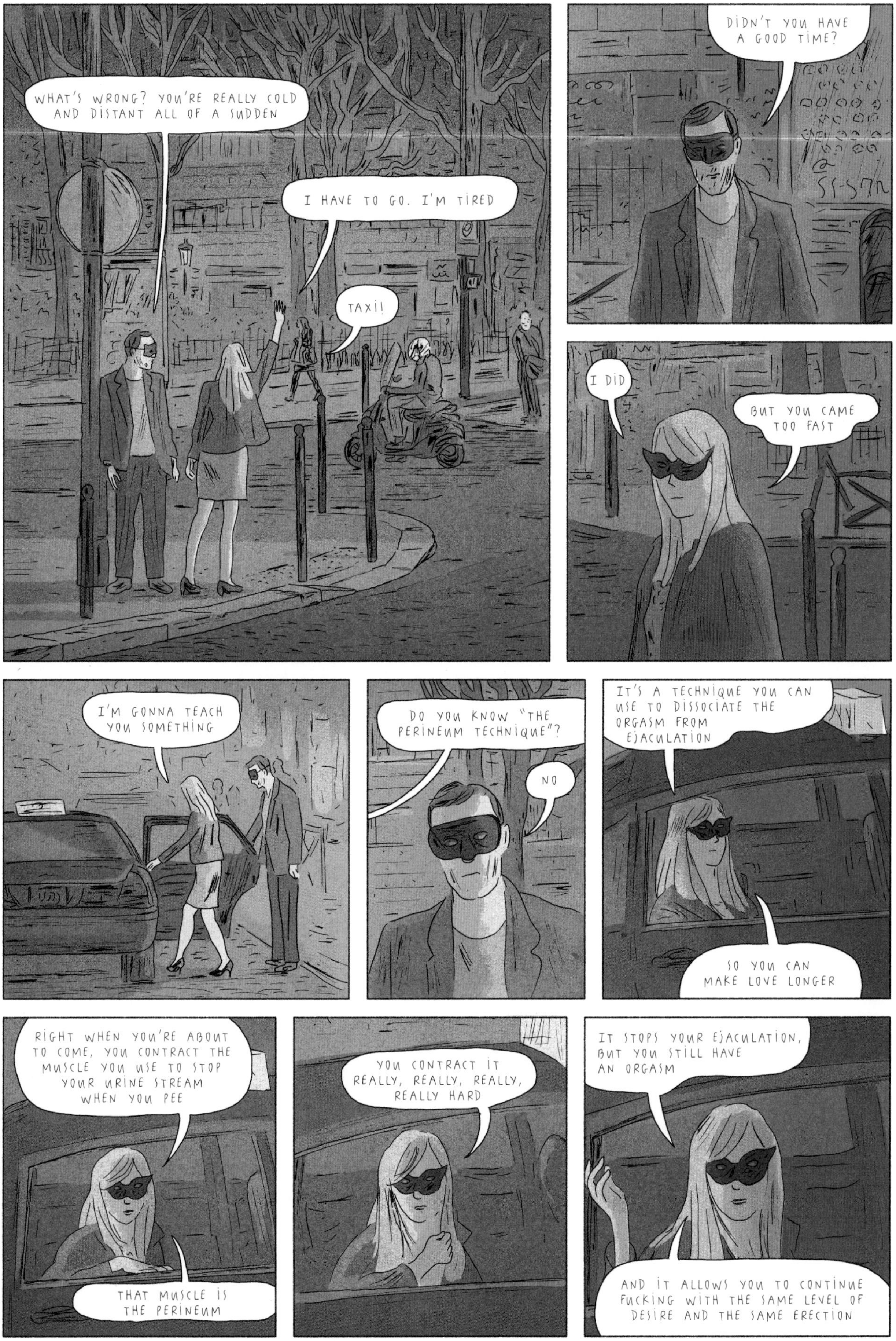
WHAT'S WRONG? YOU'RE REALLY COLD AND DISTANT ALL OF A SUDDEN
I HAVE TO GO. I'M TIRED
TAXI!
DIDN'T YOU HAVE A GOOD TIME?
I DID
BUT YOU CAME TOO FAST
I'M GONNA TEACH YOU SOMETHING
DO YOU KNOW "THE PERINEUM TECHNIQUE"?
NO
IT'S A TECHNIQUE YOU CAN USE TO DISSOCIATE THE ORGASM FROM EJACULATION
SO YOU CAN MAKE LOVE LONGER
RIGHT WHEN YOU'RE ABOUT TO COME, YOU CONTRACT THE MUSCLE YOU USE TO STOP YOUR URINE STREAM WHEN YOU PEE
THAT MUSCLE IS THE PERINEUM
YOU CONTRACT IT REALLY, REALLY, REALLY, REALLY HARD
IT STOPS YOUR EJACULATION, BUT YOU STILL HAVE AN ORGASM
AND IT ALLOWS YOU TO CONTINUE FUCKING WITH THE SAME LEVEL OF DESIRE AND THE SAME ERECTION

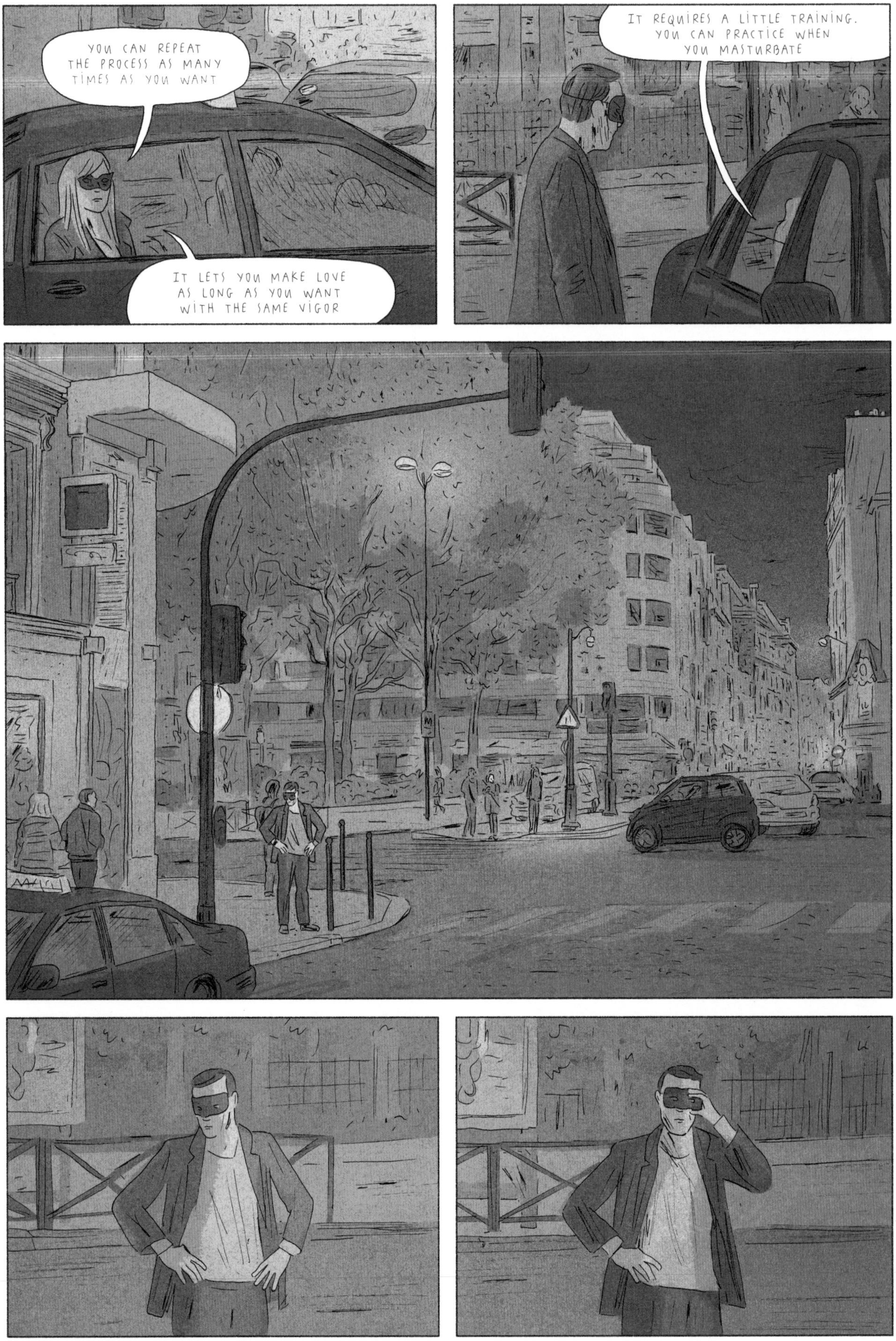
YOU CAN REPEAT THE PROCESS AS MANY TIMES AS YOU WANT
IT LETS YOU MAKE LOVE AS LONG AS YOU WANT WITH THE SAME VIGOR
IT REQUIRES A LITTLE TRAINING. YOU CAN PRACTICE WHEN YOU MASTURBATE

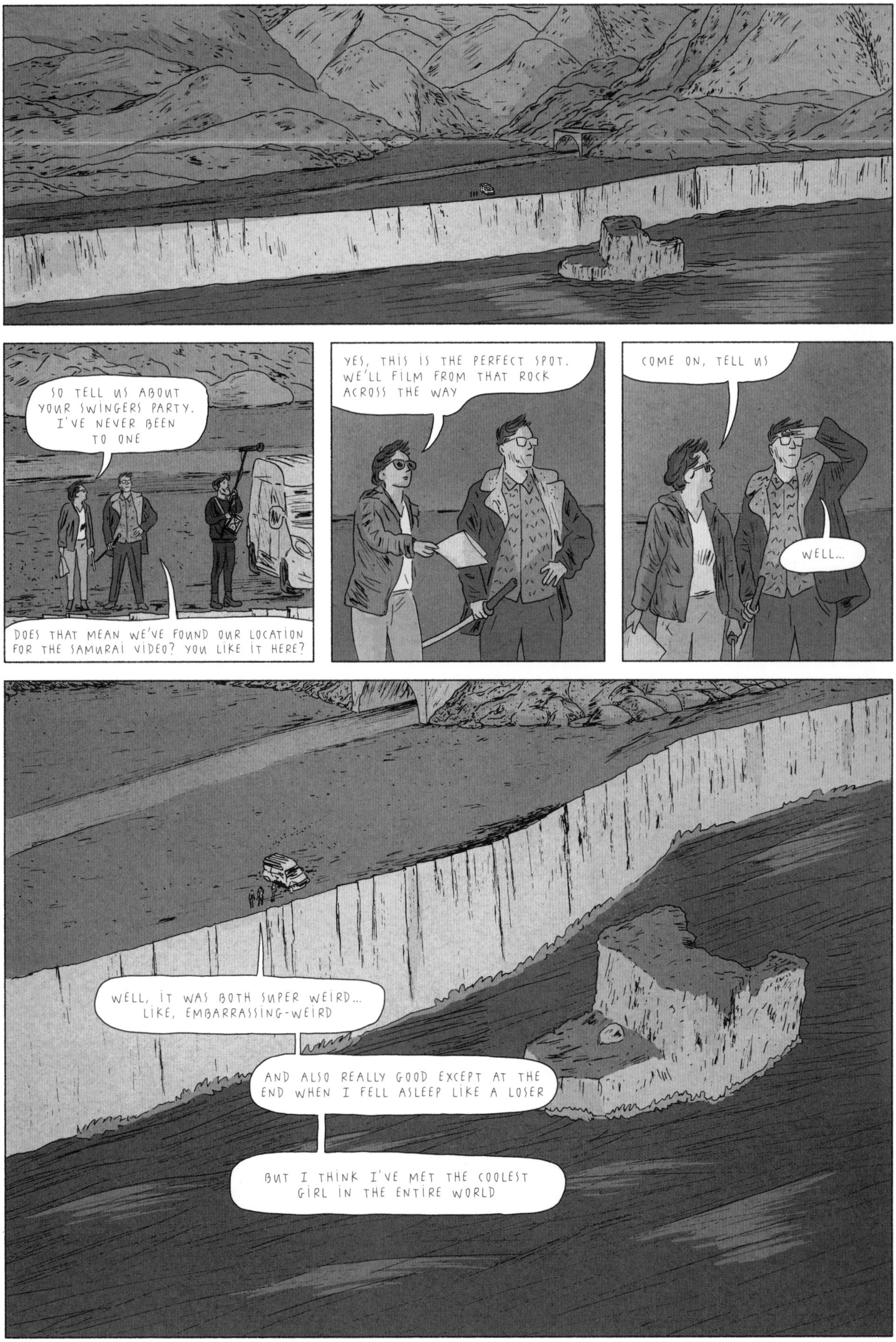

SO TELL US ABOUT YOUR SWINGERS PARTY. I'VE NEVER BEEN TO ONE
DOES THAT MEAN WE'VE FOUND OUR LOCATION FOR THE SAMURAI VIDEO? YOU LIKE IT HERE?
YES, THIS IS THE PERFECT SPOT. WE'LL FILM FROM THAT ROCK ACROSS THE WAY
COME ON, TELL US
WELL...
WELL, IT WAS BOTH SUPER WEIRD... LIKE, EMBARRASSING-WEIRD
AND ALSO REALLY GOOD EXCEPT AT THE END WHEN I FELL ASLEEP LIKE A LOSER
BUT I THINK I'VE MET THE COOLEST GIRL IN THE ENTIRE WORLD

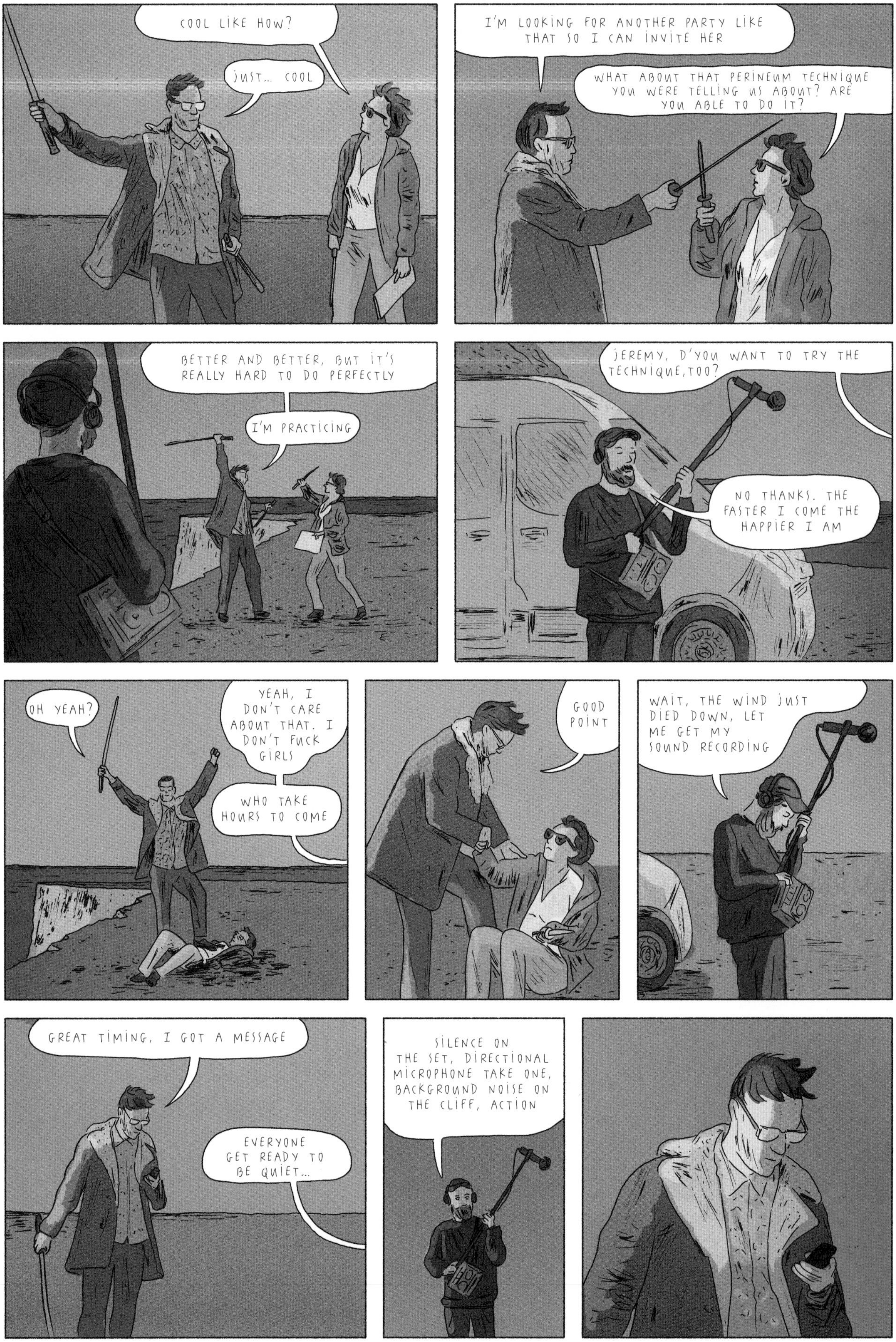
COOL LIKE HOW?
JUST... COOL
I'M LOOKING FOR ANOTHER PARTY LIKE THAT SO I CAN INVITE HER
WHAT ABOUT THAT PERINEUM TECHNIQUE YOU WERE TELLING US ABOUT? ARE YOU ABLE TO DO IT?
BETTER AND BETTER, BUT IT'S REALLY HARD TO DO PERFECTLY
I'M PRACTICING
JEREMY, D'YOU WANT TO TRY THE TECHNIQUE, TOO?
NO THANKS. THE FASTER I COME THE HAPPIER I AM
OH YEAH?
YEAH, I DON'T CARE ABOUT THAT. I DON'T FUCK GIRLS
WHO TAKE HOURS TO COME
GOOD POINT
WAIT, THE WIND JUST DIED DOWN, LET ME GET MY SOUND RECORDING
GREAT TIMING, I GOT A MESSAGE
EVERYONE GET READY TO BE QUIET...
SILENCE ON THE SET, DIRECTIONAL MICROPHONE TAKE ONE, BACKGROUND NOISE ON THE CLIFF, ACTION

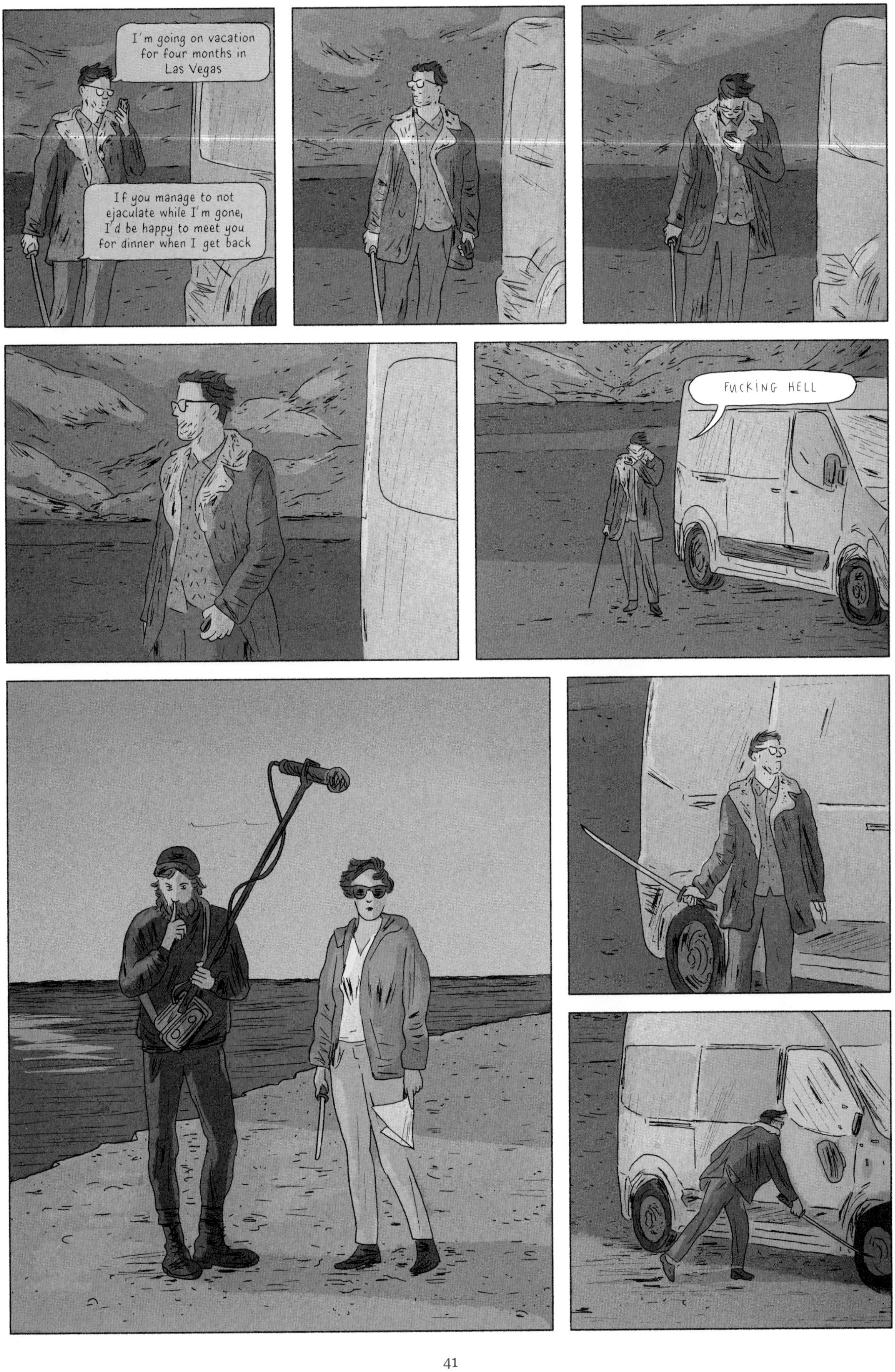
I'm going on vacation for four months in Las Vegas
If you manage to not ejaculate while I'm gone, I'd be happy to meet you for dinner when I get back
FUCKING HELL

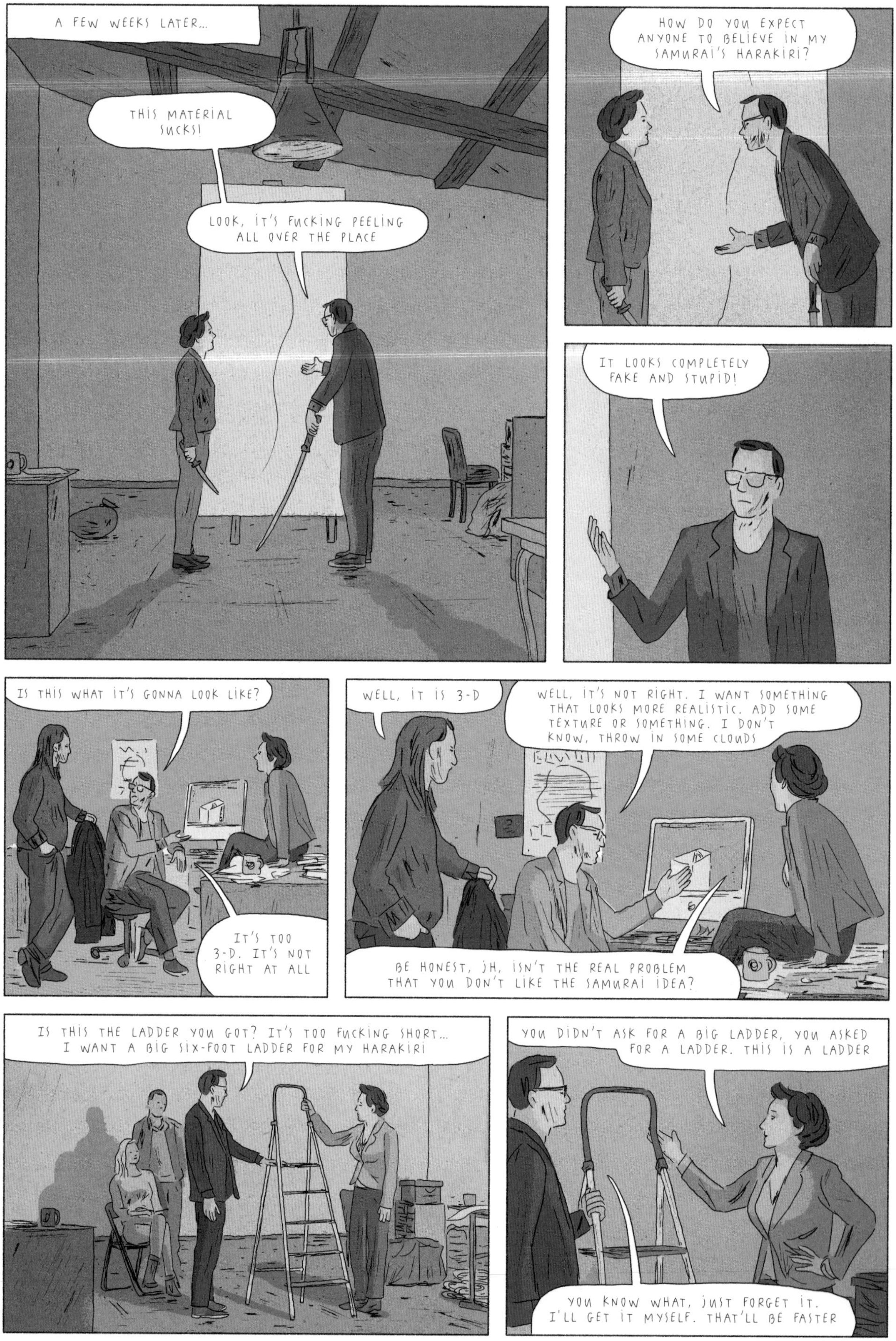
A FEW WEEKS LATER...
THIS MATERIAL SUCKS!
LOOK, IT'S FUCKING PEELING ALL OVER THE PLACE
HOW DO YOU EXPECT ANYONE TO BELIEVE IN MY SAMURAI'S HARAKIRI?
IT LOOKS COMPLETELY FAKE AND STUPID!
IS THIS WHAT IT'S GONNA LOOK LIKE?
IT'S TOO 3-D. IT'S NOT RIGHT AT ALL
WELL, IT IS 3-D
WELL, IT'S NOT RIGHT. I WANT SOMETHING THAT LOOKS MORE REALISTIC. ADD SOME TEXTURE OR SOMETHING. I DON'T KNOW, THROW IN SOME CLOUDS
BE HONEST, JH, ISN'T THE REAL PROBLEM THAT YOU DON'T LIKE THE SAMURAI IDEA?
IS THIS THE LADDER YOU GOT? IT'S TOO FUCKING SHORT... I WANT A BIG SIX-FOOT LADDER FOR MY HARAKIRI
YOU DIDN'T ASK FOR A BIG LADDER, YOU ASKED FOR A LADDER. THIS IS A LADDER
YOU KNOW WHAT, JUST FORGET IT. I'LL GET IT MYSELF. THAT'LL BE FASTER

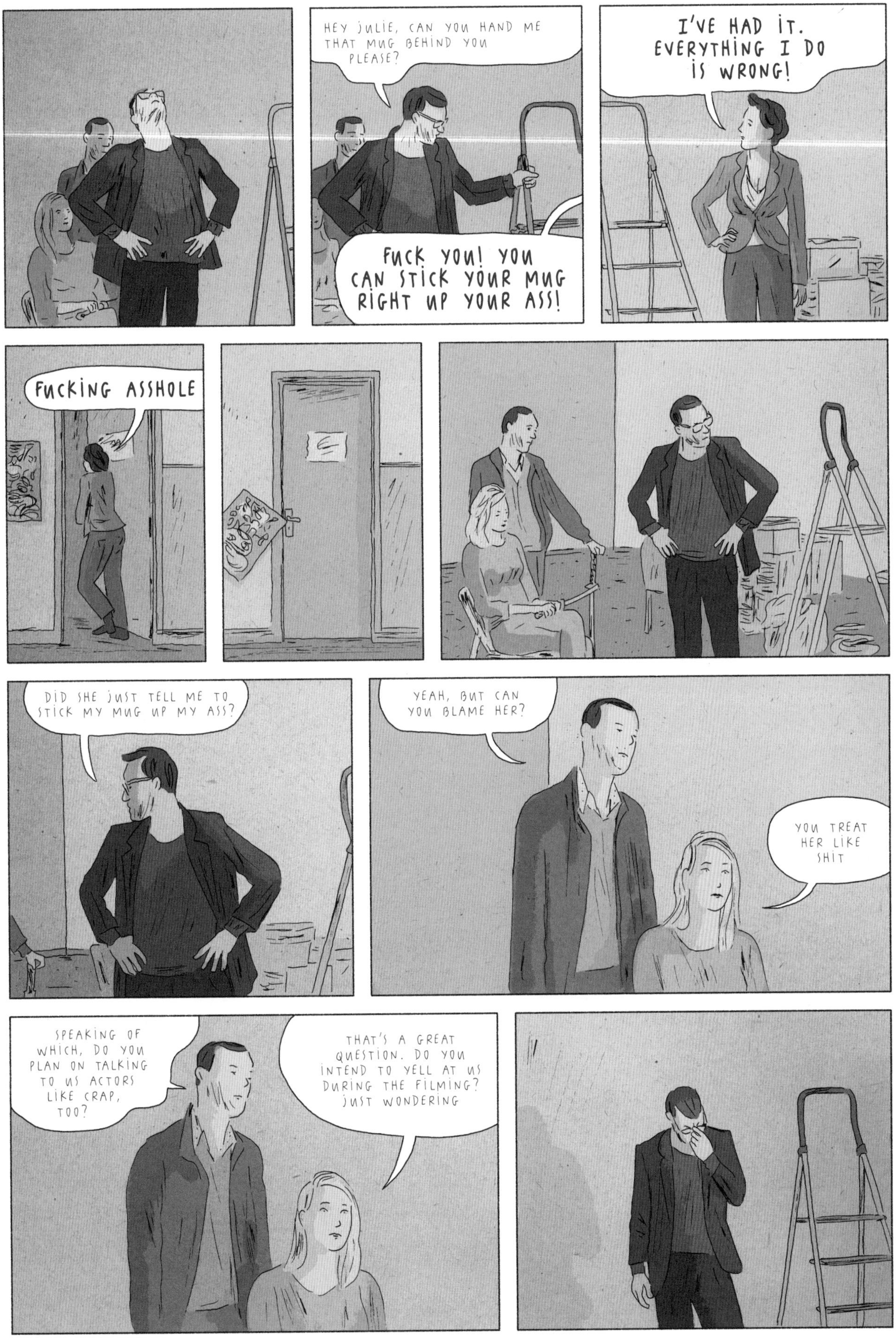
HEY JULIE, CAN YOU HAND ME THAT MUG BEHIND YOU PLEASE?
FUCK YOU! YOU CAN STICK YOUR MUG RIGHT UP YOUR ASS!
I'VE HAD IT. EVERYTHING I DO IS WRONG!
FUCKING ASSHOLE
DID SHE JUST TELL ME TO STICK MY MUG UP MY ASS?
YEAH, BUT CAN YOU BLAME HER?
YOU TREAT HER LIKE SHIT
SPEAKING OF WHICH, DO YOU PLAN ON TALKING TO US ACTORS LIKE CRAP, TOO?
THAT'S A GREAT QUESTION. DO YOU INTEND TO YELL AT US DURING THE FILMING? JUST WONDERING

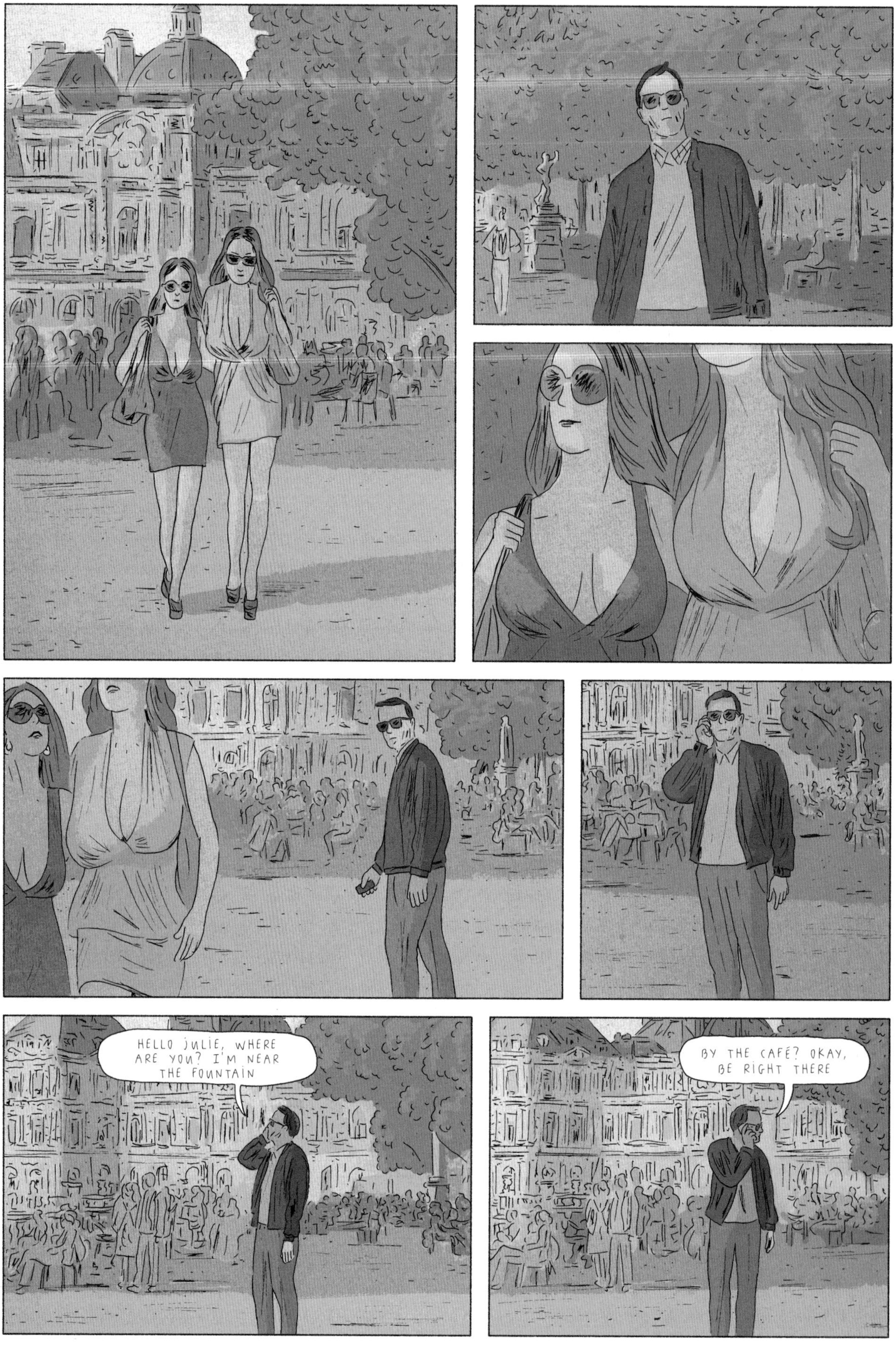
HELLO JULIE, WHERE ARE YOU? I'M NEAR THE FOUNTAIN
BY THE CAFÉ? OKAY, BE RIGHT THERE

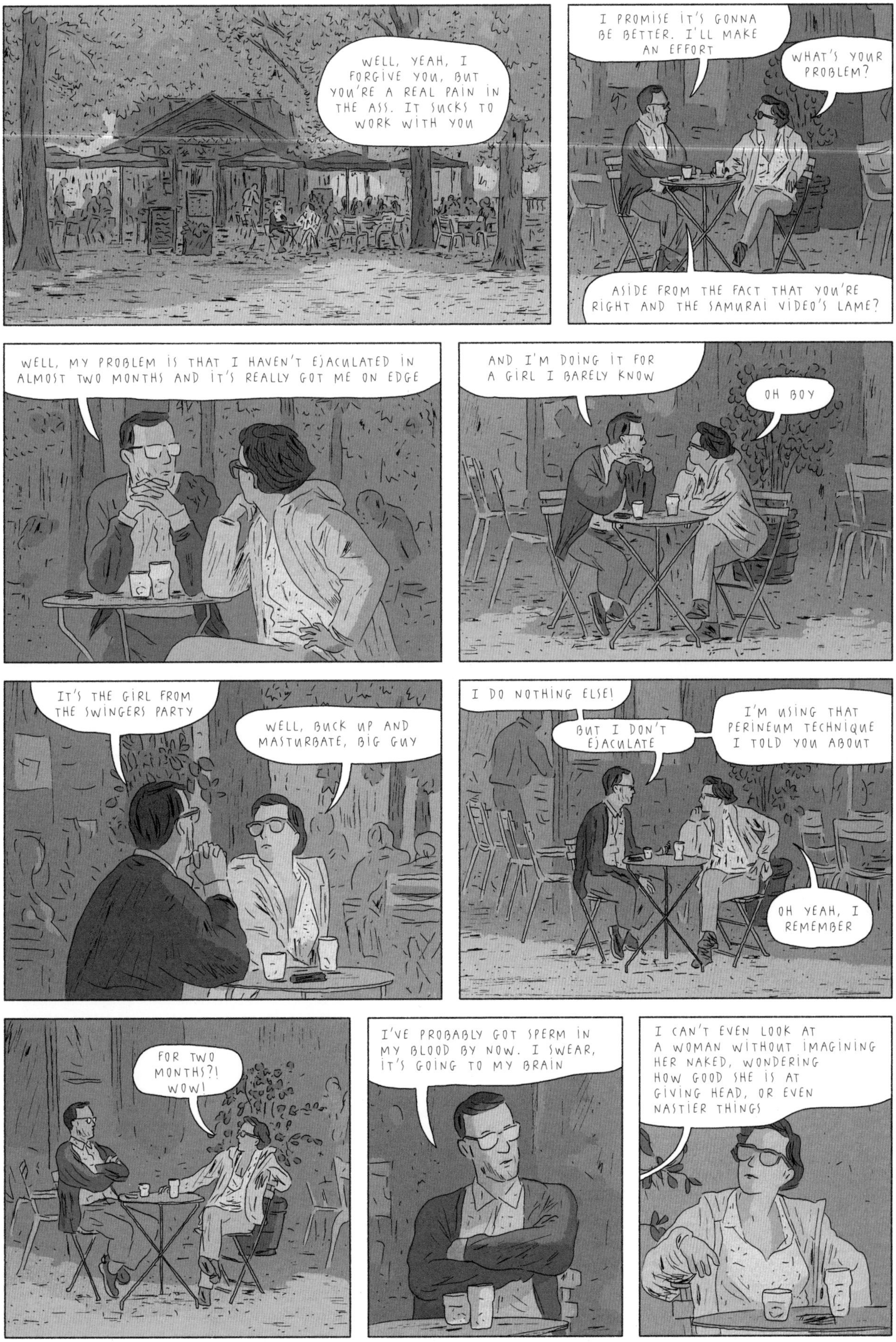
WELL, YEAH, I FORGIVE YOU, BUT YOU'RE A REAL PAIN IN THE ASS. IT SUCKS TO WORK WITH YOU
I PROMISE IT'S GONNA BE BETTER. I'LL MAKE AN EFFORT
WHAT'S YOUR PROBLEM?
ASIDE FROM THE FACT THAT YOU'RE RIGHT AND THE SAMURAI VIDEO'S LAME?
WELL, MY PROBLEM IS THAT I HAVEN'T EJACULATED IN ALMOST TWO MONTHS AND IT'S REALLY GOT ME ON EDGE
AND I'M DOING IT FOR A GIRL I BARELY KNOW
OH BOY
IT'S THE GIRL FROM THE SWINGERS PARTY
WELL, BUCK UP AND MASTURBATE, BIG GUY
I DO NOTHING ELSE!
BUT I DON'T EJACULATE
I'M USING THAT PERINEUM TECHNIQUE I TOLD YOU ABOUT
OH YEAH, I REMEMBER
FOR TWO MONTHS?! WOW!
I'VE PROBABLY GOT SPERM IN MY BLOOD BY NOW. I SWEAR, IT'S GOING TO MY BRAIN
I CAN'T EVEN LOOK AT A WOMAN WITHOUT IMAGINING HER NAKED, WONDERING HOW GOOD SHE IS AT GIVING HEAD, OR EVEN NASTIER THINGS

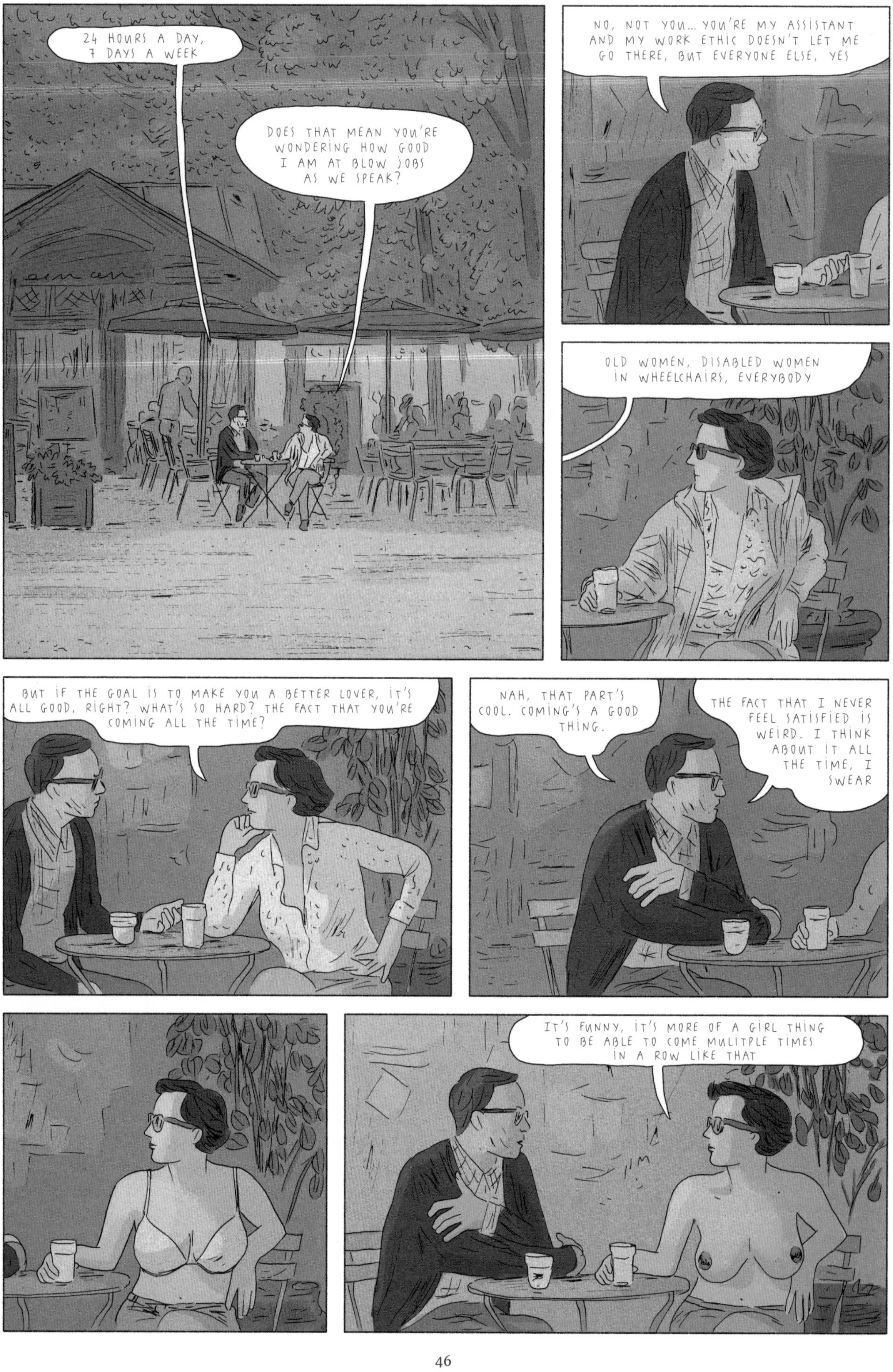
24 HOURS A DAY, 7 DAYS A WEEK
DOES THAT MEAN YOU'RE WONDERING HOW GOOD I AM AT BLOW JOBS AS WE SPEAK?
NO, NOT YOU... YOU'RE MY ASSISTANT AND MY WORK ETHIC DOESN'T LET ME GO THERE, BUT EVERYONE ELSE, YES
OLD WOMEN, DISABLED WOMEN IN WHEELCHAIRS, EVERYBODY
BUT IF THE GOAL IS TO MAKE YOU A BETTER LOVER, IT'S ALL GOOD, RIGHT? WHAT'S SO HARD? THE FACT THAT YOU'RE COMING ALL THE TIME?
NAH, THAT PART'S COOL. COMING'S A GOOD THING.
THE FACT THAT I NEVER FEEL SATISFIED IS WEIRD. I THINK ABOUT IT ALL THE TIME, I SWEAR
IT'S FUNNY, IT'S MORE OF A GIRL THING TO BE ABLE TO COME MULITPLE TIMES IN A ROW LIKE THAT

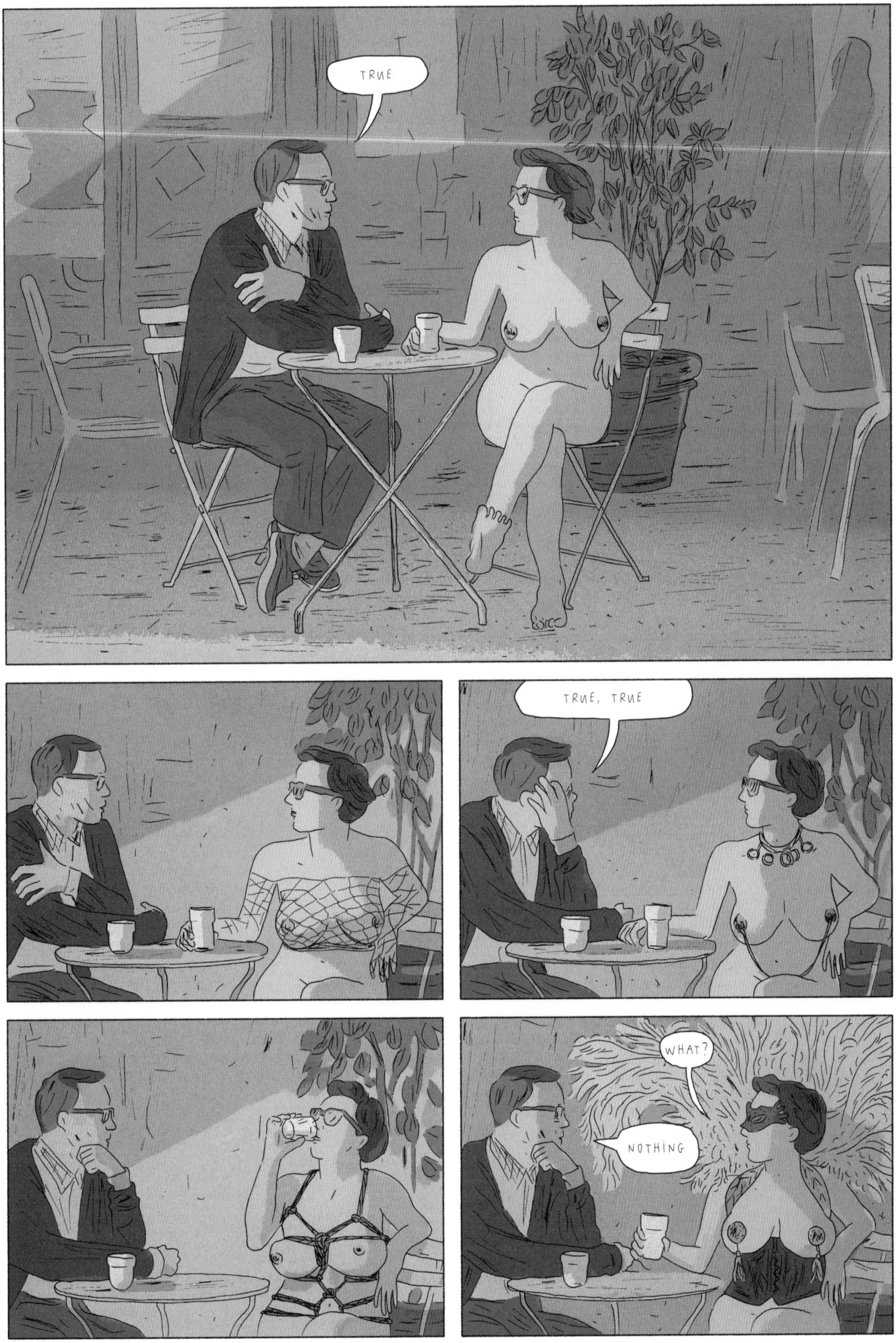
TRUE
TRUE, TRUE
WHAT?
NOTHING

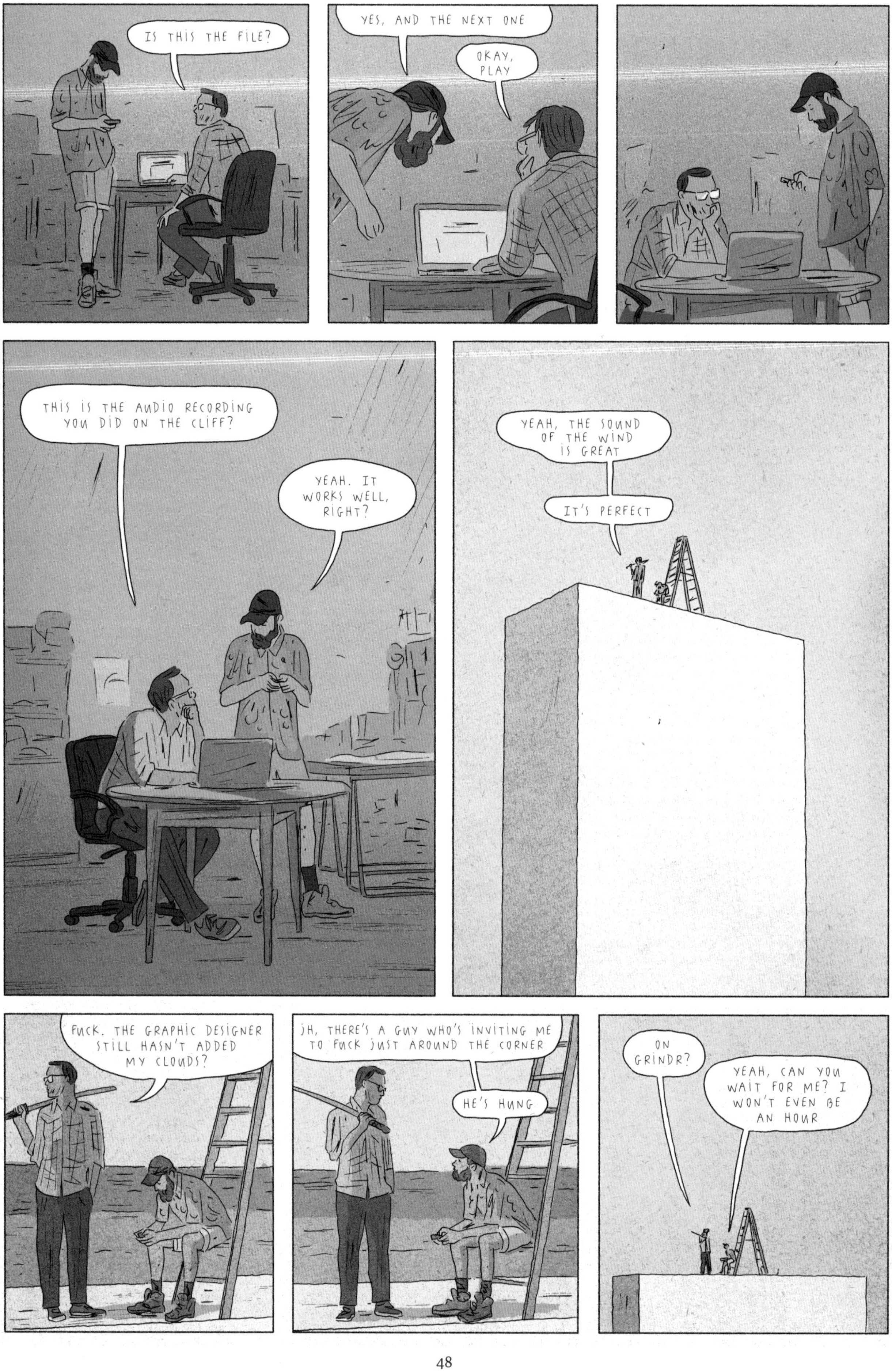
IS THIS THE FILE?
YES, AND THE NEXT ONE
OKAY, PLAY
THIS IS THE AUDIO RECORDING YOU DID ON THE CLIFF?
YEAH. IT WORKS WELL, RIGHT?
YEAH, THE SOUND OF THE WIND IS GREAT
IT'S PERFECT
FUCK. THE GRAPHIC DESIGNER STILL HASN'T ADDED MY CLOUDS?
JH, THERE'S A GUY WHO'S INVITING ME TO FUCK JUST AROUND THE CORNER
HE'S HUNG
ON GRINDR?
YEAH, CAN YOU WAIT FOR ME? I WON'T EVEN BE AN HOUR

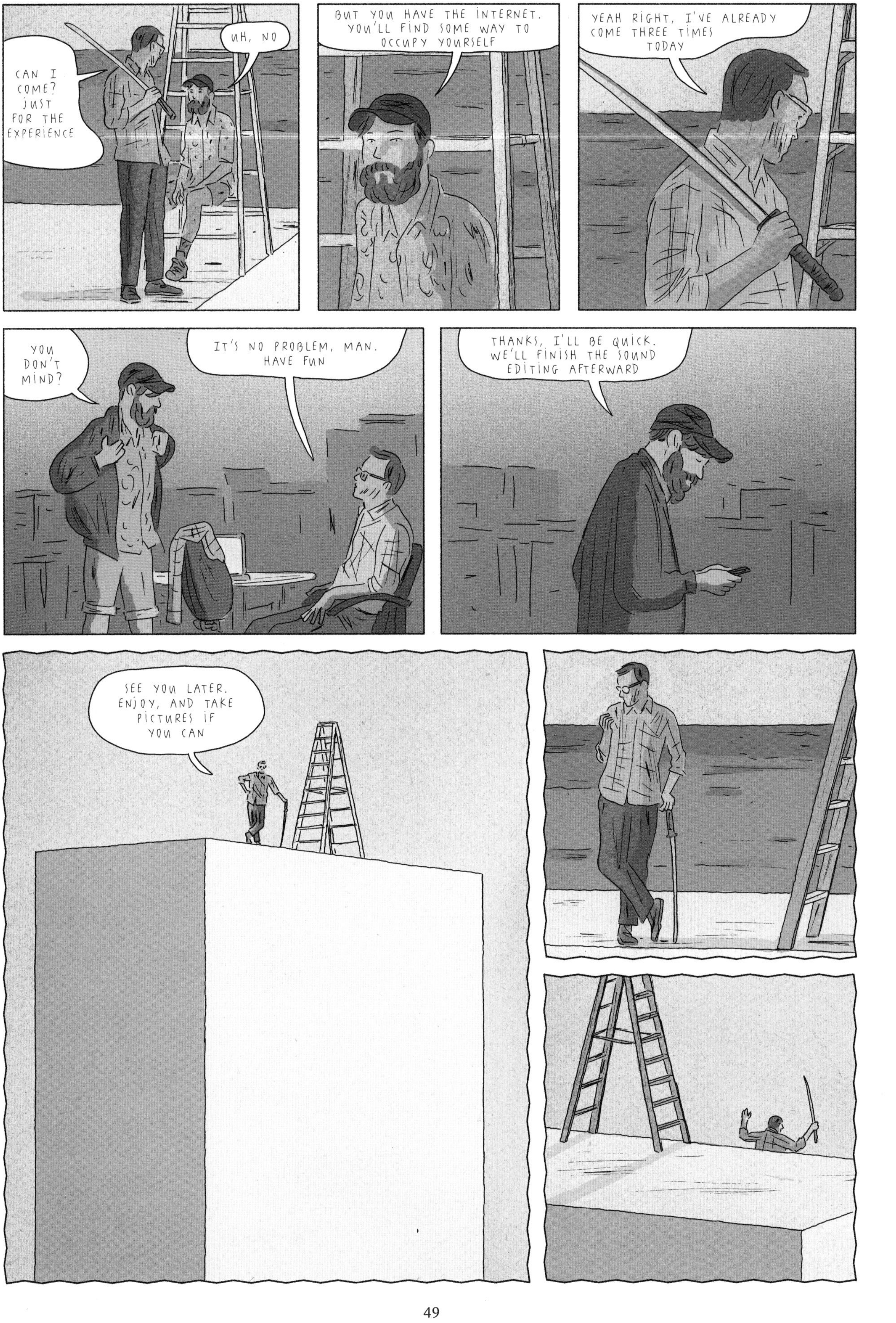
CAN I COME? JUST FOR THE EXPERIENCE
UH, NO
BUT YOU HAVE THE INTERNET. YOU'LL FIND SOME WAY TO OCCUPY YOURSELF
YEAH RIGHT, I'VE ALREADY COME THREE TIMES TODAY
YOU DON'T MIND?
IT'S NO PROBLEM, MAN. HAVE FUN
THANKS, I'LL BE QUICK. WE'LL FINISH THE SOUND EDITING AFTERWARD
SEE YOU LATER. ENJOY, AND TAKE PICTURES IF YOU CAN

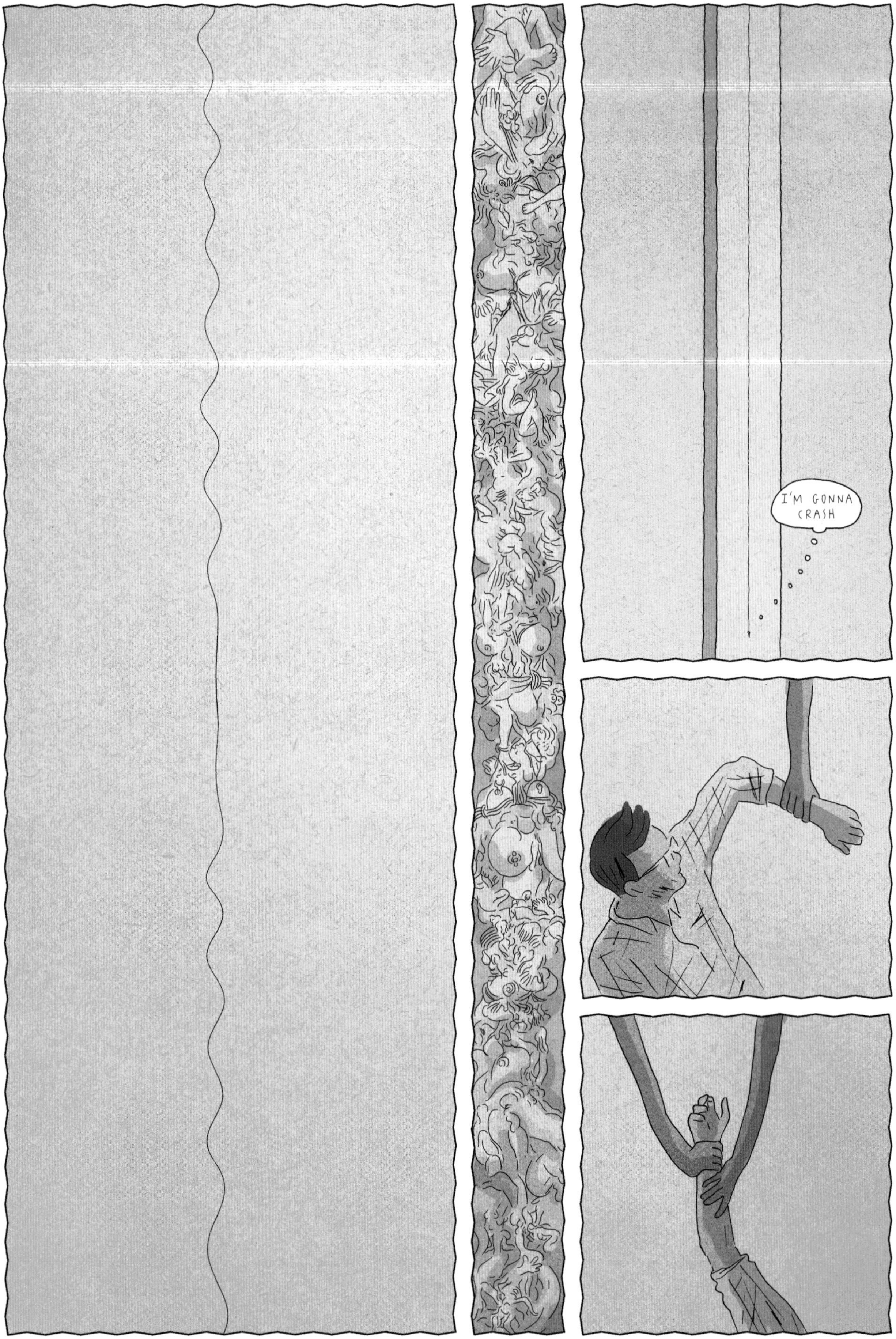
I'M GONNA CRASH

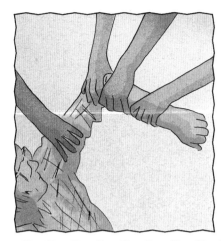
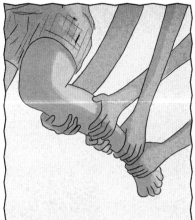

YEAH, HI JEREMY

I JUST HAD A REVELATION. LET'S SCRATCH THE SAMURAI VIDEO. WE'LL DO ANOTHER VIDEO INSTEAD

A VIDEO ABOUT YOUR INTERNET GIRLFRIEND? YOU SURE ABOUT THAT?

YEAH, KINDA LIKE A MUSE...

D'YOU WANNA KEEP THE FINGERS VIDEO?

WAIT, CALM DOWN. THAT MAKES FIVE VIDEOS. YOU ONLY WANTED TWO BEFORE

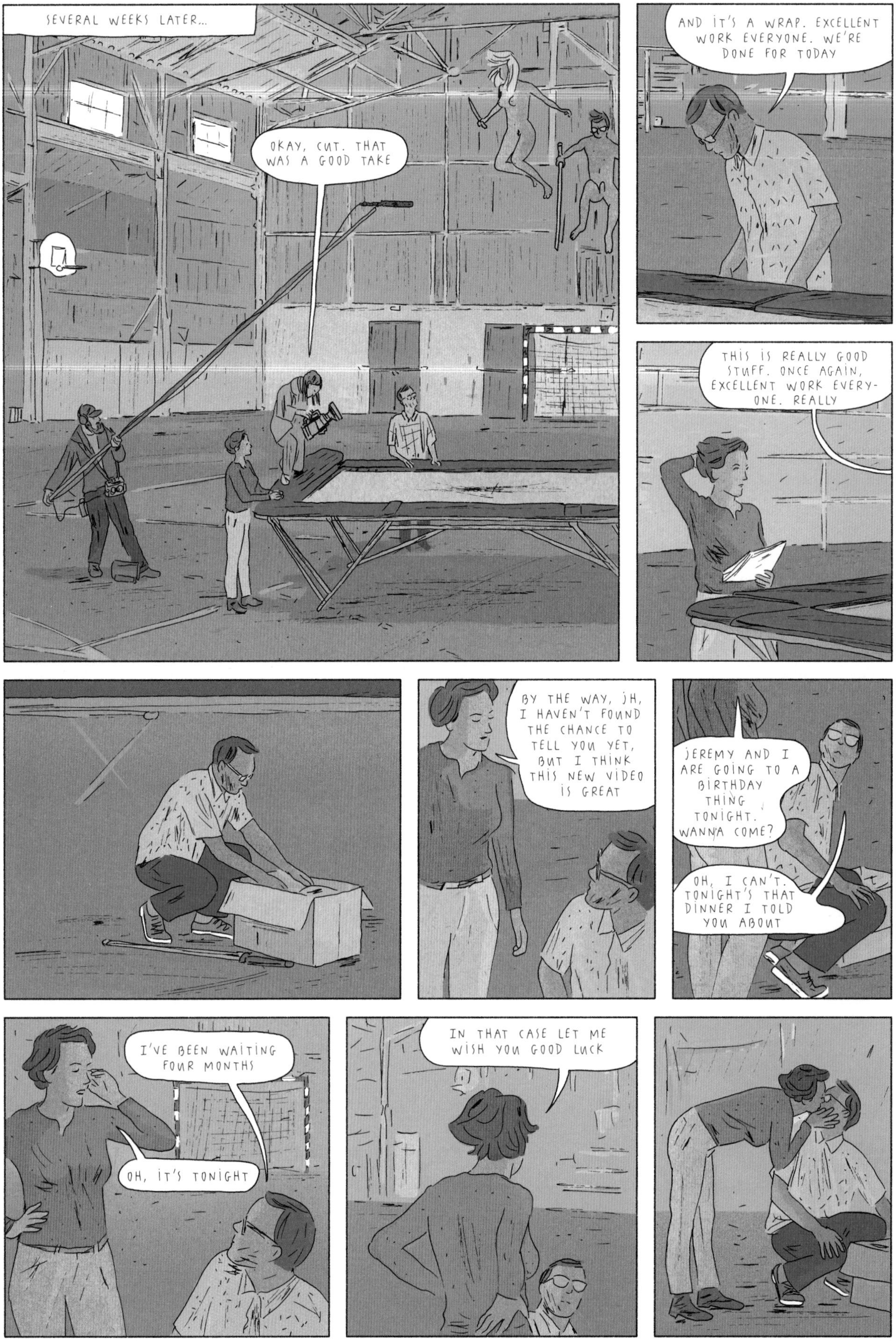
SEVERAL WEEKS LATER...
OKAY, CUT. THAT WAS A GOOD TAKE
AND IT'S A WRAP. EXCELLENT WORK EVERYONE. WE'RE DONE FOR TODAY
THIS IS REALLY GOOD STUFF. ONCE AGAIN, EXCELLENT WORK EVERY-ONE. REALLY
BY THE WAY, JH, I HAVEN'T FOUND THE CHANCE TO TELL YOU YET, BUT I THINK THIS NEW VIDEO IS GREAT
JEREMY AND I ARE GOING TO A BIRTHDAY THING TONIGHT. WANNA COME?
OH, I CAN'T. TONIGHT'S THAT DINNER I TOLD YOU ABOUT
I'VE BEEN WAITING FOUR MONTHS
OH, IT'S TONIGHT
IN THAT CASE LET ME WISH YOU GOOD LUCK

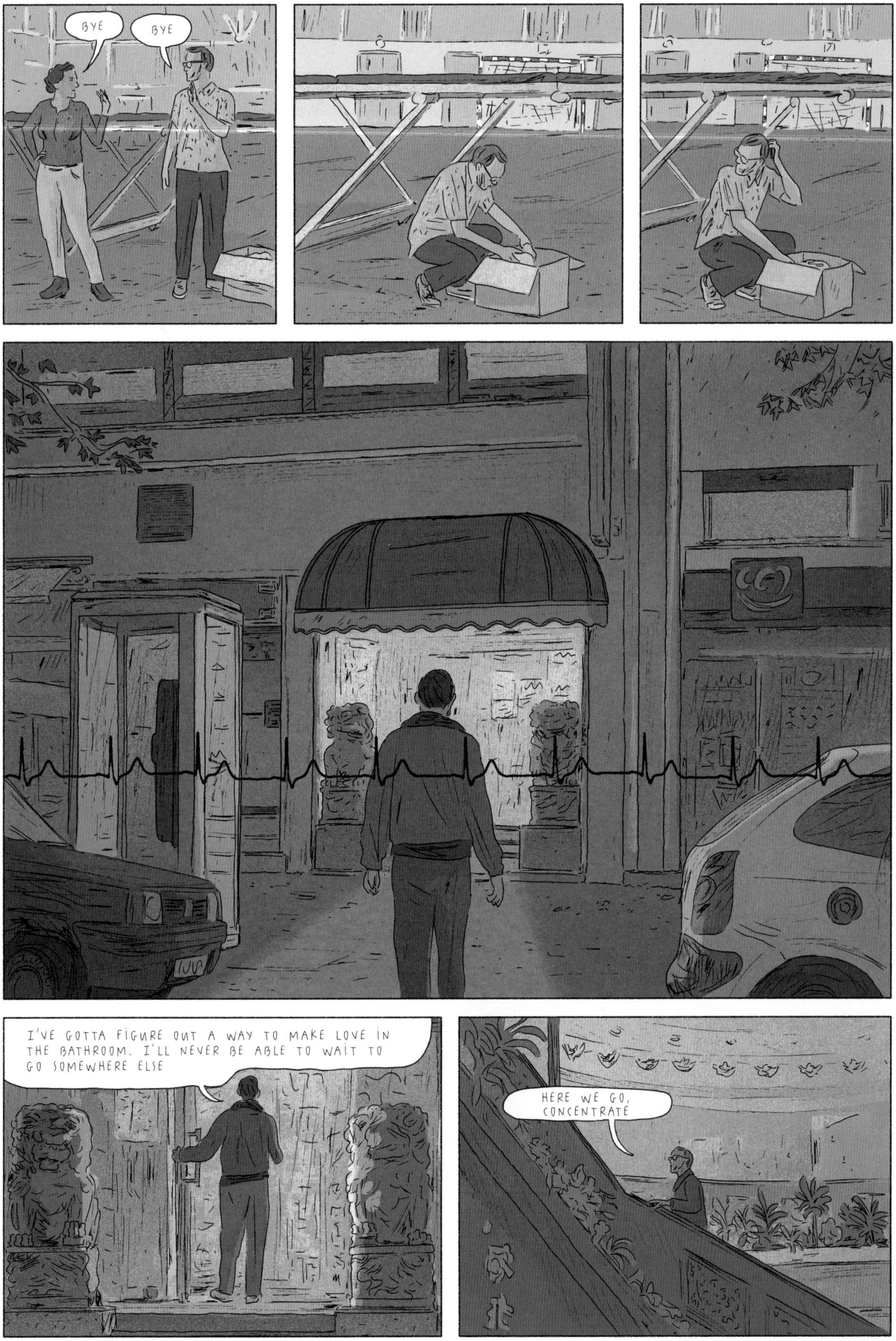
BYE
BYE
I'VE GOTTA FIGURE OUT A WAY TO MAKE LOVE IN THE BATHROOM. I'LL NEVER BE ABLE TO WAIT TO GO SOMEWHERE ELSE
HERE WE GO, CONCENTRATE

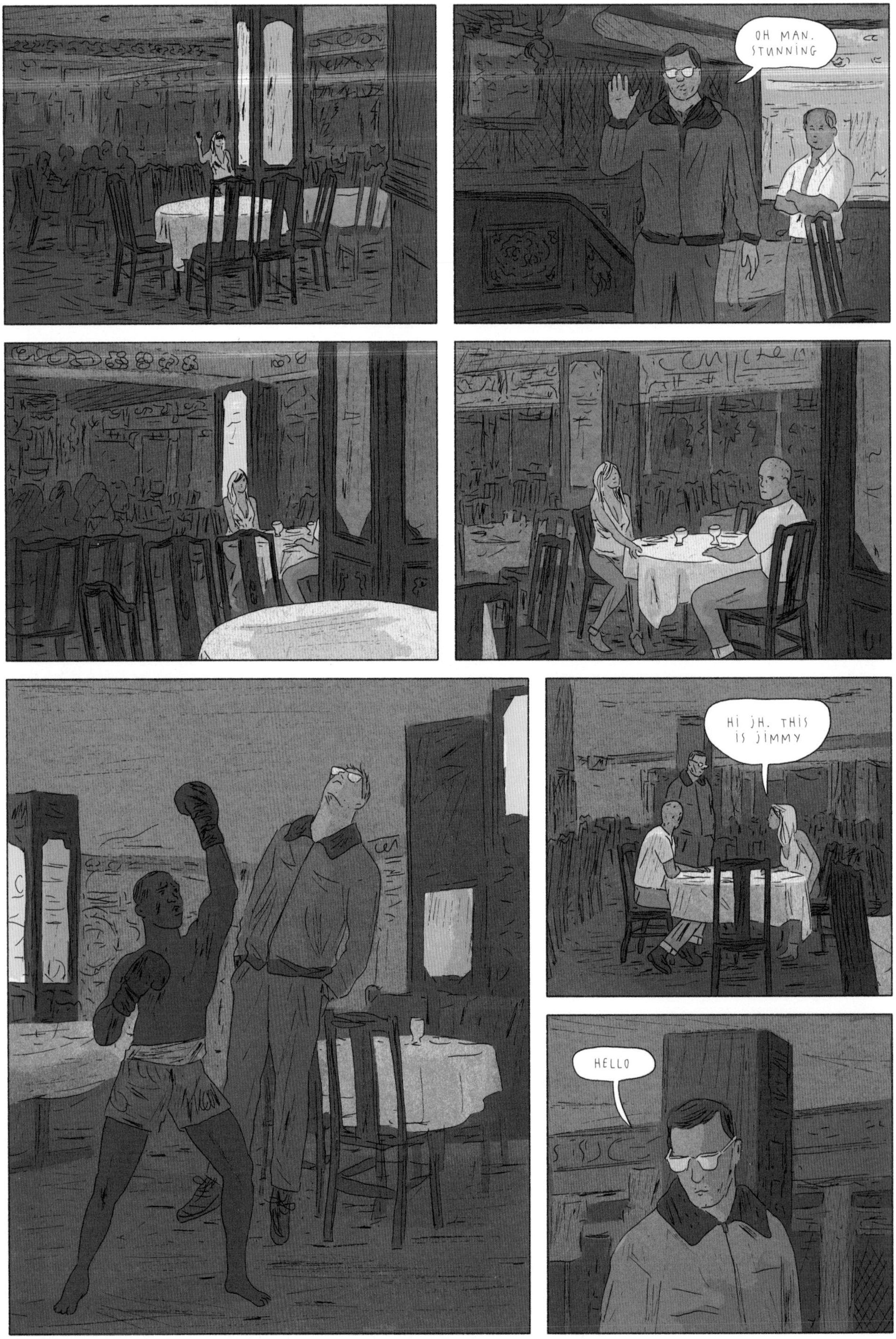
OH MAN. STUNNING
HI JH. THIS IS JIMMY
HELLO

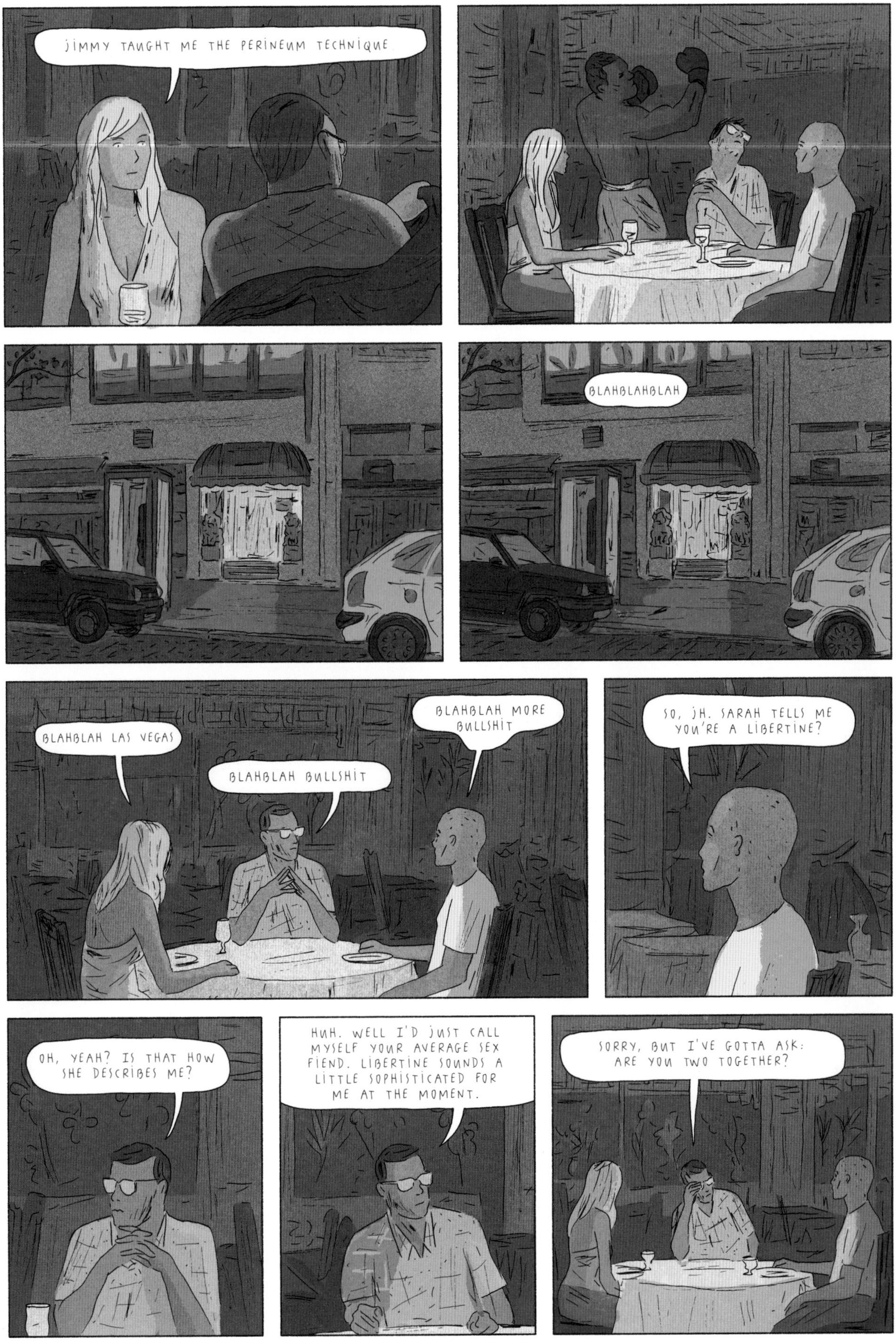
JIMMY TAUGHT ME THE PERINEUM TECHNIQUE
BLAHBLAHBLAH
BLAHBLAH LAS VEGAS
BLAHBLAH BULLSHIT
BLAHBLAH MORE BULLSHIT
SO, JH. SARAH TELLS ME YOU'RE A LIBERTINE?
OH, YEAH? IS THAT HOW SHE DESCRIBES ME?
HUH. WELL I'D JUST CALL MYSELF YOUR AVERAGE SEX FIEND. LIBERTINE SOUNDS A LITTLE SOPHISTICATED FOR ME AT THE MOMENT.
SORRY, BUT I'VE GOTTA ASK: ARE YOU TWO TOGETHER?

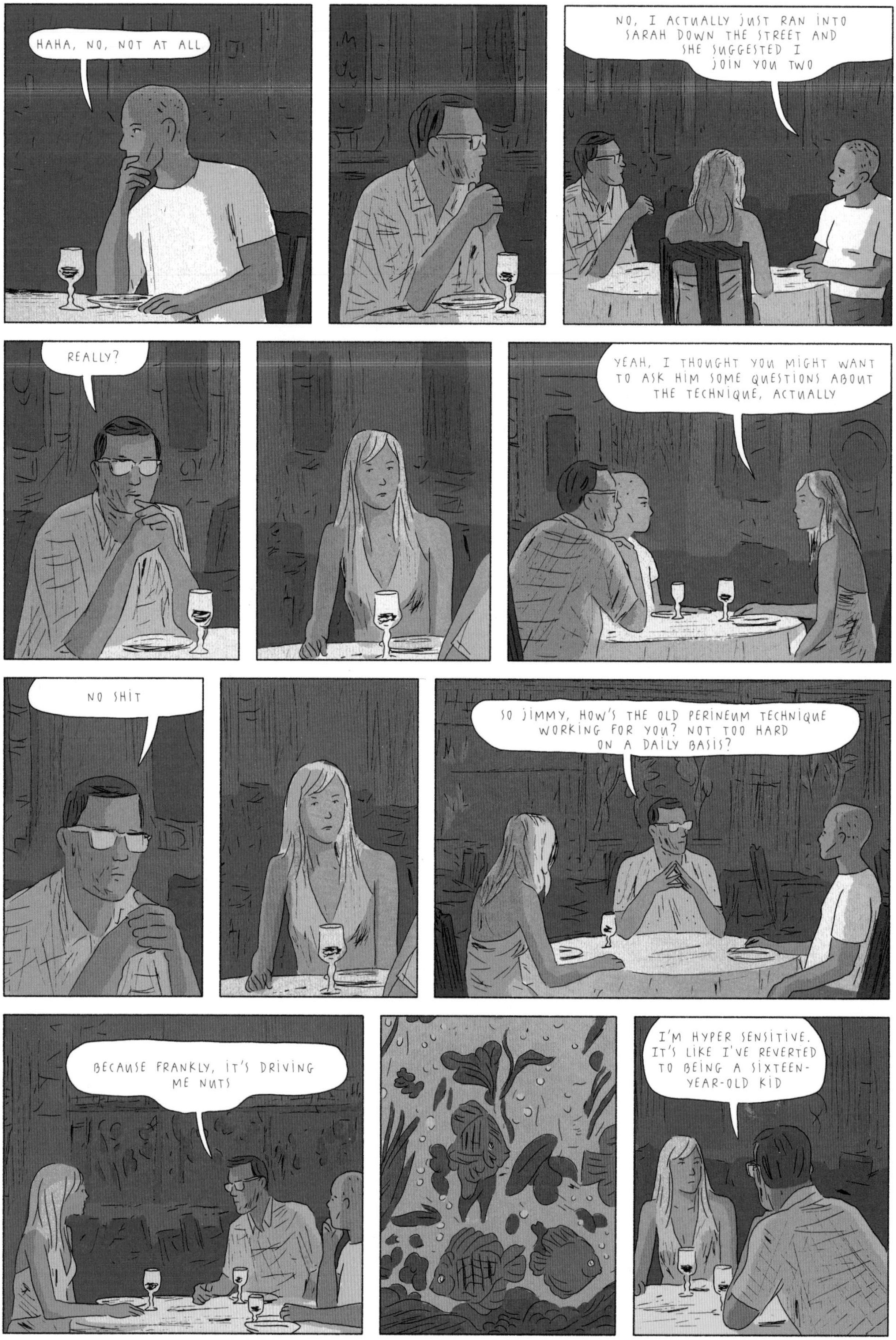
HAHA, NO, NOT AT ALL
NO, I ACTUALLY JUST RAN INTO SARAH DOWN THE STREET AND SHE SUGGESTED I JOIN YOU TWO
REALLY?
YEAH, I THOUGHT YOU MIGHT WANT TO ASK HIM SOME QUESTIONS ABOUT THE TECHNIQUE, ACTUALLY
NO SHIT
SO JIMMY, HOW'S THE OLD PERINEUM TECHNIQUE WORKING FOR YOU? NOT TOO HARD ON A DAILY BASIS?
BECAUSE FRANKLY, IT'S DRIVING ME NUTS
I'M HYPER SENSITIVE. IT'S LIKE I'VE REVERTED TO BEING A SIXTEEN-YEAR-OLD KID

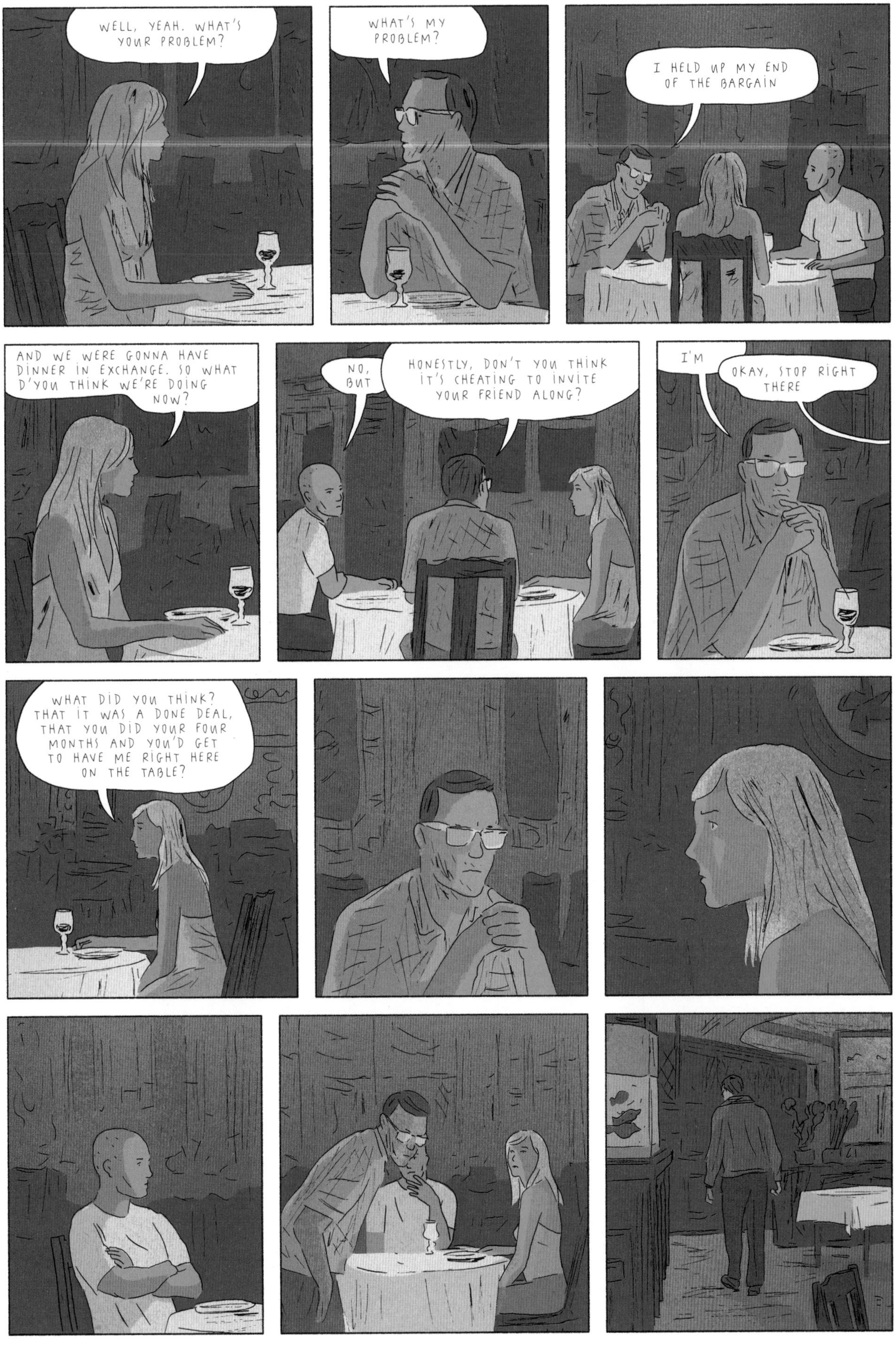
WELL, YEAH. WHAT'S YOUR PROBLEM?
WHAT'S MY PROBLEM?
I HELD UP MY END OF THE BARGAIN
AND WE WERE GONNA HAVE DINNER IN EXCHANGE. SO WHAT D'YOU THINK WE'RE DOING NOW?
NO, BUT
HONESTLY, DON'T YOU THINK IT'S CHEATING TO INVITE YOUR FRIEND ALONG?
I'M
OKAY, STOP RIGHT THERE
WHAT DID YOU THINK? THAT IT WAS A DONE DEAL, THAT YOU DID YOUR FOUR MONTHS AND YOU'D GET TO HAVE ME RIGHT HERE ON THE TABLE?

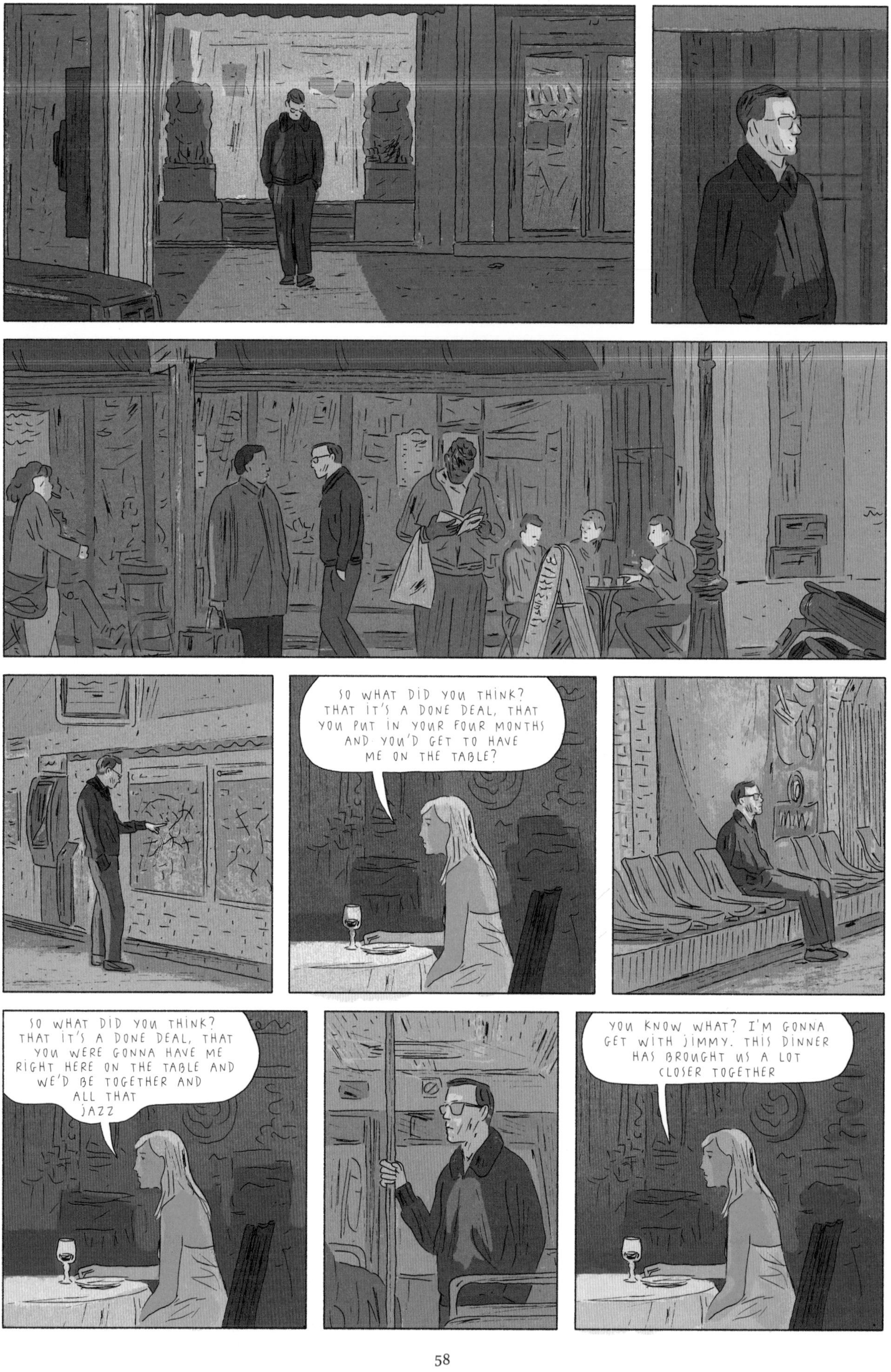
SO WHAT DID YOU THINK? THAT IT'S A DONE DEAL, THAT YOU PUT IN YOUR FOUR MONTHS AND YOU'D GET TO HAVE ME ON THE TABLE?
SO WHAT DID YOU THINK? THAT IT'S A DONE DEAL, THAT YOU WERE GONNA HAVE ME RIGHT HERE ON THE TABLE AND WE'D BE TOGETHER AND ALL THAT JAZZ
YOU KNOW WHAT? I'M GONNA GET WITH JIMMY. THIS DINNER HAS BROUGHT US A LOT CLOSER TOGETHER

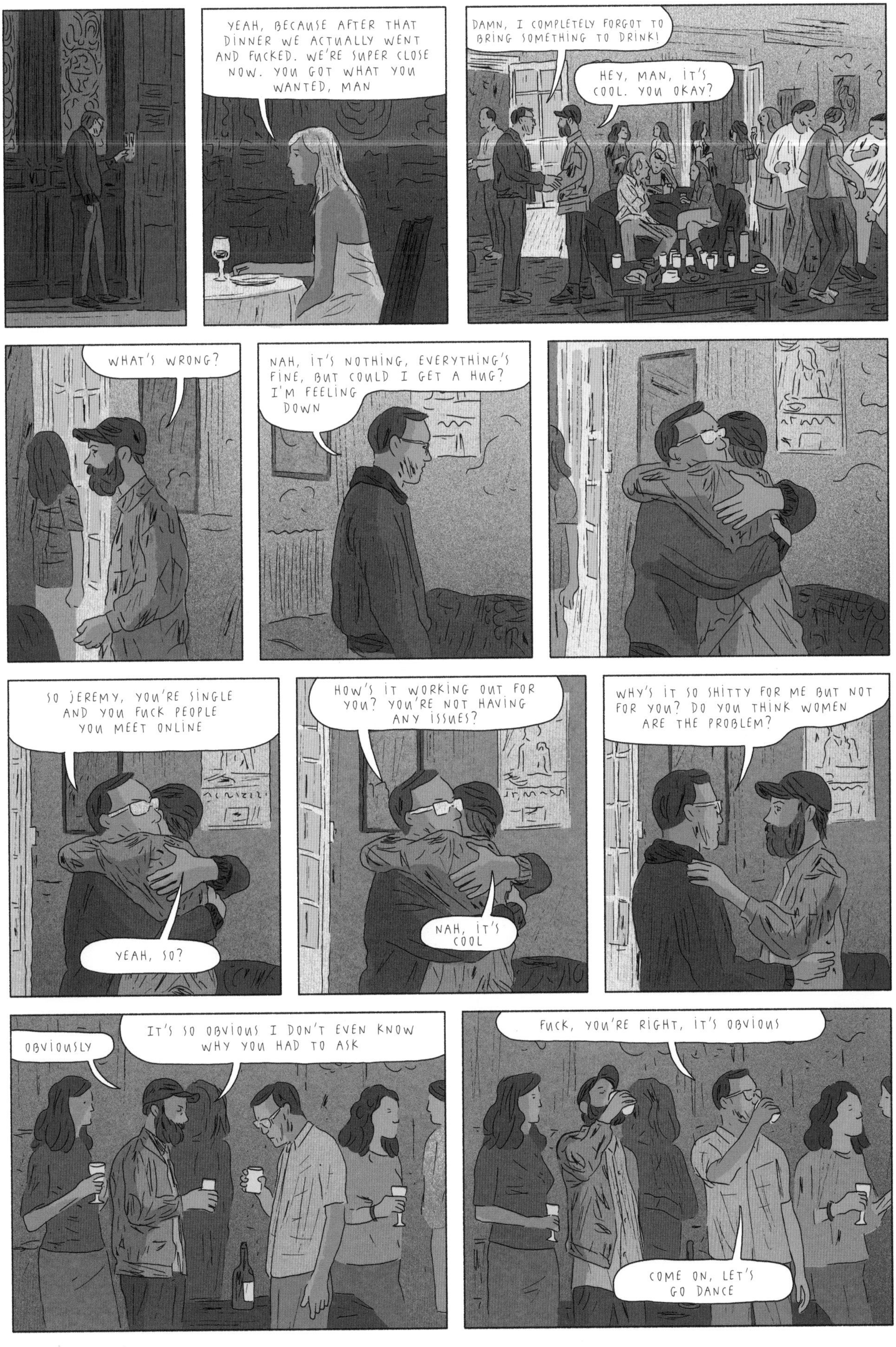
YEAH, BECAUSE AFTER THAT DINNER WE ACTUALLY WENT AND FUCKED. WE'RE SUPER CLOSE NOW. YOU GOT WHAT YOU WANTED, MAN
DAMN, I COMPLETELY FORGOT TO BRING SOMETHING TO DRINK!
HEY, MAN, IT'S COOL. YOU OKAY?
WHAT'S WRONG?
NAH, IT'S NOTHING, EVERYTHING'S FINE, BUT COULD I GET A HUG? I'M FEELING DOWN
SO JEREMY, YOU'RE SINGLE AND YOU FUCK PEOPLE YOU MEET ONLINE
YEAH, SO?
HOW'S IT WORKING OUT FOR YOU? YOU'RE NOT HAVING ANY ISSUES?
NAH, IT'S COOL
WHY'S IT SO SHITTY FOR ME BUT NOT FOR YOU? DO YOU THINK WOMEN ARE THE PROBLEM?
OBVIOUSLY
IT'S SO OBVIOUS I DON'T EVEN KNOW WHY YOU HAD TO ASK
FUCK, YOU'RE RIGHT, IT'S OBVIOUS
COME ON, LET'S GO DANCE

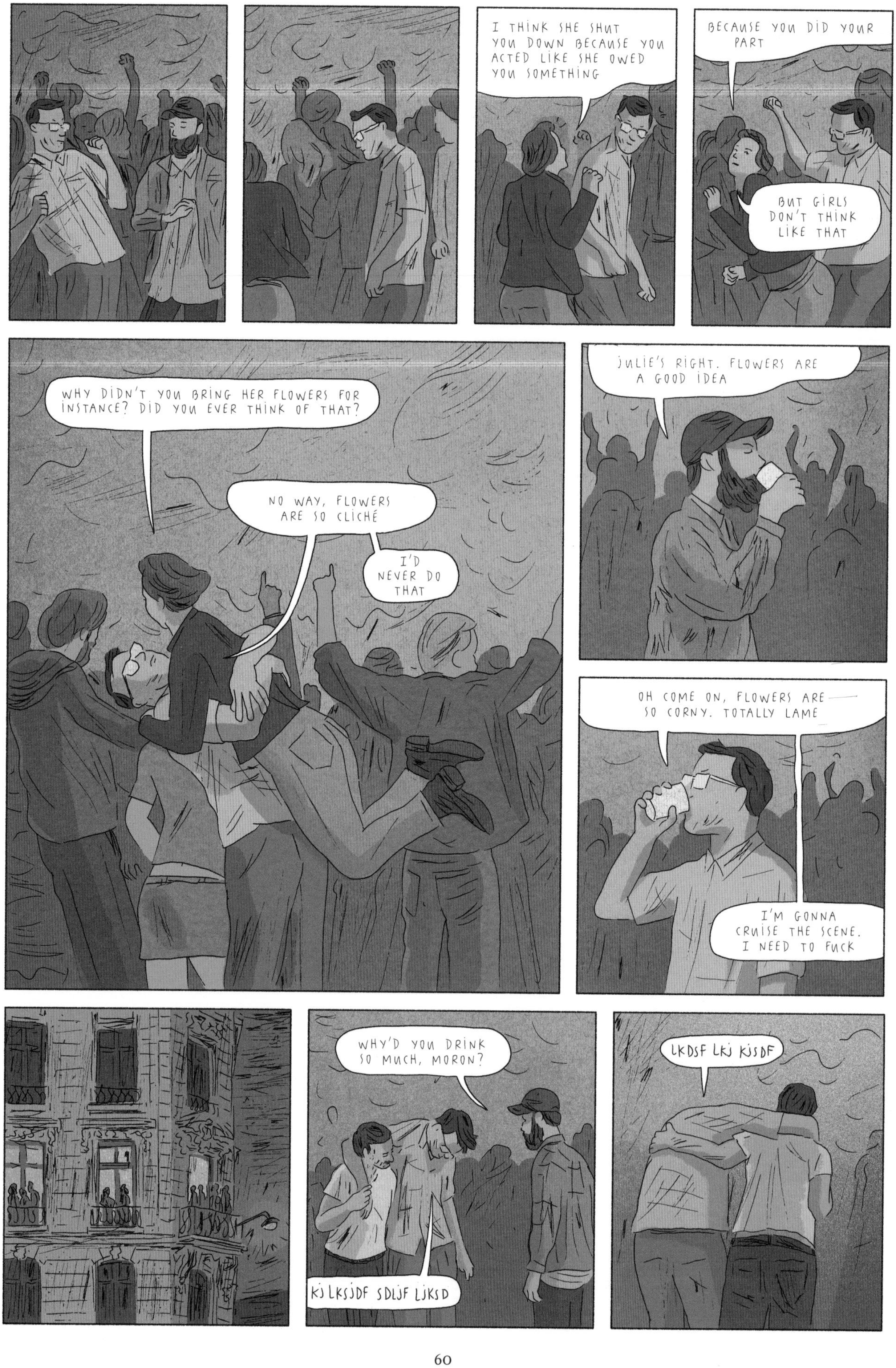
I THINK SHE SHUT YOU DOWN BECAUSE YOU ACTED LIKE SHE OWED YOU SOMETHING
BECAUSE YOU DID YOUR PART
BUT GIRLS DON'T THINK LIKE THAT
WHY DIDN'T YOU BRING HER FLOWERS FOR INSTANCE? DID YOU EVER THINK OF THAT?
NO WAY, FLOWERS ARE SO CLICHÉ
I'D NEVER DO THAT
JULIE'S RIGHT. FLOWERS ARE A GOOD IDEA
OH COME ON, FLOWERS ARE SO CORNY. TOTALLY LAME
I'M GONNA CRUISE THE SCENE. I NEED TO FUCK
WHY'D YOU DRINK SO MUCH, MORON?
KJ LKSJDF SDLJF LJKSD
LKDSF LKJ KJSDF

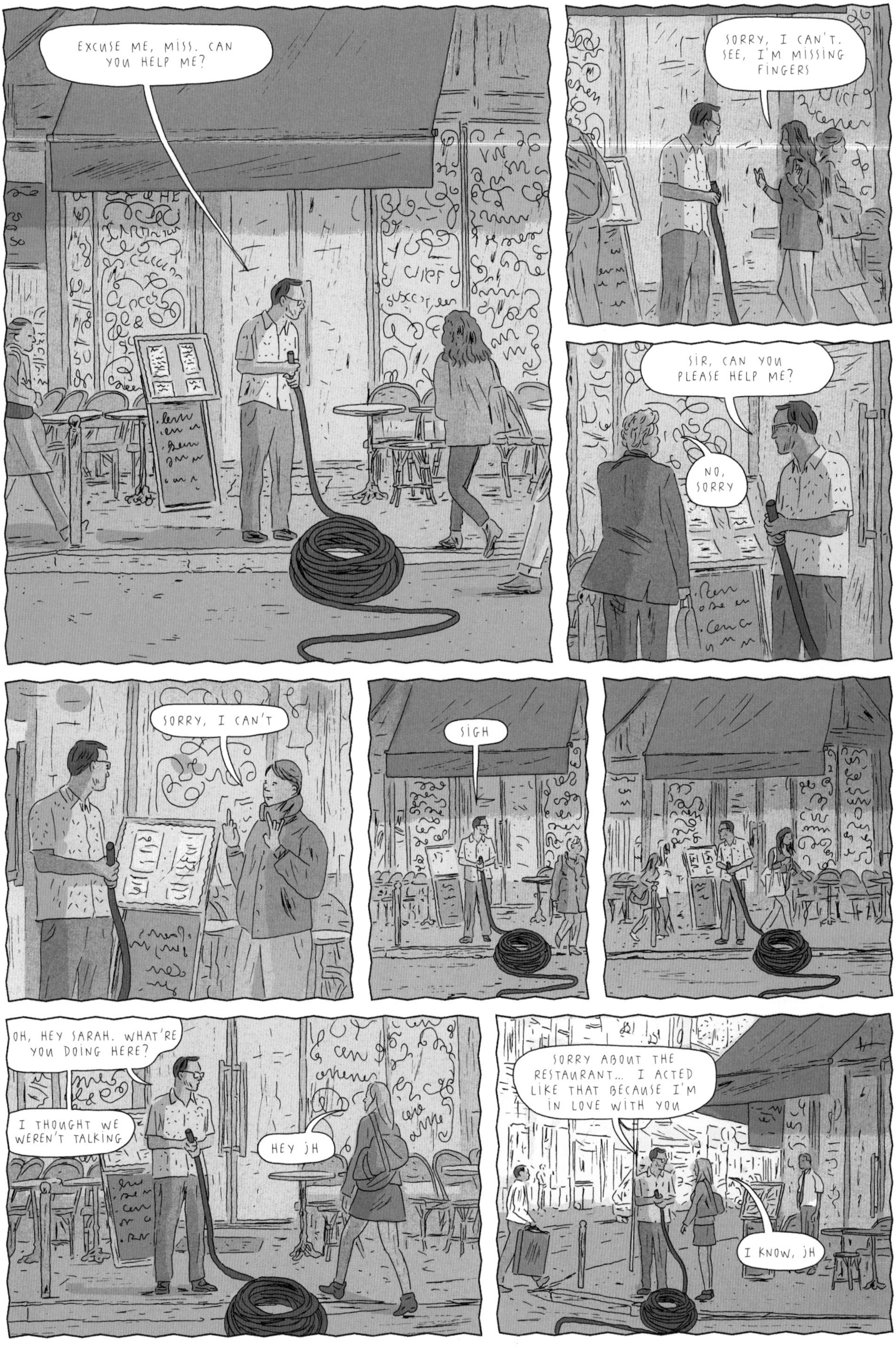
EXCUSE ME, MISS. CAN YOU HELP ME?
SORRY, I CAN'T. SEE, I'M MISSING FINGERS
SIR, CAN YOU PLEASE HELP ME?
NO, SORRY
SORRY, I CAN'T
SIGH
OH, HEY SARAH. WHAT'RE YOU DOING HERE?
I THOUGHT WE WEREN'T TALKING
HEY JH
SORRY ABOUT THE RESTAURANT... I ACTED LIKE THAT BECAUSE I'M IN LOVE WITH YOU
I KNOW, JH

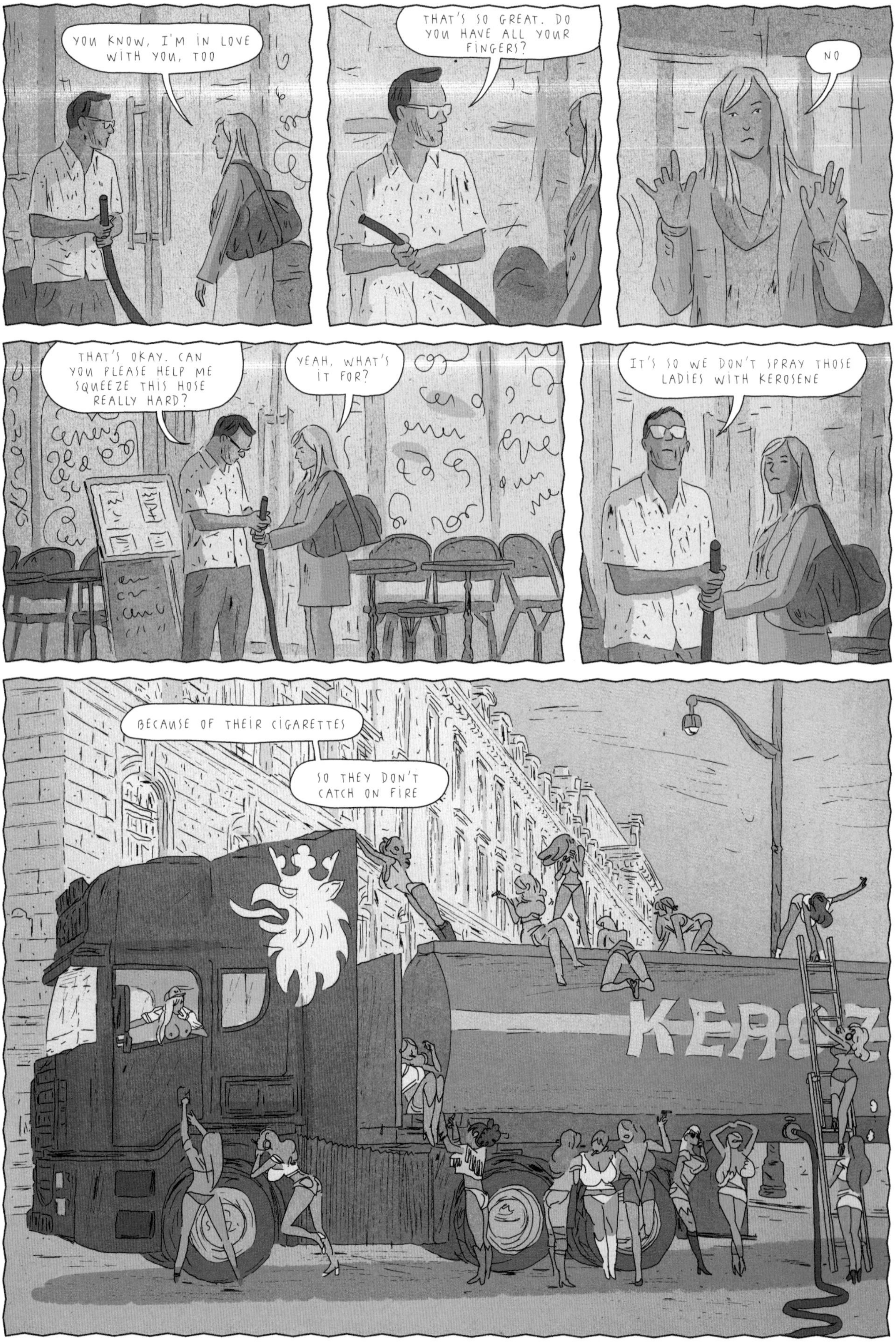
YOU KNOW, I'M IN LOVE WITH YOU, TOO
THAT'S SO GREAT. DO YOU HAVE ALL YOUR FINGERS?
NO
THAT'S OKAY. CAN YOU PLEASE HELP ME SQUEEZE THIS HOSE REALLY HARD?
YEAH, WHAT'S IT FOR?
IT'S SO WE DON'T SPRAY THOSE LADIES WITH KEROSENE
BECAUSE OF THEIR CIGARETTES
SO THEY DON'T CATCH ON FIRE
KEROZ

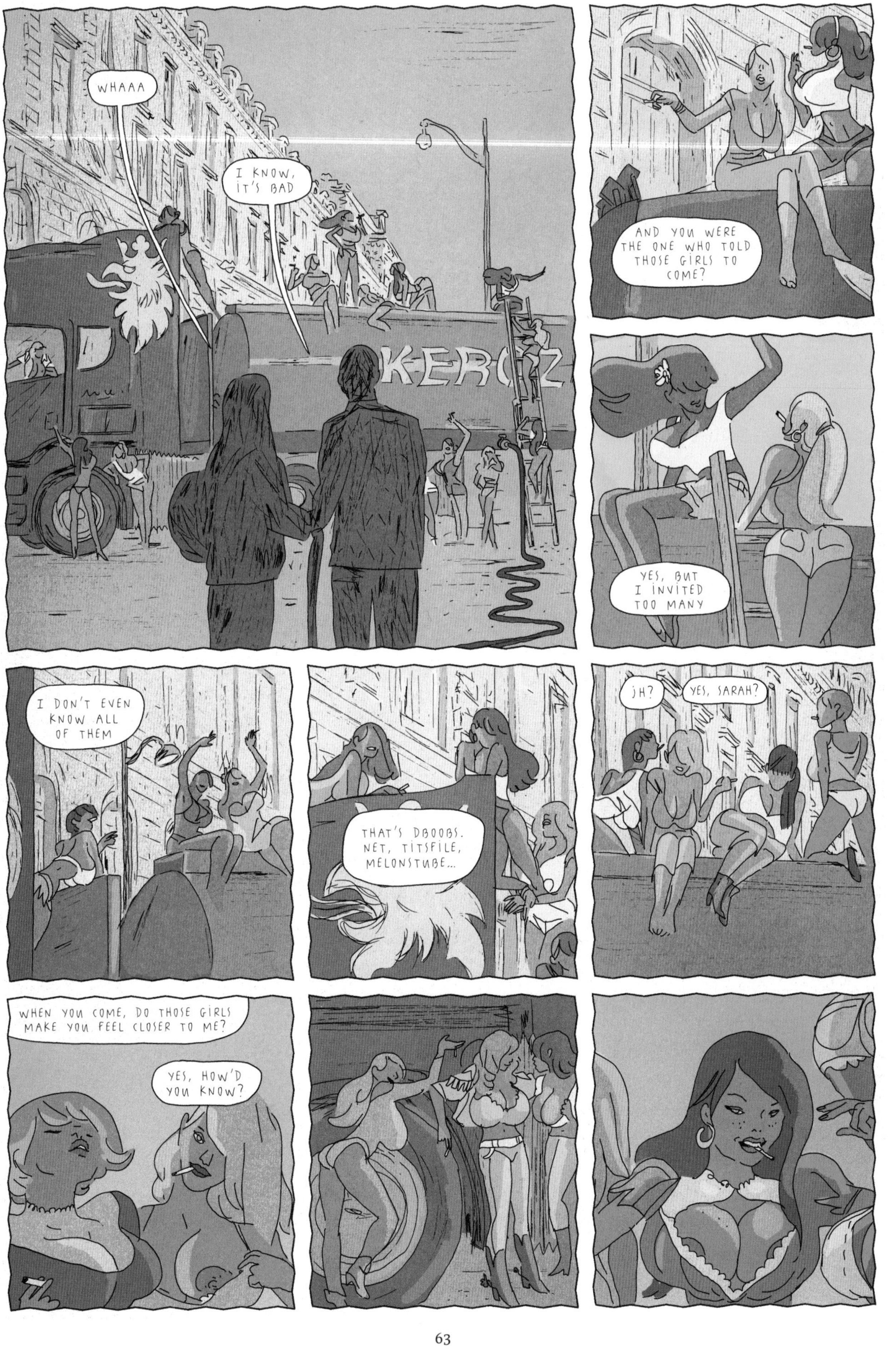
WHAAA
I KNOW, IT'S BAD
AND YOU WERE THE ONE WHO TOLD THOSE GIRLS TO COME?
YES, BUT I INVITED TOO MANY
I DON'T EVEN KNOW ALL OF THEM
THAT'S DBOOBS. NET, TITSFILE, MELONSTUBE...
JH?
YES, SARAH?
WHEN YOU COME, DO THOSE GIRLS MAKE YOU FEEL CLOSER TO ME?
YES, HOW'D YOU KNOW?

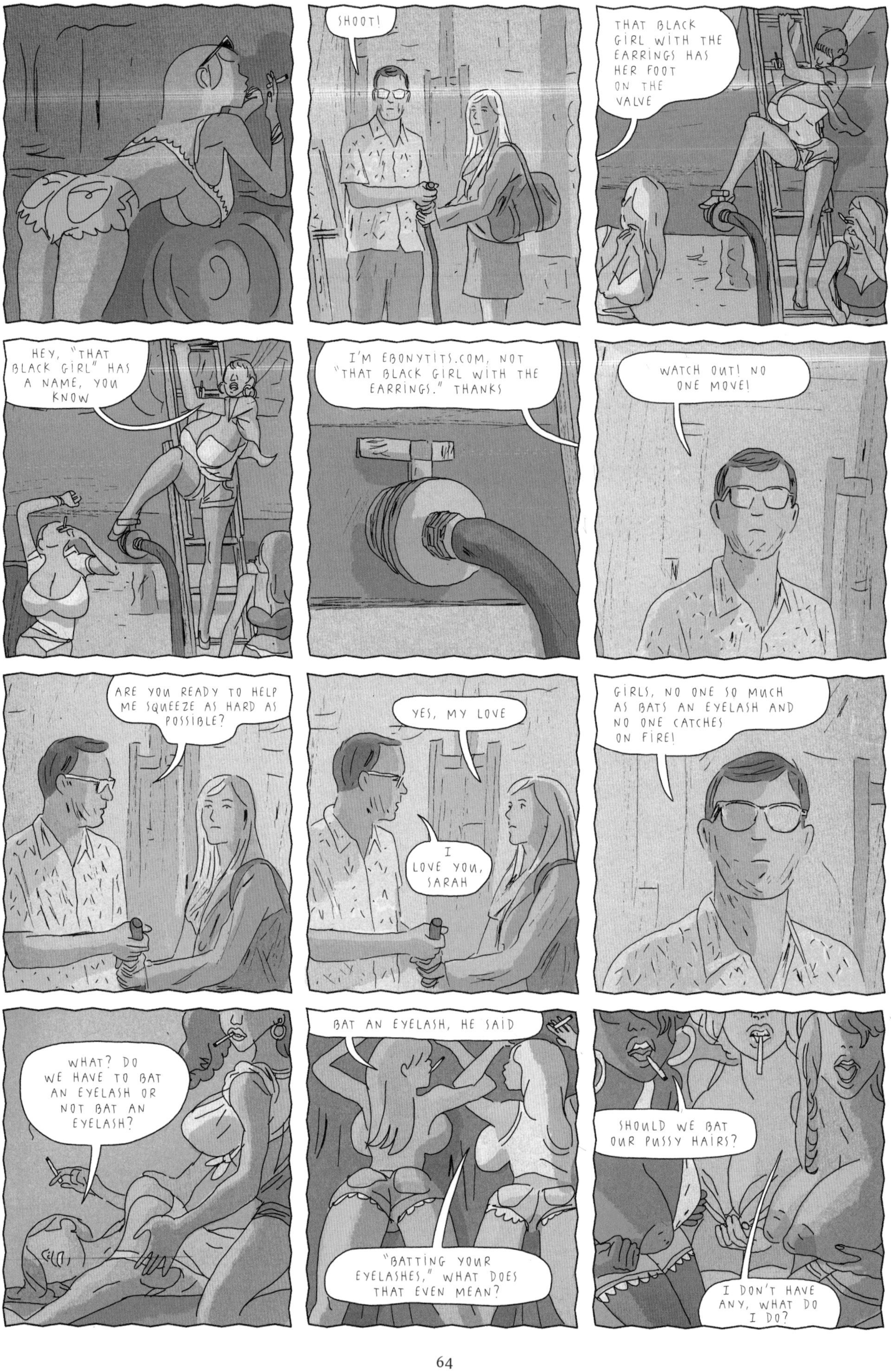
SHOOT!
THAT BLACK GIRL WITH THE EARRINGS HAS HER FOOT ON THE VALVE
HEY, "THAT BLACK GIRL" HAS A NAME, YOU KNOW
I'M EBONYTITS.COM, NOT "THAT BLACK GIRL WITH THE EARRINGS." THANKS
WATCH OUT! NO ONE MOVE!
ARE YOU READY TO HELP ME SQUEEZE AS HARD AS POSSIBLE?
YES, MY LOVE
I LOVE YOU, SARAH
GIRLS, NO ONE SO MUCH AS BATS AN EYELASH AND NO ONE CATCHES ON FIRE!
WHAT? DO WE HAVE TO BAT AN EYELASH OR NOT BAT AN EYELASH?
BAT AN EYELASH, HE SAID
"BATTING YOUR EYELASHES," WHAT DOES THAT EVEN MEAN?
SHOULD WE BAT OUR PUSSY HAIRS?
I DON'T HAVE ANY, WHAT DO I DO?

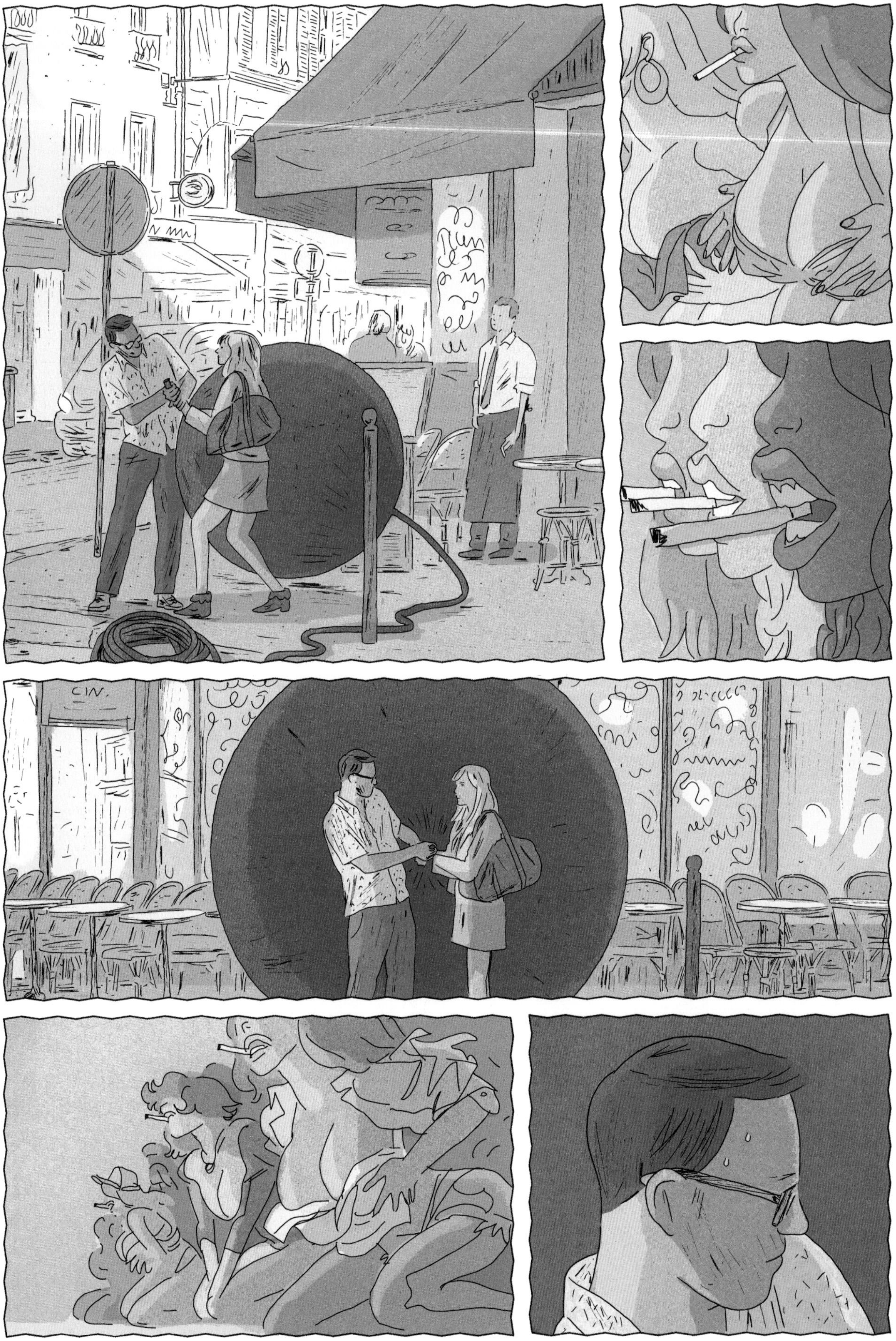

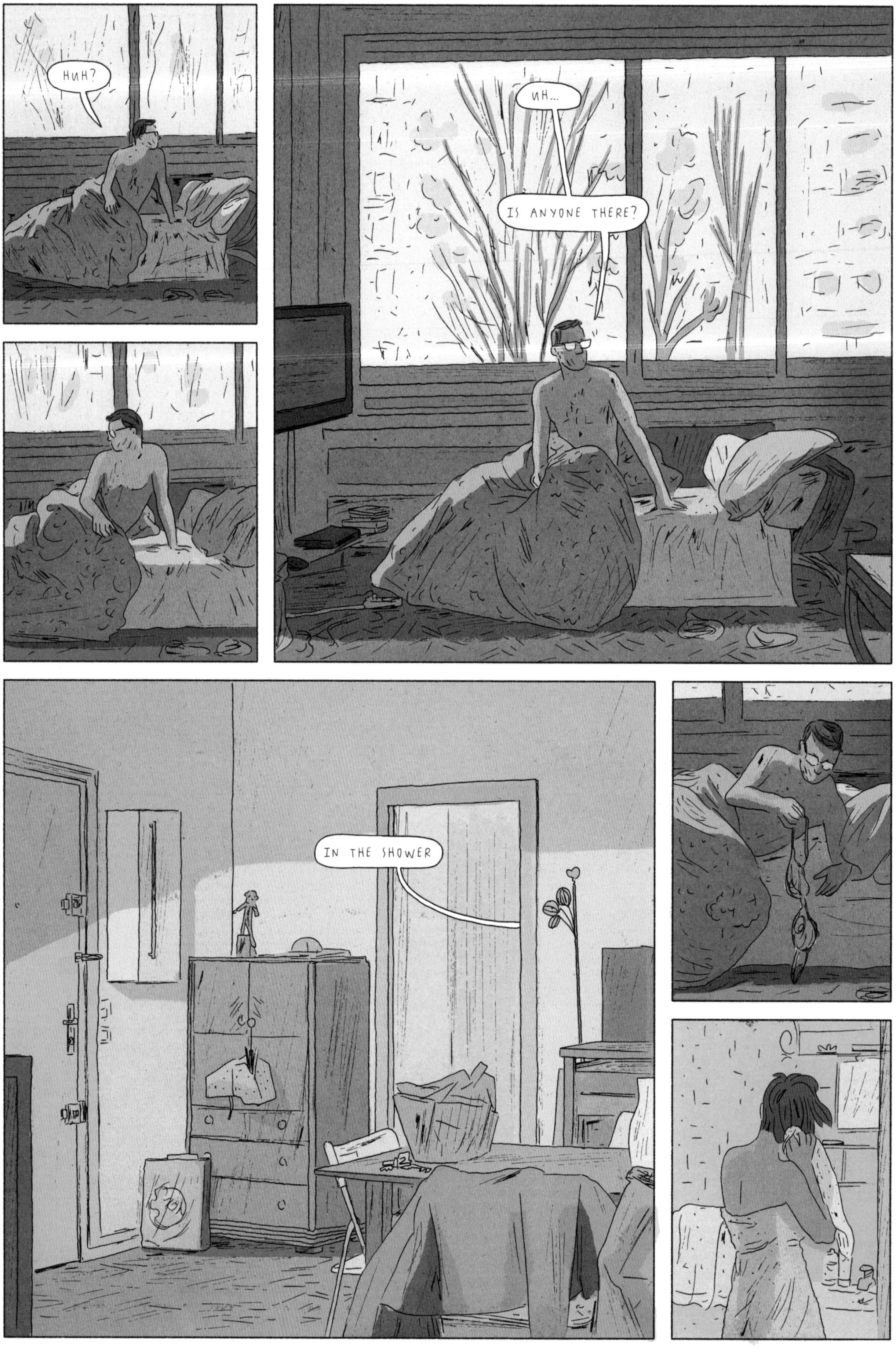
HUH?
UH...
IS ANYONE THERE?
IN THE SHOWER

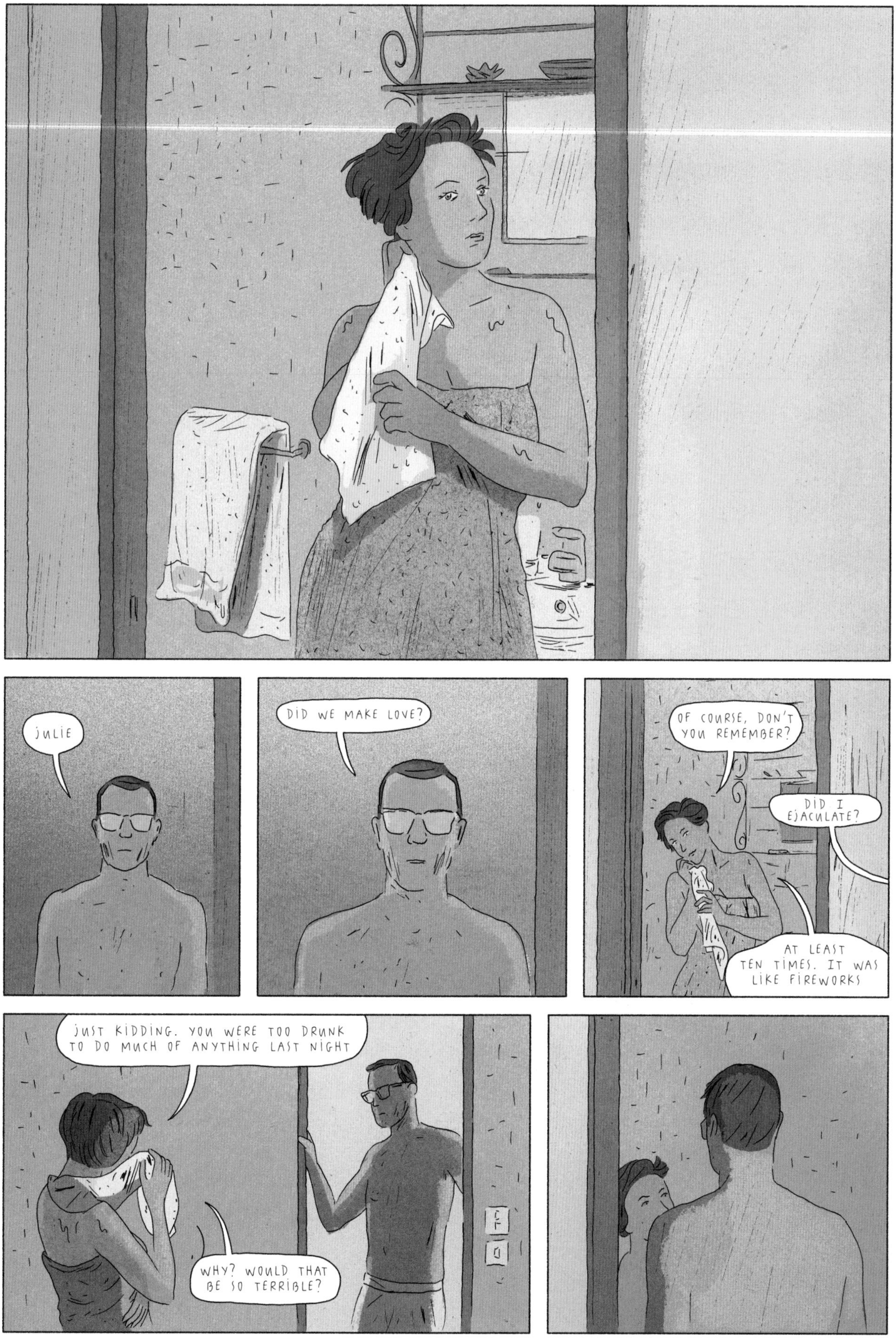

JULIE
DID WE MAKE LOVE?
OF COURSE, DON'T YOU REMEMBER?
DID I EJACULATE?
AT LEAST TEN TIMES. IT WAS LIKE FIREWORKS
JUST KIDDING. YOU WERE TOO DRUNK TO DO MUCH OF ANYTHING LAST NIGHT
WHY? WOULD THAT BE SO TERRIBLE?

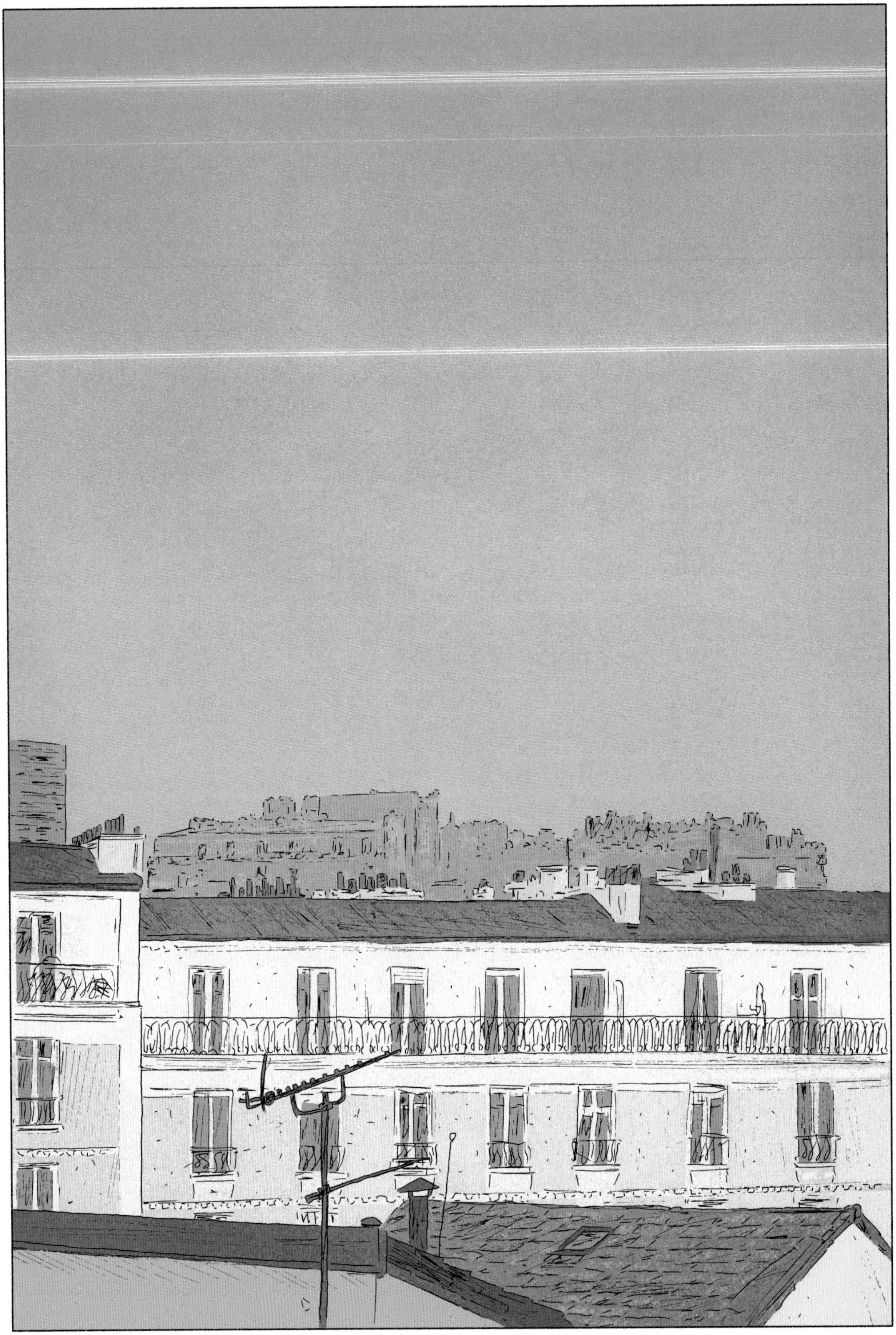

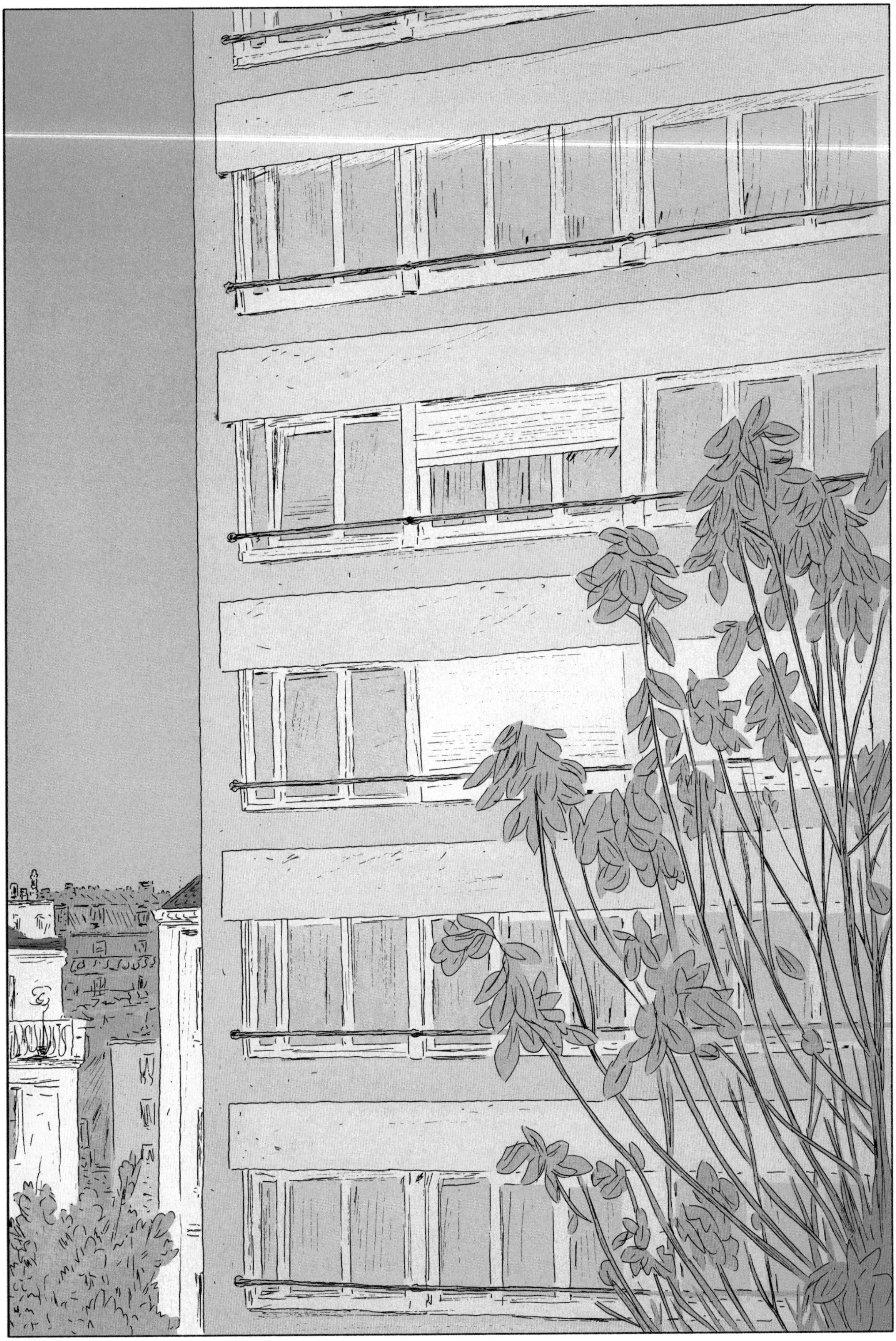

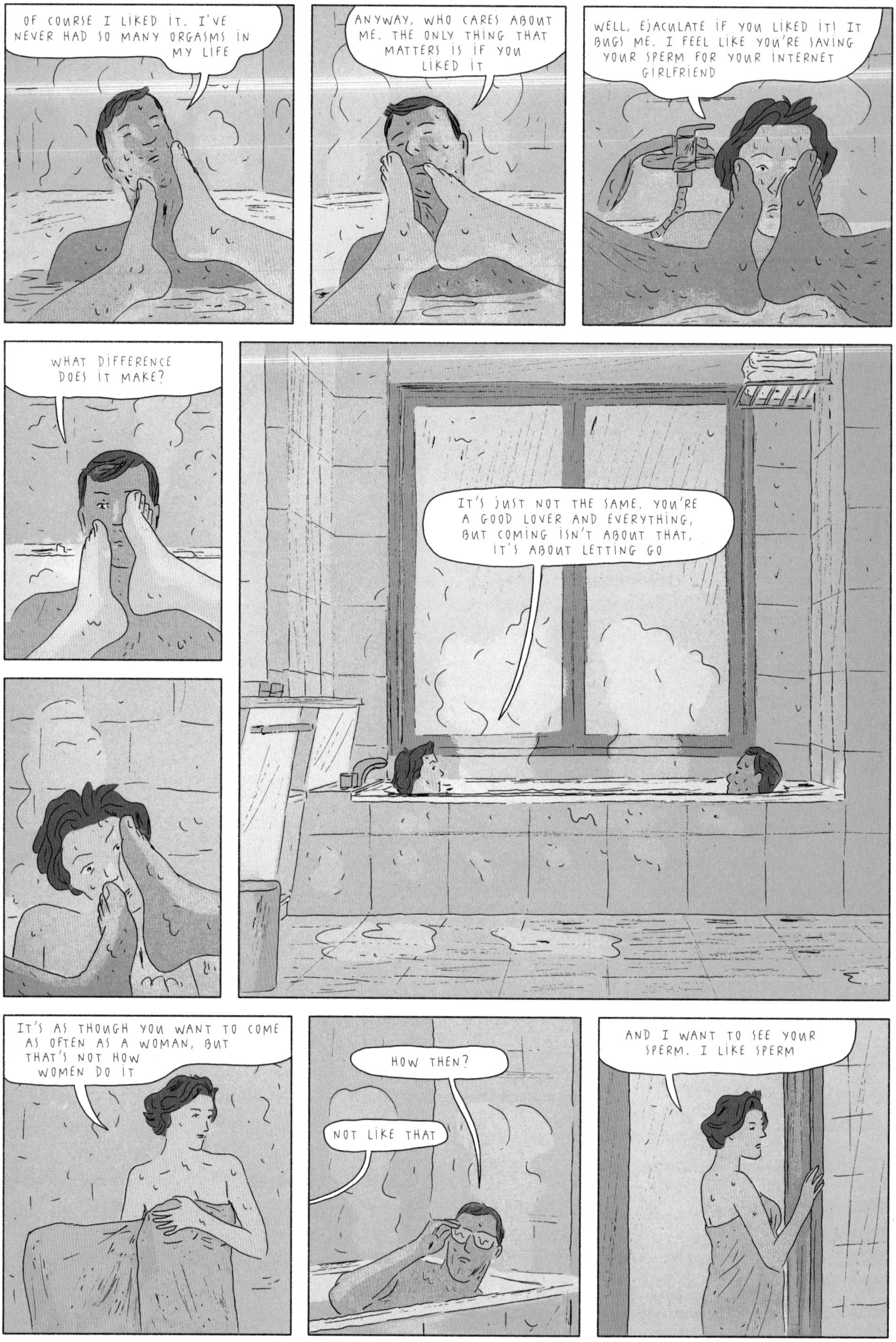
OF COURSE I LIKED IT. I'VE NEVER HAD SO MANY ORGASMS IN MY LIFE
ANYWAY, WHO CARES ABOUT ME. THE ONLY THING THAT MATTERS IS IF YOU LIKED IT
WELL, EJACULATE IF YOU LIKED IT! IT BUGS ME. I FEEL LIKE YOU'RE SAVING YOUR SPERM FOR YOUR INTERNET GIRLFRIEND
WHAT DIFFERENCE DOES IT MAKE?
IT'S JUST NOT THE SAME. YOU'RE A GOOD LOVER AND EVERYTHING, BUT COMING ISN'T ABOUT THAT, IT'S ABOUT LETTING GO
IT'S AS THOUGH YOU WANT TO COME AS OFTEN AS A WOMAN, BUT THAT'S NOT HOW WOMEN DO IT
HOW THEN?
NOT LIKE THAT
AND I WANT TO SEE YOUR SPERM. I LIKE SPERM

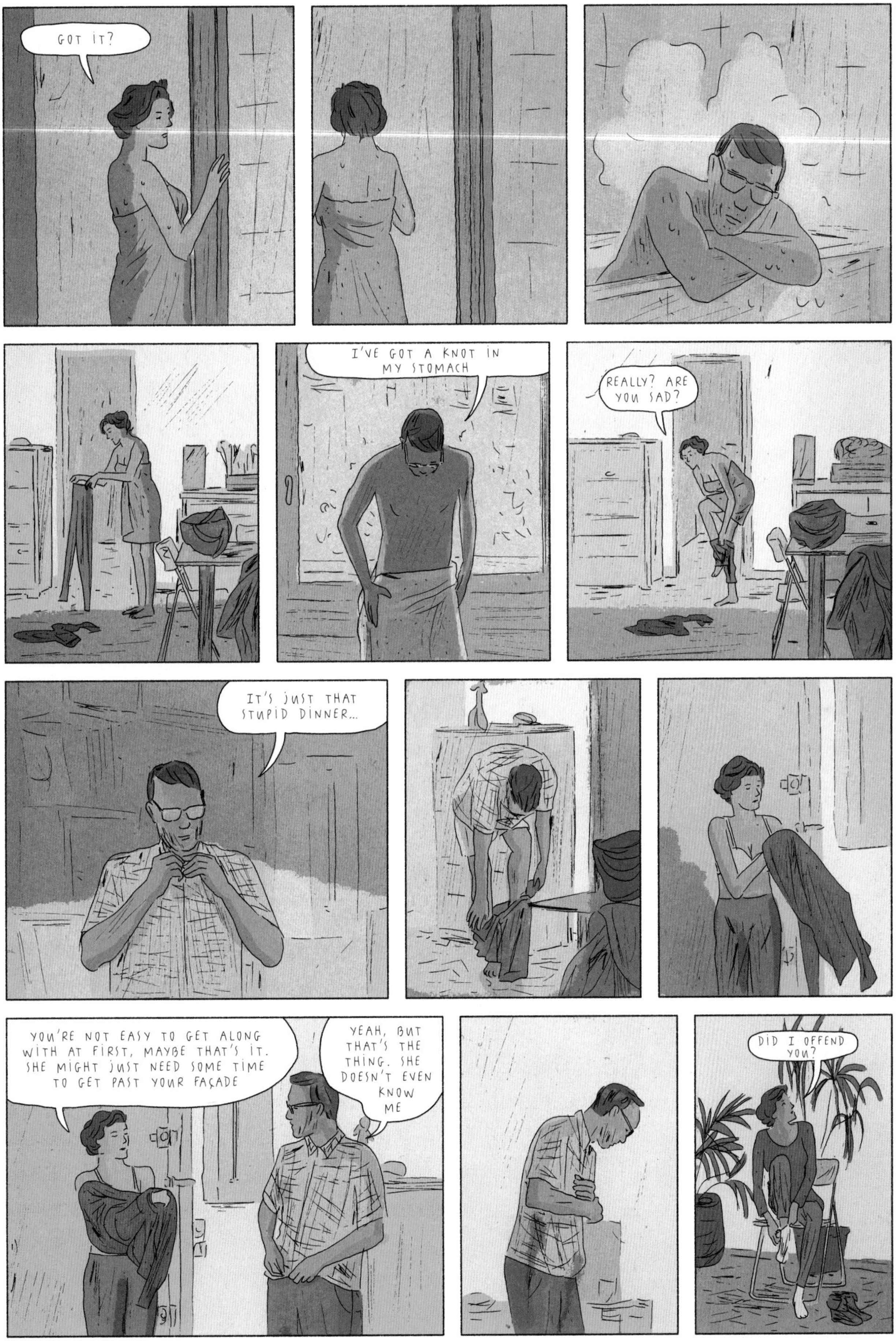
GOT IT?
I'VE GOT A KNOT IN MY STOMACH
REALLY? ARE YOU SAD?
IT'S JUST THAT STUPID DINNER...
YOU'RE NOT EASY TO GET ALONG WITH AT FIRST, MAYBE THAT'S IT. SHE MIGHT JUST NEED SOME TIME TO GET PAST YOUR FAÇADE
YEAH, BUT THAT'S THE THING. SHE DOESN'T EVEN KNOW ME
DID I OFFEND YOU?

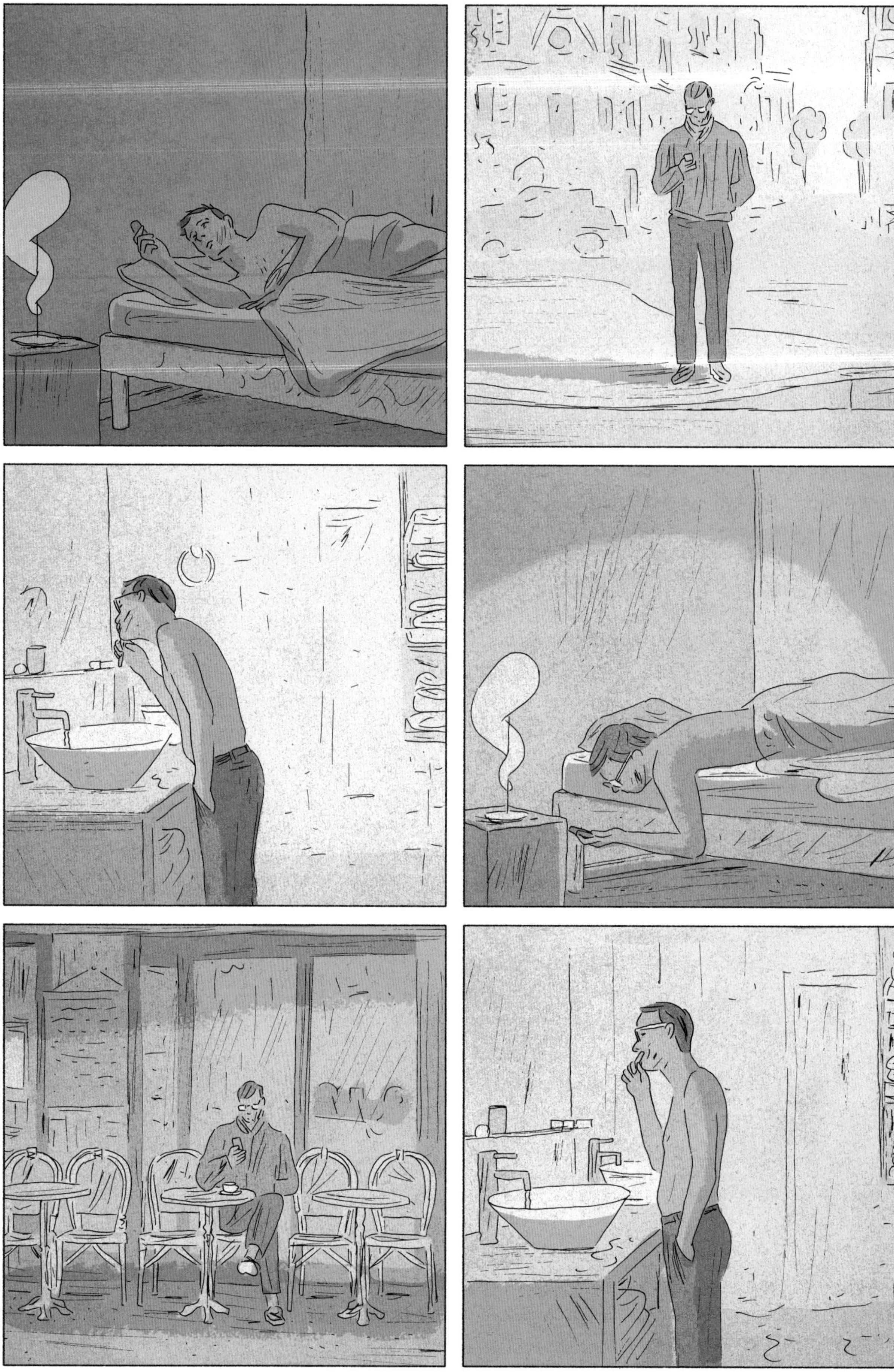

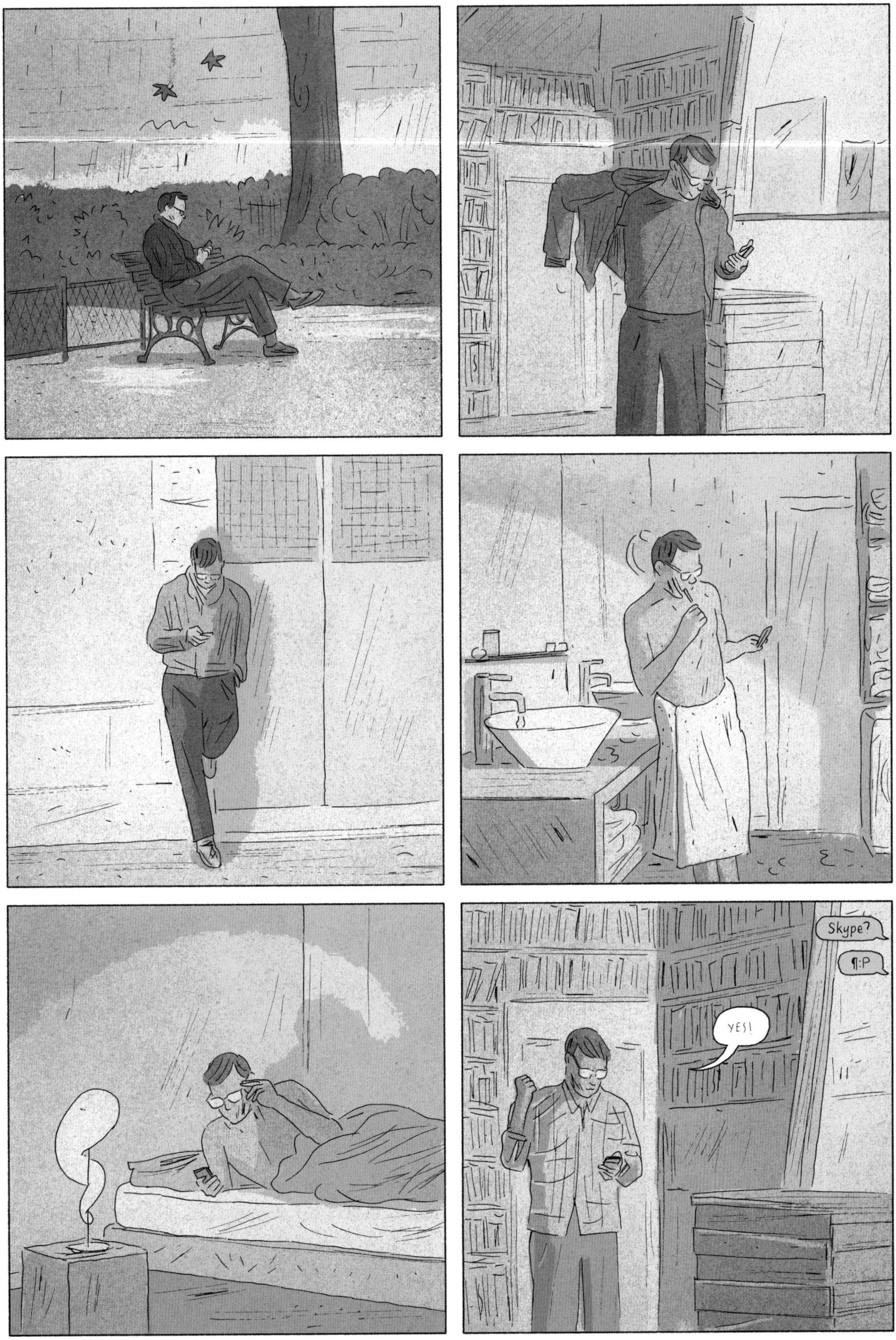
Skype?
¶:P
YES!

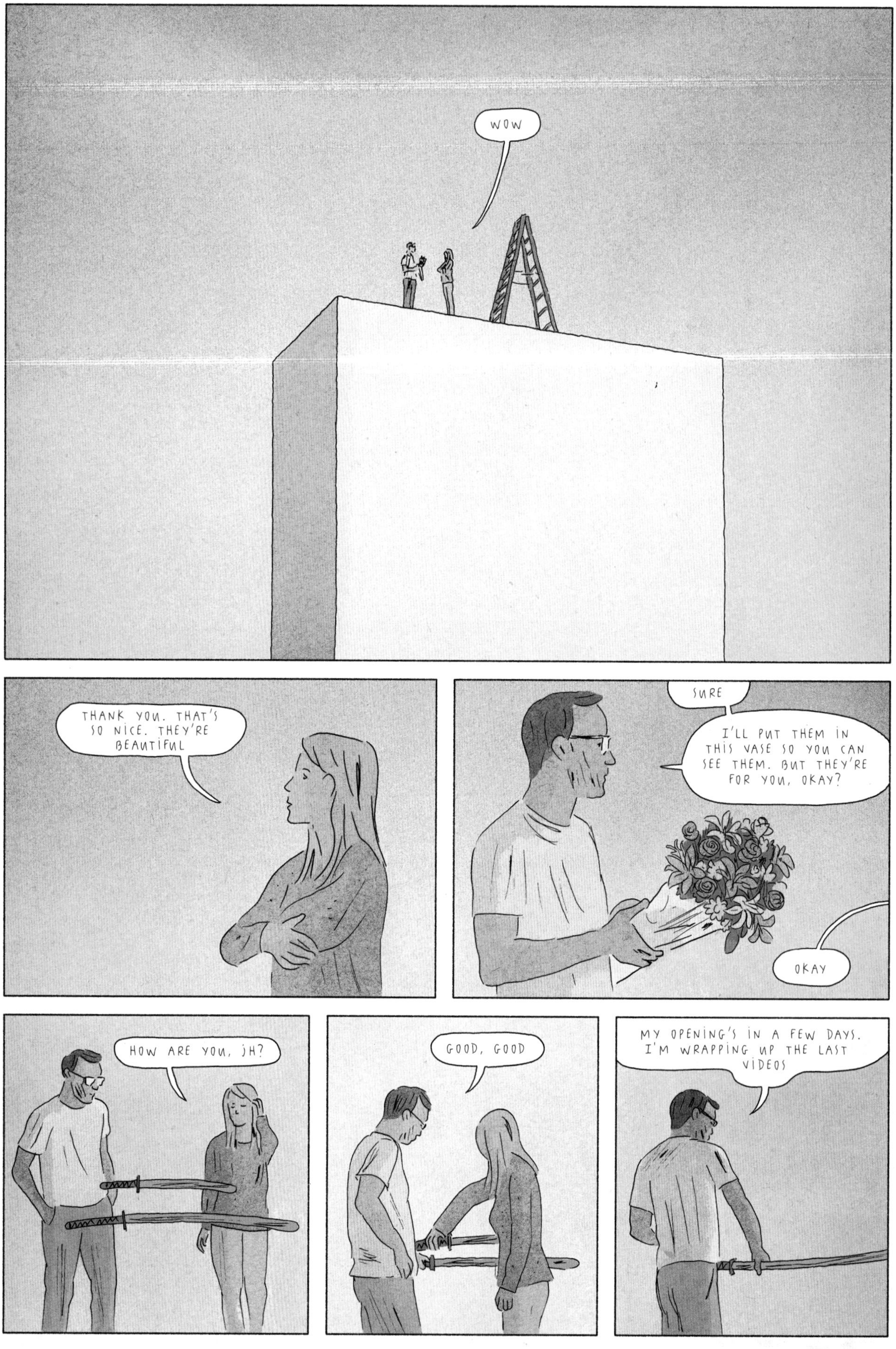
WOW
THANK YOU. THAT'S SO NICE. THEY'RE BEAUTIFUL
SURE
I'LL PUT THEM IN THIS VASE SO YOU CAN SEE THEM. BUT THEY'RE FOR YOU, OKAY?
OKAY
HOW ARE YOU, JH?
GOOD, GOOD
MY OPENING'S IN A FEW DAYS. I'M WRAPPING UP THE LAST VIDEOS

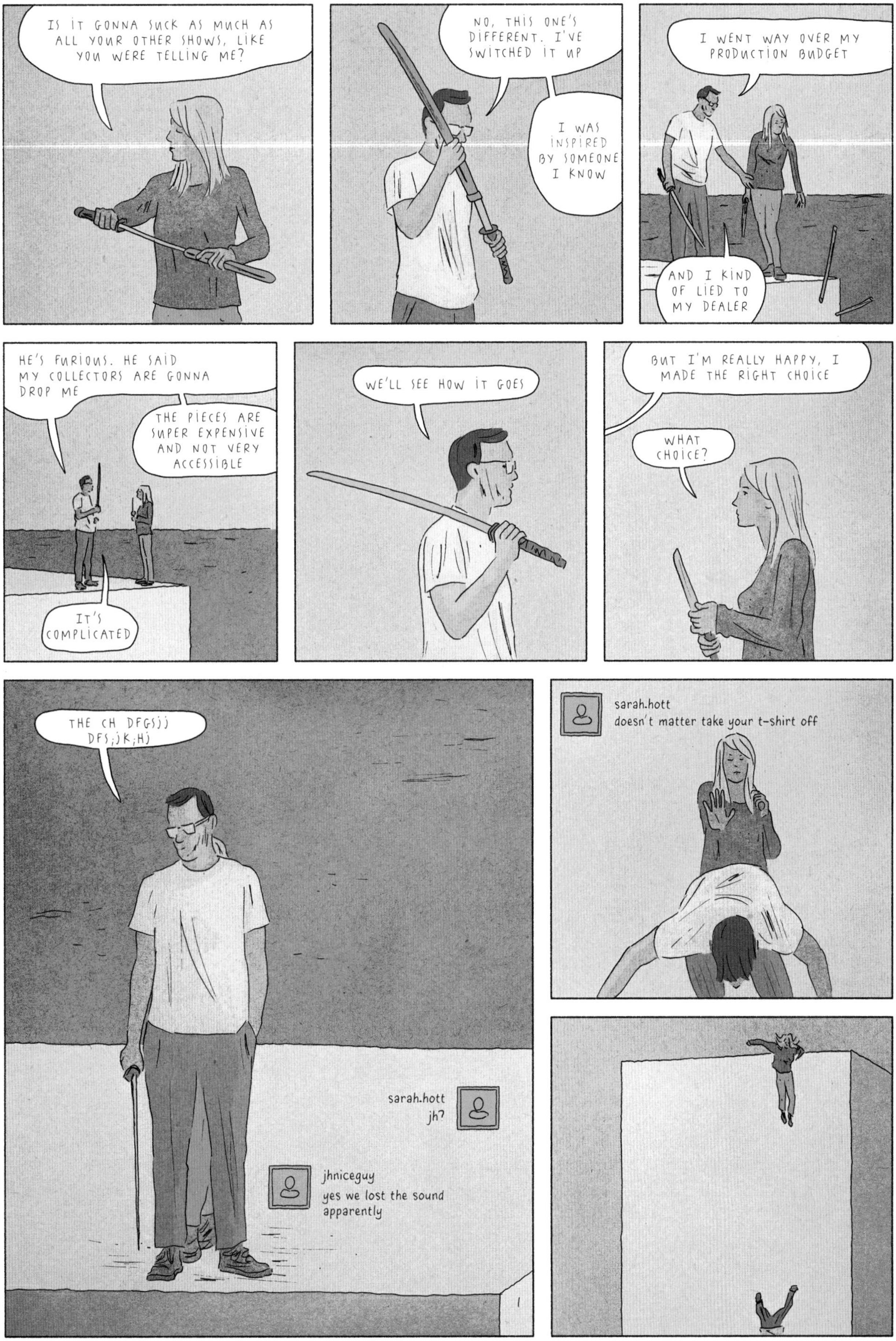
IS IT GONNA SUCK AS MUCH AS ALL YOUR OTHER SHOWS, LIKE YOU WERE TELLING ME?
NO, THIS ONE'S DIFFERENT. I'VE SWITCHED IT UP
I WAS INSPIRED BY SOMEONE I KNOW
I WENT WAY OVER MY PRODUCTION BUDGET
AND I KIND OF LIED TO MY DEALER
HE'S FURIOUS. HE SAID MY COLLECTORS ARE GONNA DROP ME
THE PIECES ARE SUPER EXPENSIVE AND NOT VERY ACCESSIBLE
IT'S COMPLICATED
WE'LL SEE HOW IT GOES
BUT I'M REALLY HAPPY, I MADE THE RIGHT CHOICE
WHAT CHOICE?
THE CH DFGSjj DFS;jK;Hj
sarah.hott
jh?
jhniceguy
yes we lost the sound apparently
sarah.hott
doesn't matter take your t-shirt off

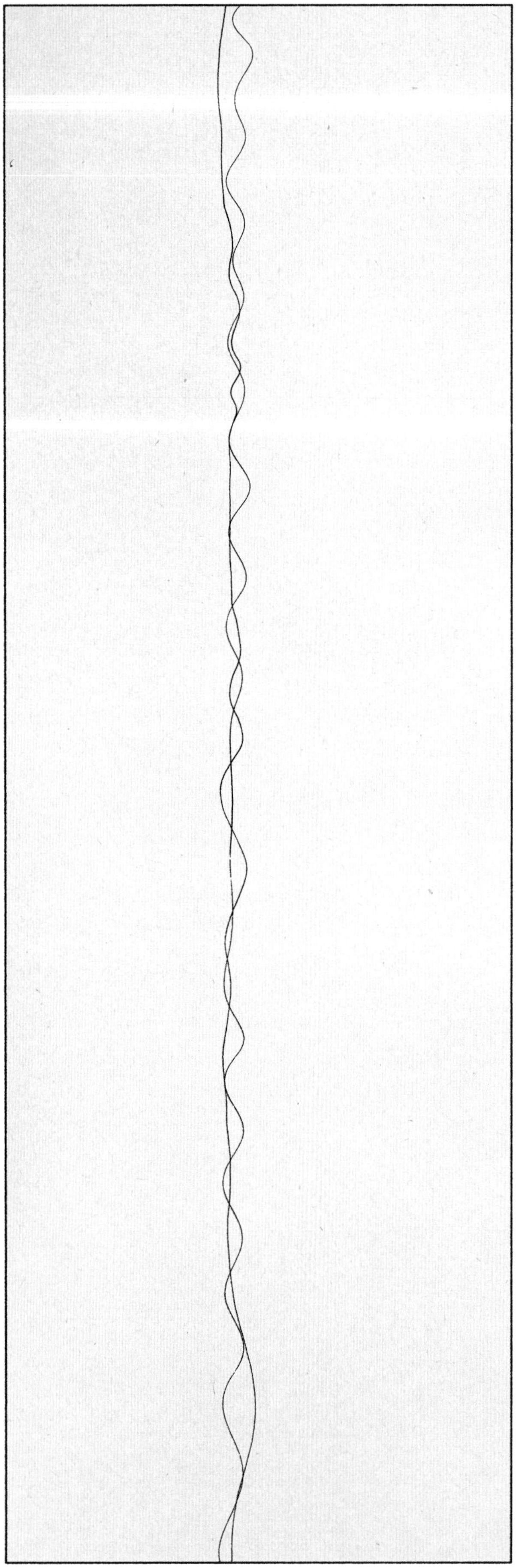
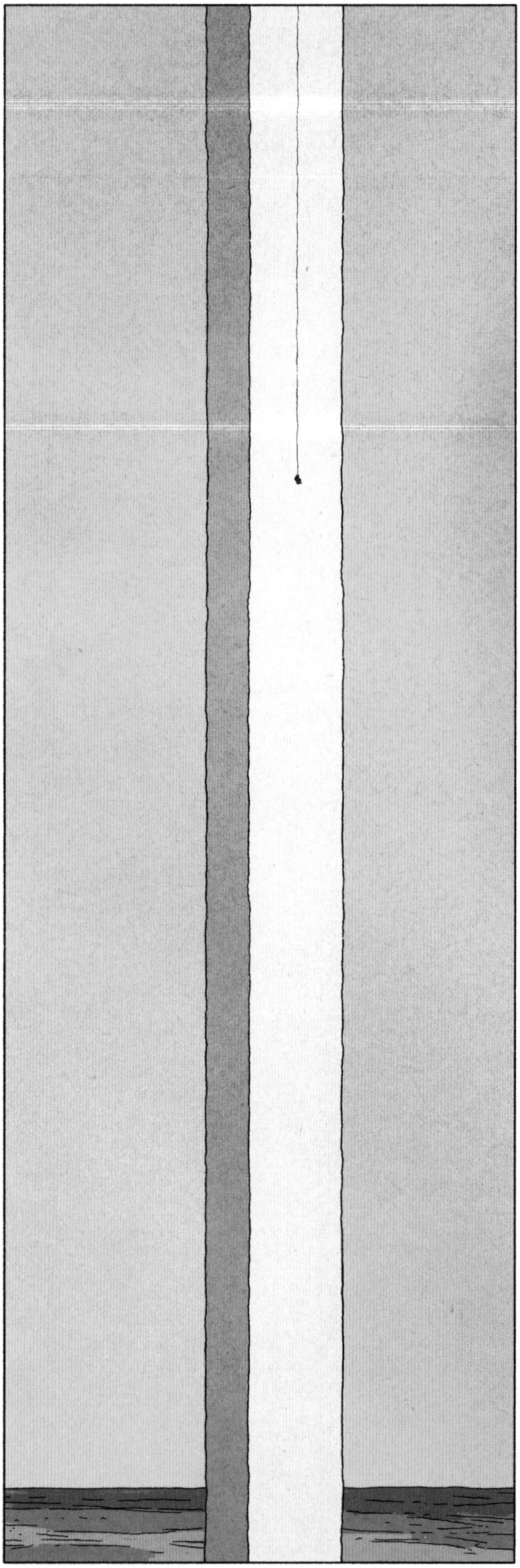

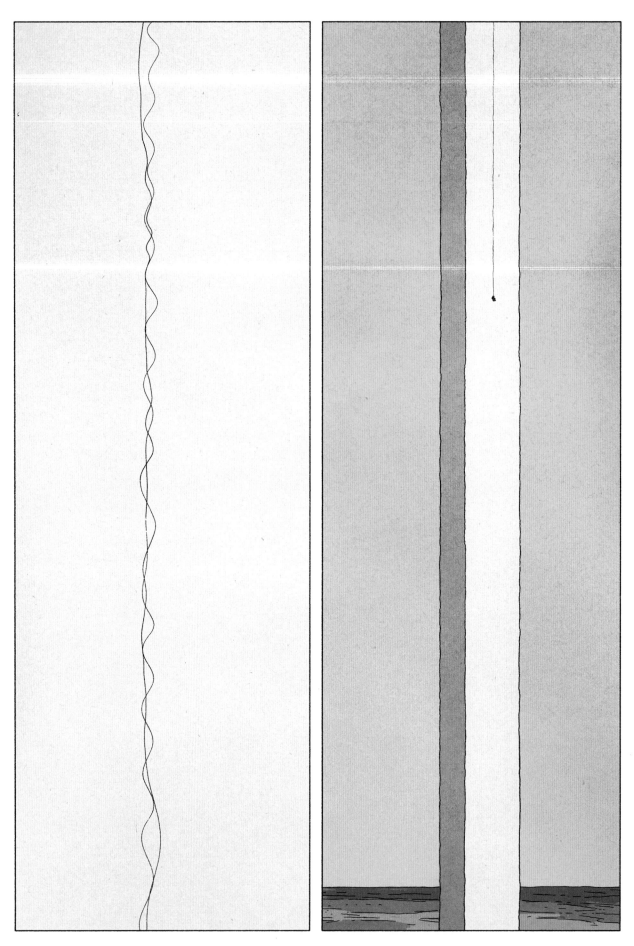

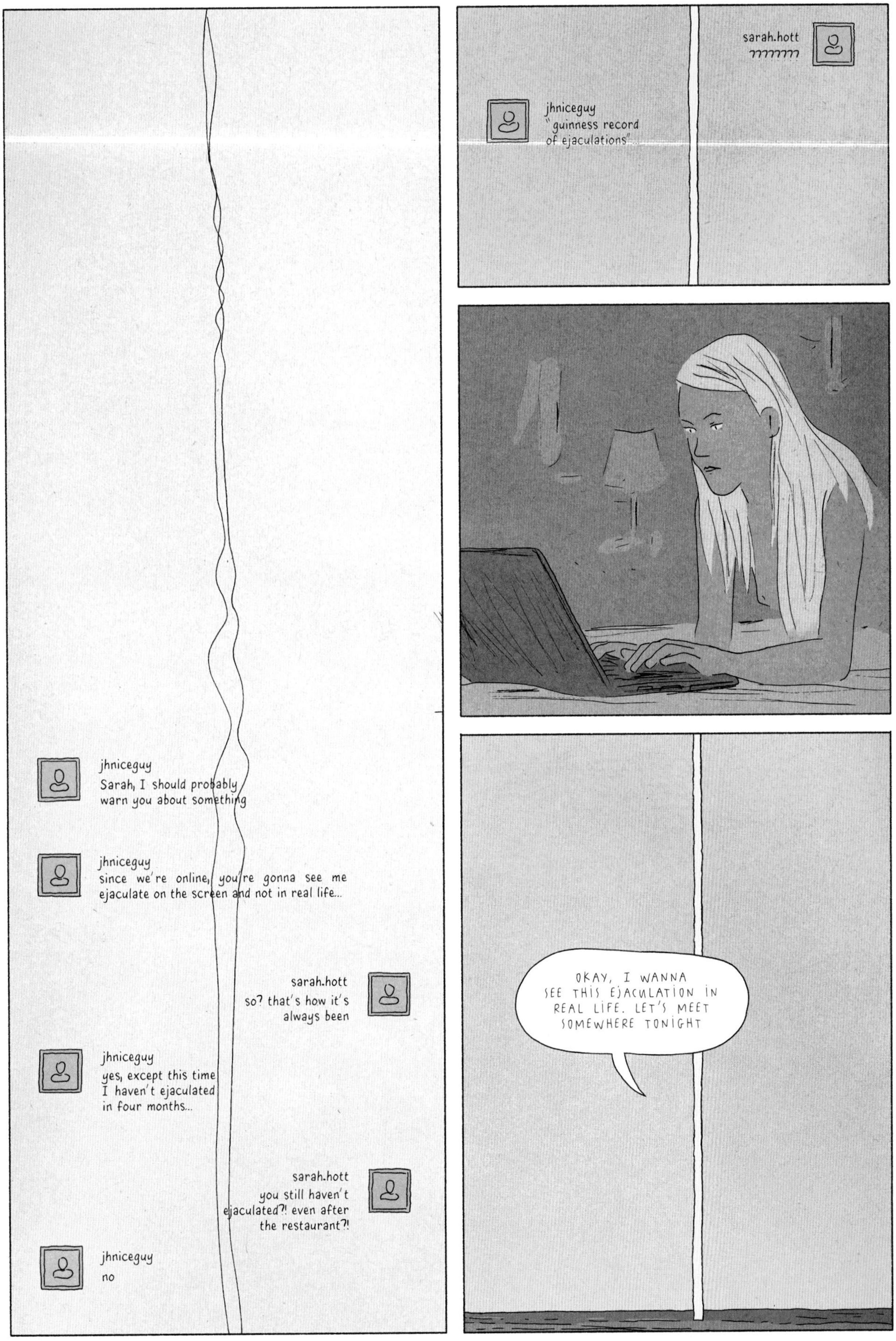
jhniceguy
Sarah, I should probably warn you about something
jhniceguy
since we're online, you're gonna see me ejaculate on the screen and not in real life...
sarah.hott
so? that's how it's always been
jhniceguy
yes, except this time I haven't ejaculated in four months...
sarah.hott
you still haven't ejaculated?! even after the restaurant?!
jhniceguy
no
sarah.hott
???????
jhniceguy
"guinness record of ejaculations"...
OKAY, I WANNA SEE THIS EJACULATION IN REAL LIFE. LET'S MEET SOMEWHERE TONIGHT

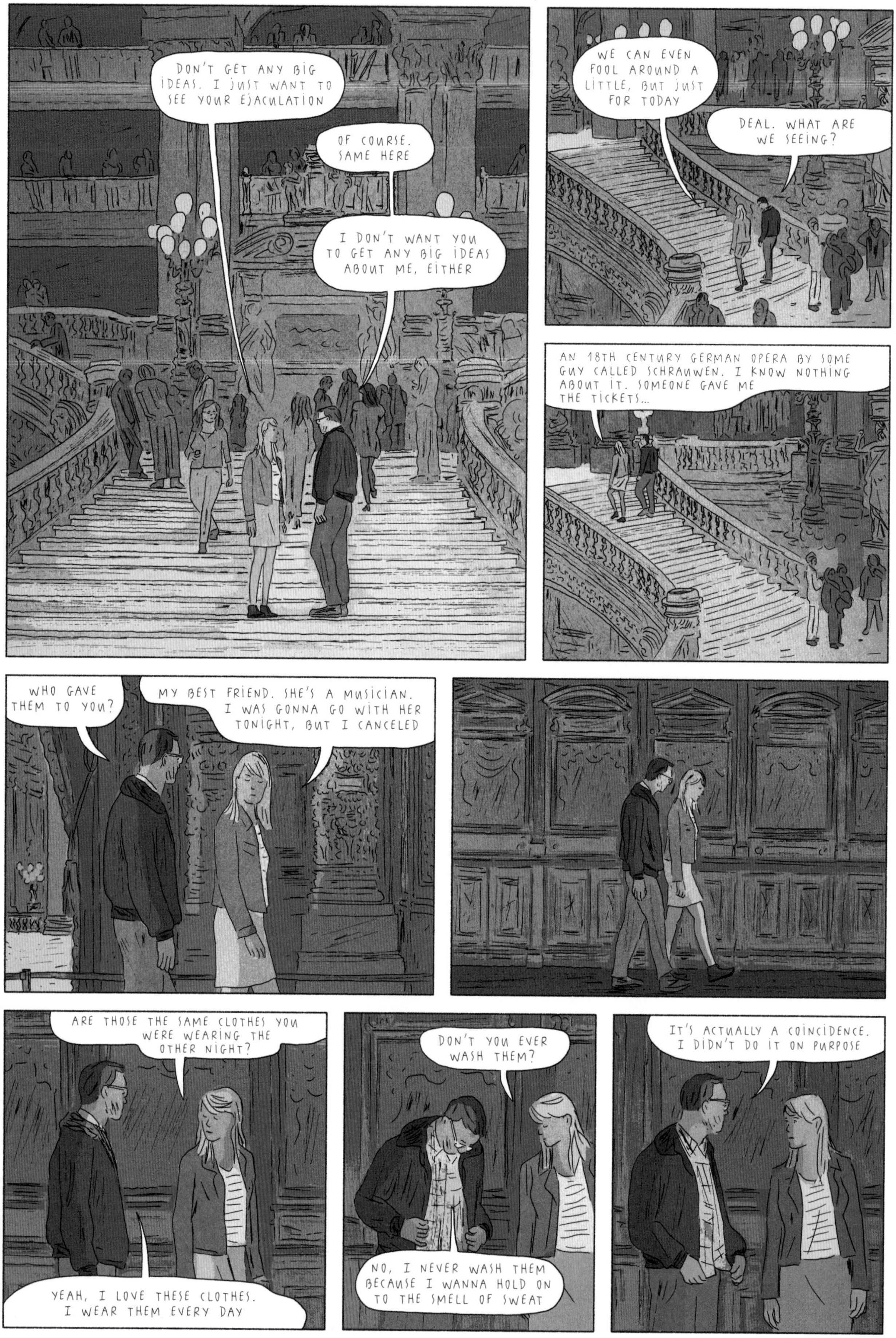
DON'T GET ANY BIG IDEAS. I JUST WANT TO SEE YOUR EJACULATION
OF COURSE. SAME HERE
I DON'T WANT YOU TO GET ANY BIG IDEAS ABOUT ME, EITHER
WE CAN EVEN FOOL AROUND A LITTLE, BUT JUST FOR TODAY
DEAL. WHAT ARE WE SEEING?
AN 18TH CENTURY GERMAN OPERA BY SOME GUY CALLED SCHRAUWEN. I KNOW NOTHING ABOUT IT. SOMEONE GAVE ME THE TICKETS...
WHO GAVE THEM TO YOU?
MY BEST FRIEND. SHE'S A MUSICIAN. I WAS GONNA GO WITH HER TONIGHT, BUT I CANCELED
ARE THOSE THE SAME CLOTHES YOU WERE WEARING THE OTHER NIGHT?
YEAH, I LOVE THESE CLOTHES. I WEAR THEM EVERY DAY
DON'T YOU EVER WASH THEM?
NO, I NEVER WASH THEM BECAUSE I WANNA HOLD ON TO THE SMELL OF SWEAT
IT'S ACTUALLY A COINCIDENCE. I DIDN'T DO IT ON PURPOSE

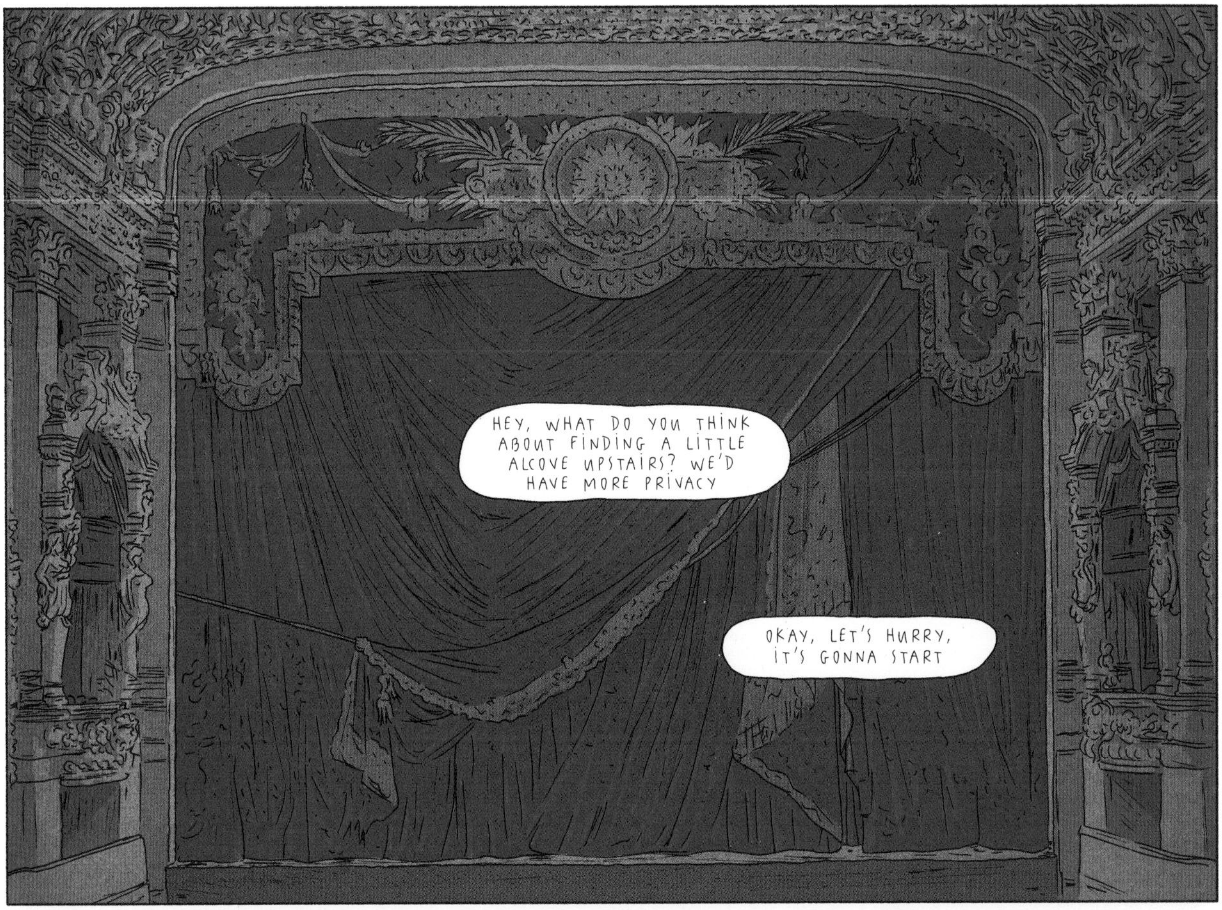
HEY, WHAT DO YOU THINK ABOUT FINDING A LITTLE ALCOVE UPSTAIRS? WE'D HAVE MORE PRIVACY
OKAY, LET'S HURRY, IT'S GONNA START

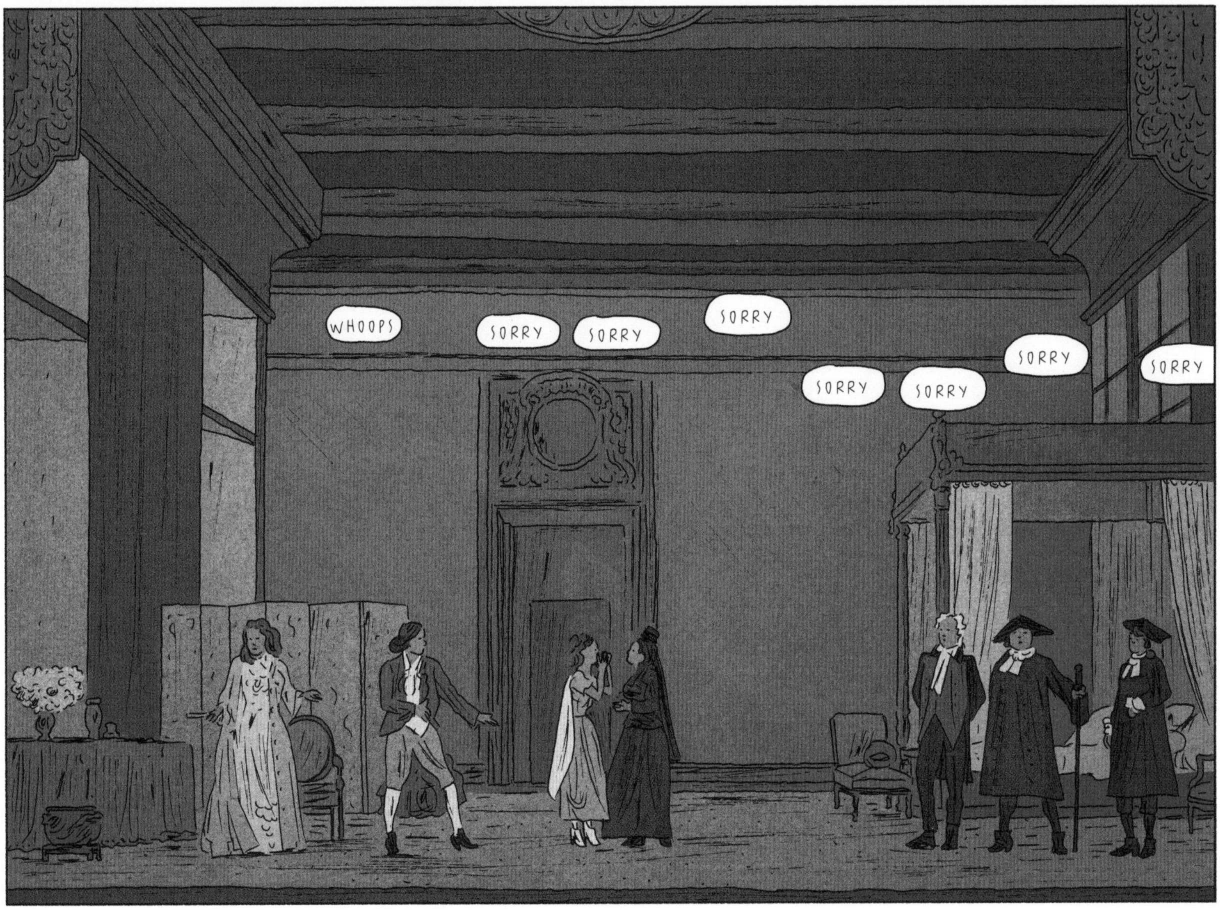
WHOOPS
SORRY
SORRY
SORRY
SORRY
SORRY
SORRY
SORRY

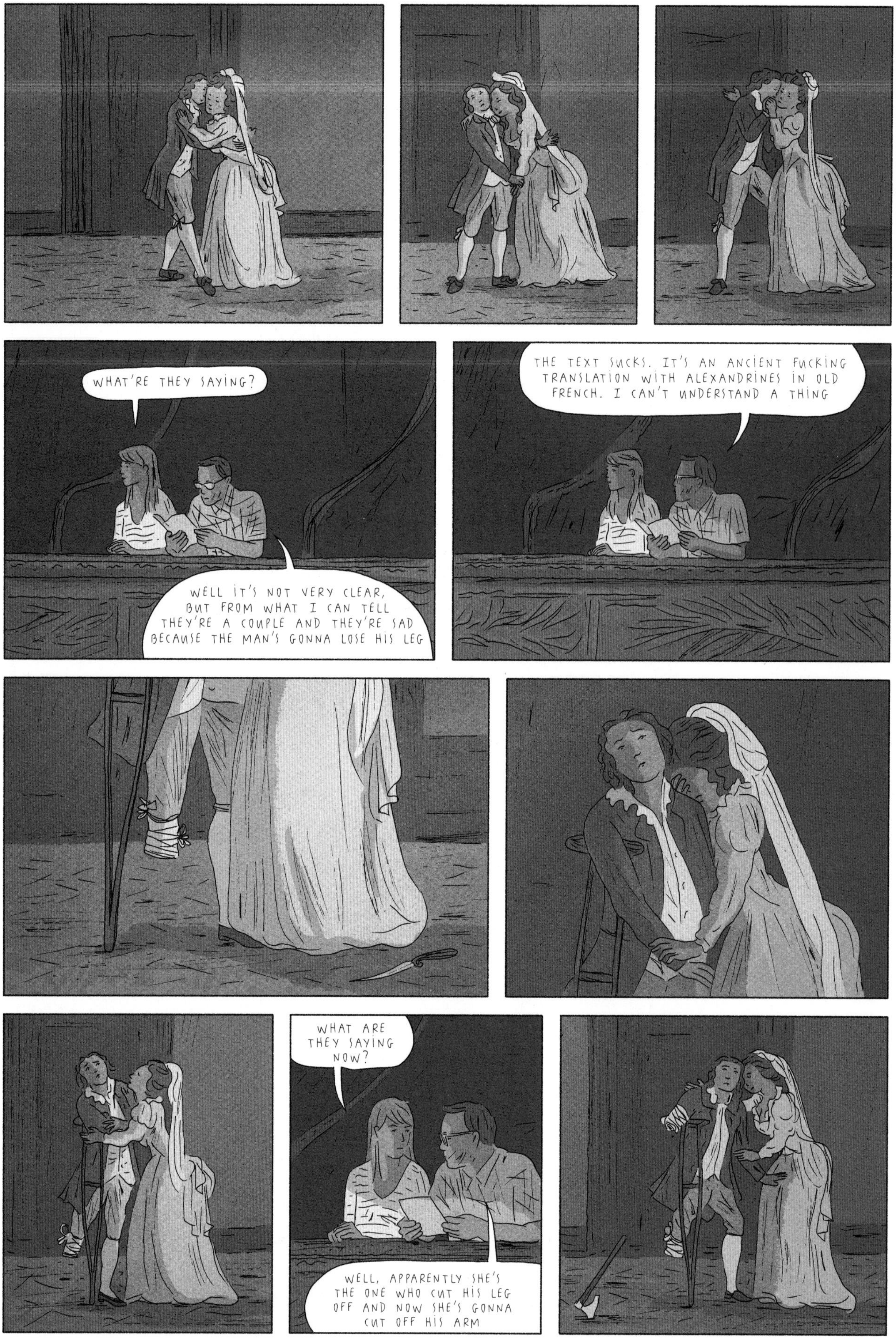
WHAT'RE THEY SAYING?
WELL IT'S NOT VERY CLEAR, BUT FROM WHAT I CAN TELL THEY'RE A COUPLE AND THEY'RE SAD BECAUSE THE MAN'S GONNA LOSE HIS LEG
THE TEXT SUCKS. IT'S AN ANCIENT FUCKING TRANSLATION WITH ALEXANDRINES IN OLD FRENCH. I CAN'T UNDERSTAND A THING
WHAT ARE THEY SAYING NOW?
WELL, APPARENTLY SHE'S THE ONE WHO CUT HIS LEG OFF AND NOW SHE'S GONNA CUT OFF HIS ARM

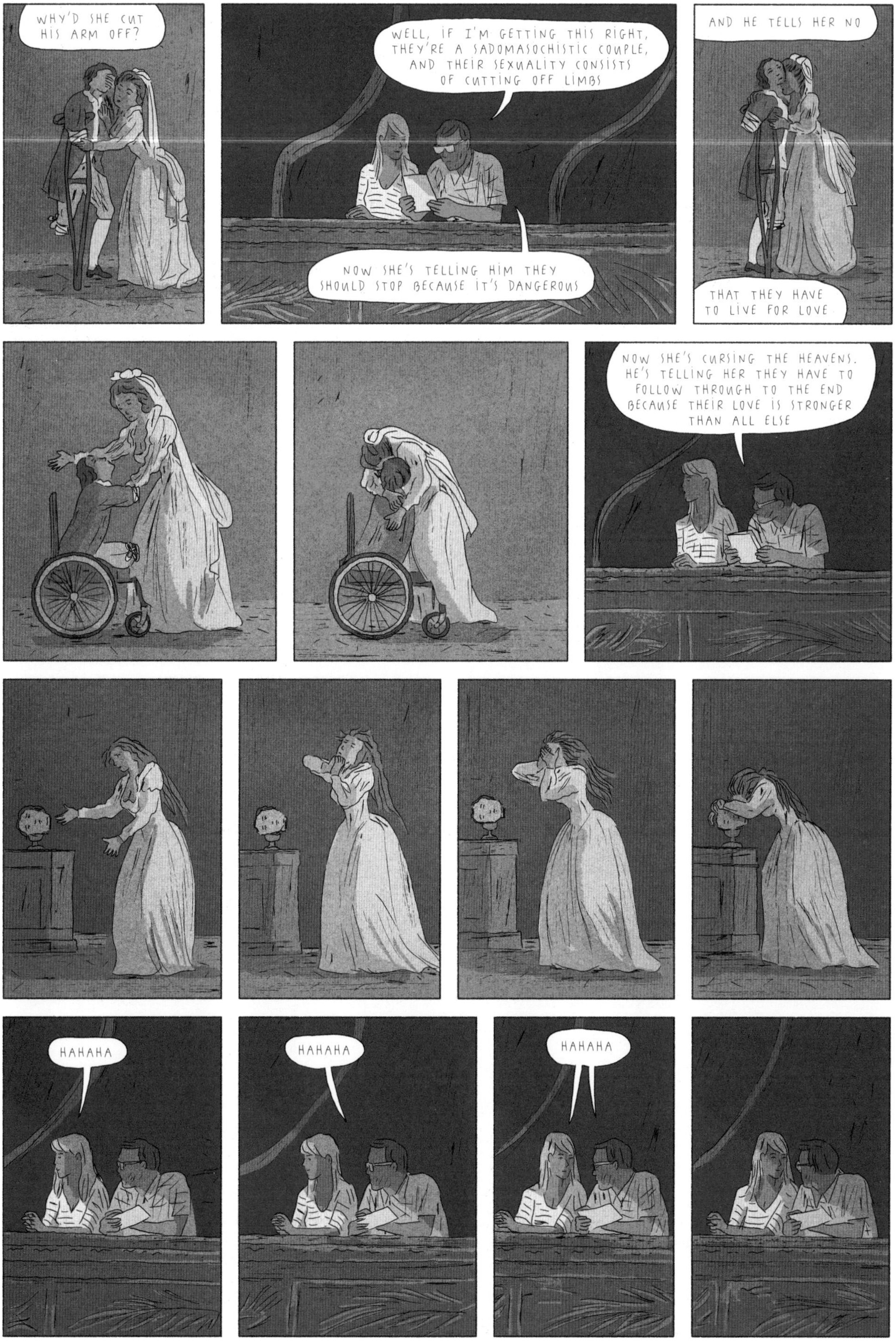
WHY'D SHE CUT HIS ARM OFF?
WELL, IF I'M GETTING THIS RIGHT, THEY'RE A SADOMASOCHISTIC COUPLE, AND THEIR SEXUALITY CONSISTS OF CUTTING OFF LIMBS
NOW SHE'S TELLING HIM THEY SHOULD STOP BECAUSE IT'S DANGEROUS
AND HE TELLS HER NO
THAT THEY HAVE TO LIVE FOR LOVE
NOW SHE'S CURSING THE HEAVENS. HE'S TELLING HER THEY HAVE TO FOLLOW THROUGH TO THE END BECAUSE THEIR LOVE IS STRONGER THAN ALL ELSE
HAHAHA
HAHAHA
HAHAHA

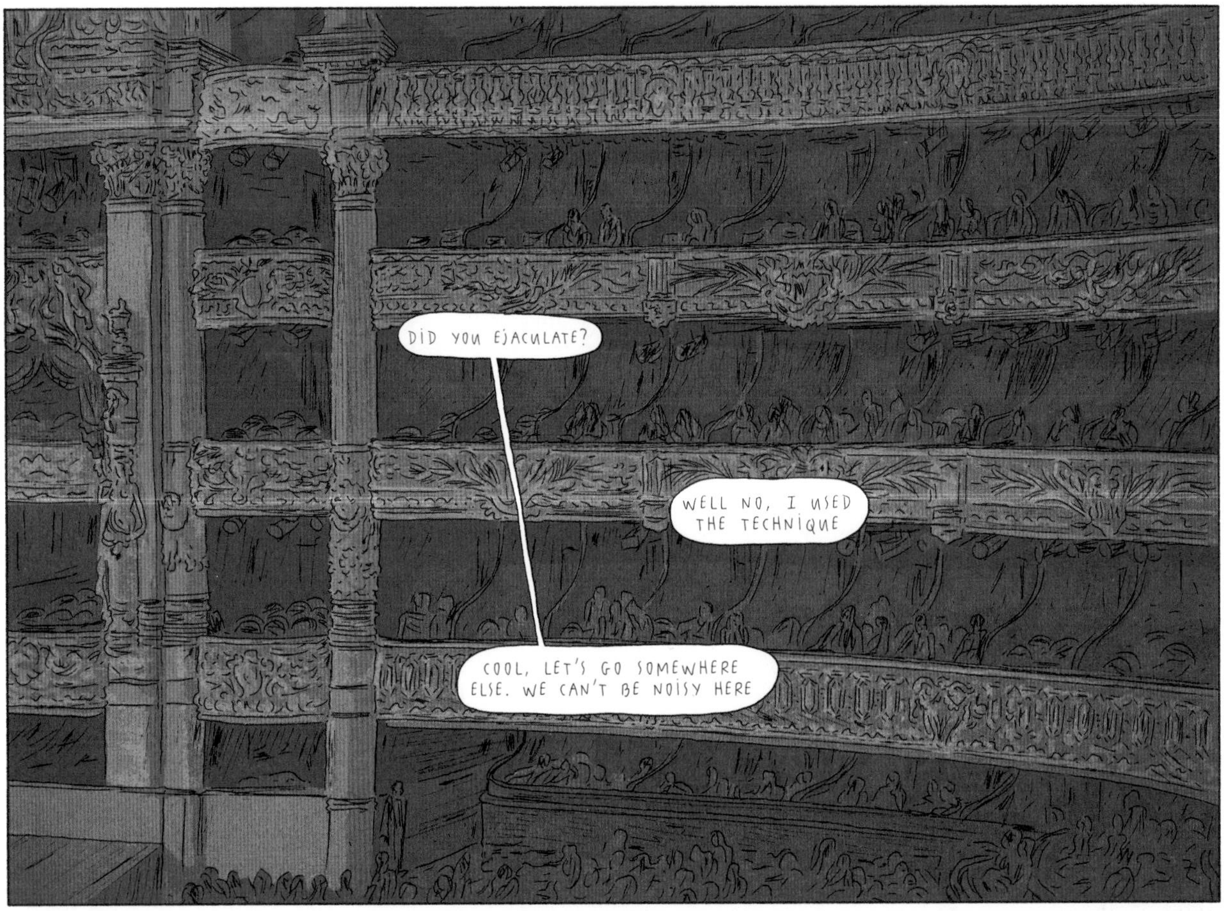
DID YOU EJACULATE?
WELL NO, I USED THE TECHNIQUE
COOL, LET'S GO SOMEWHERE ELSE. WE CAN'T BE NOISY HERE

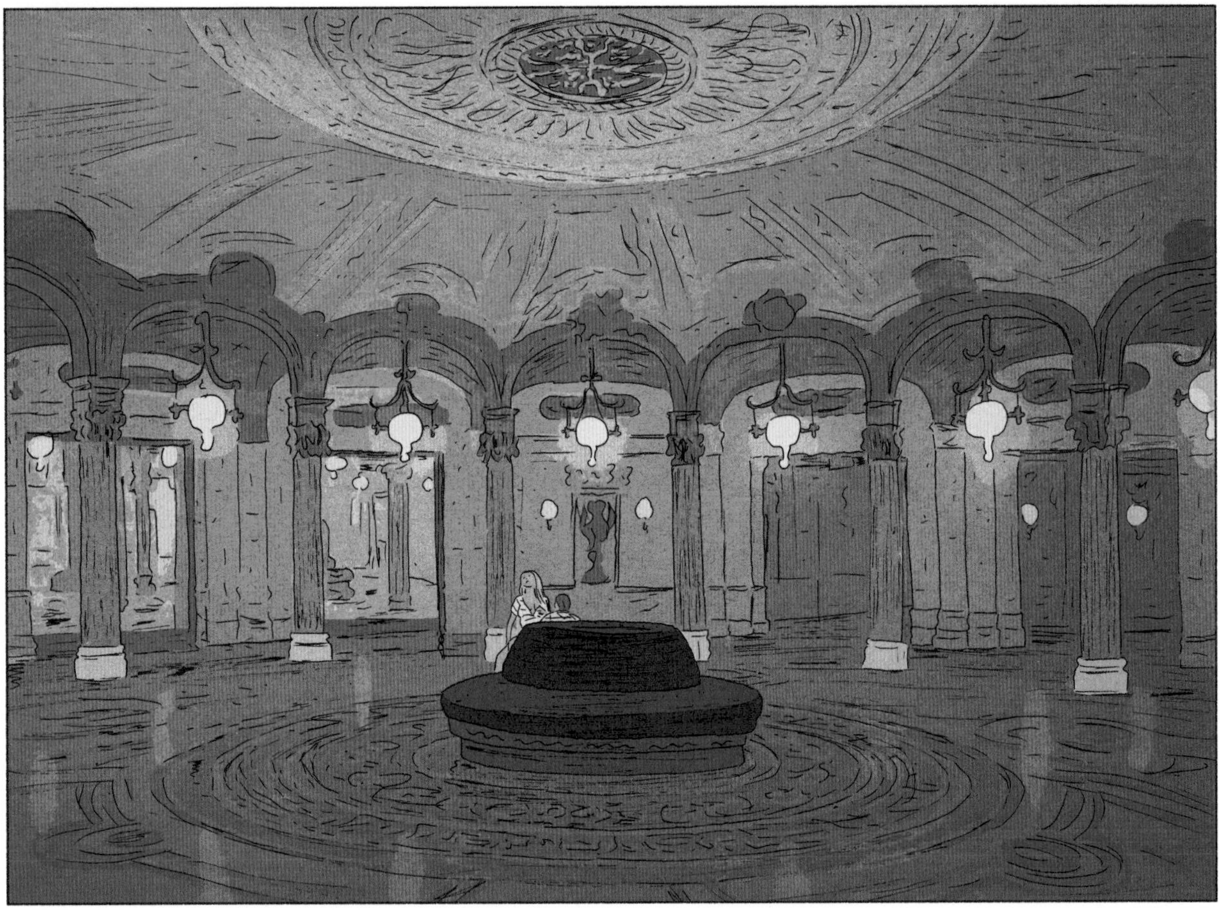

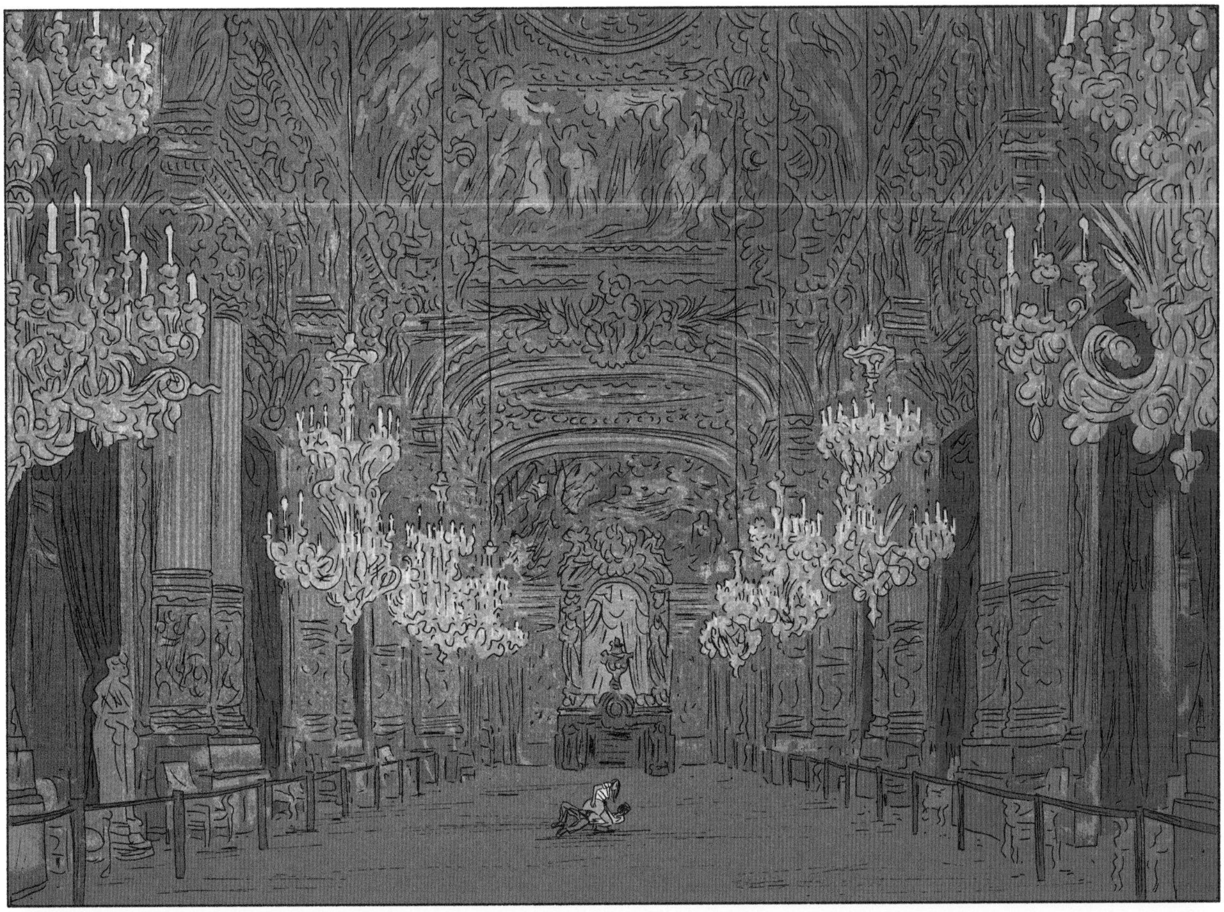

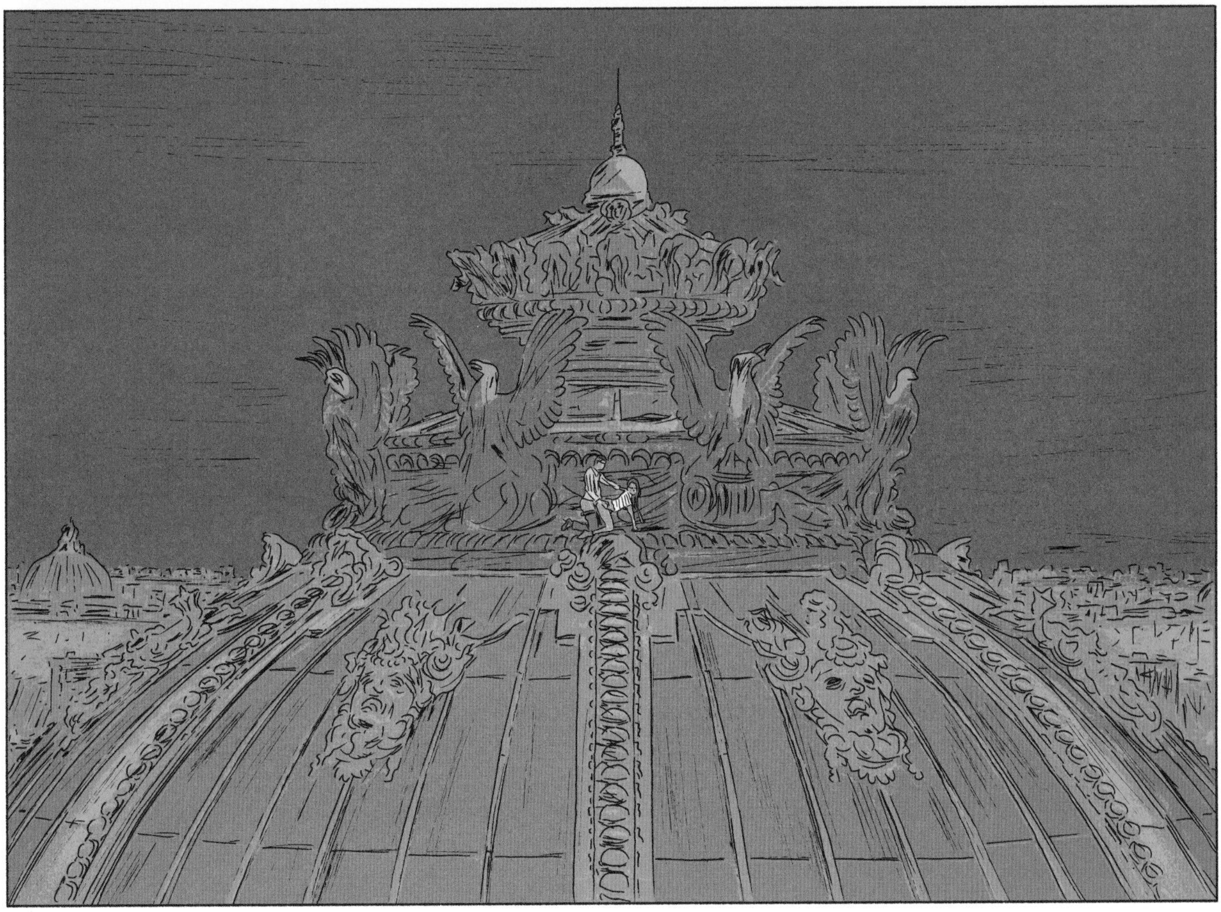

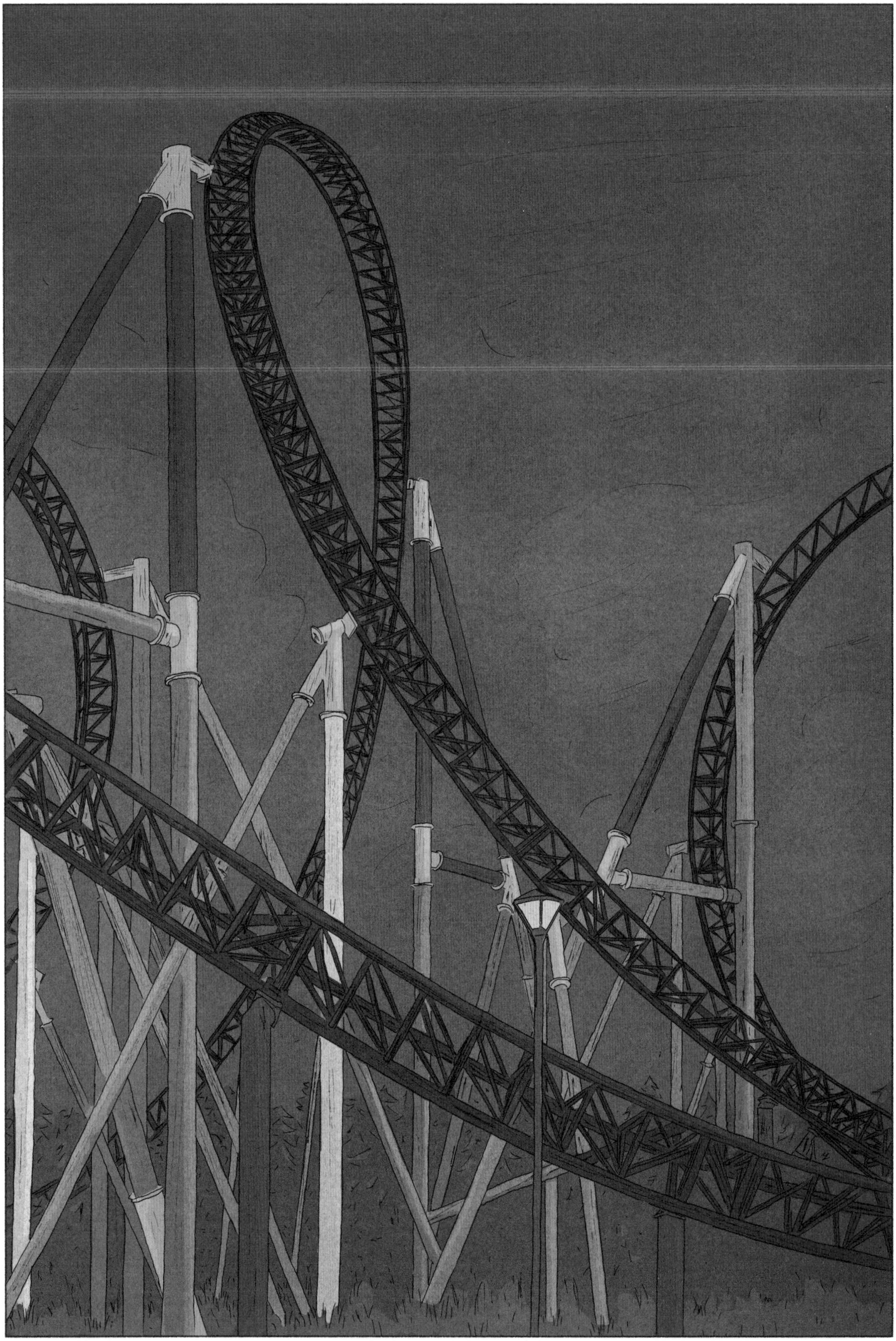

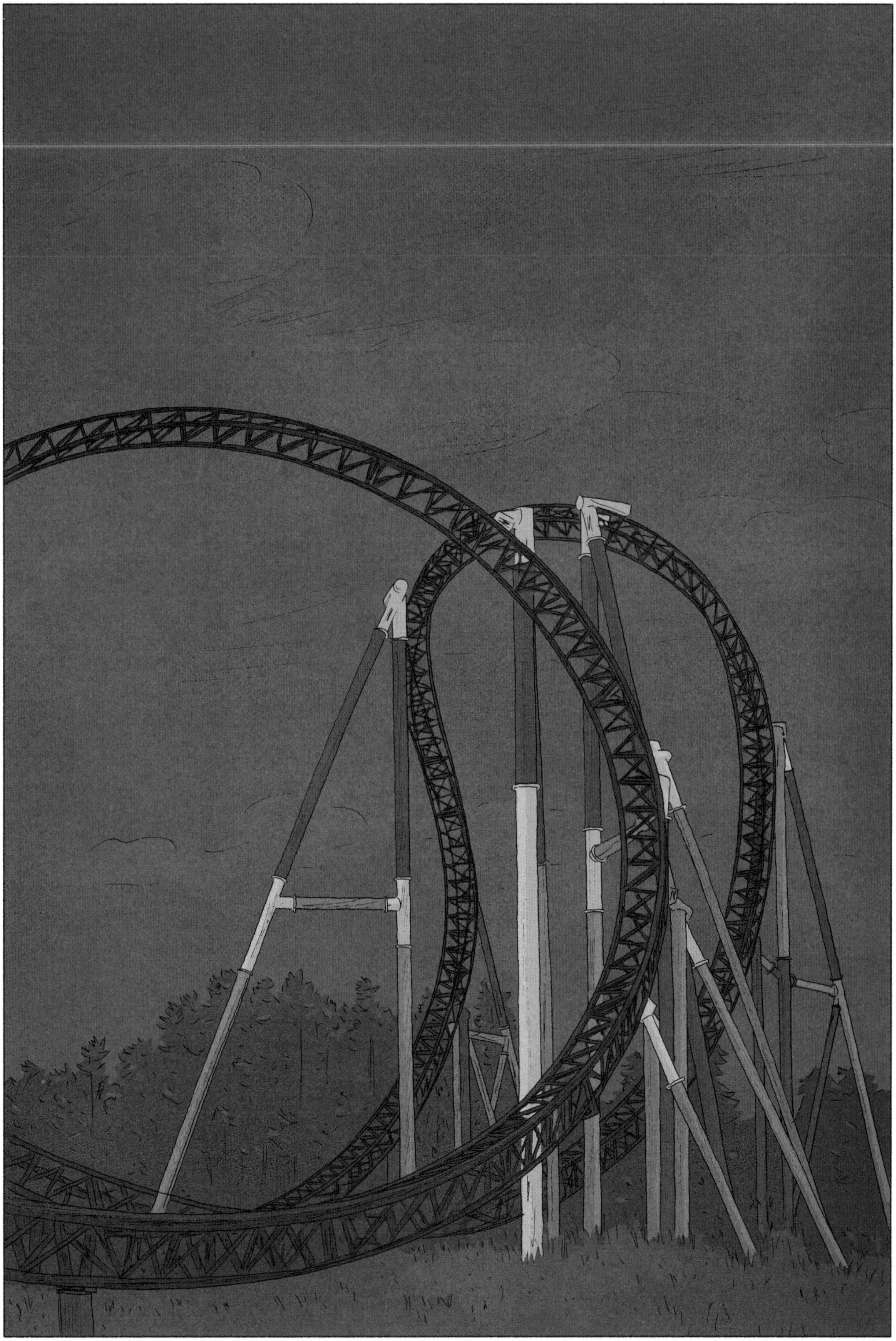

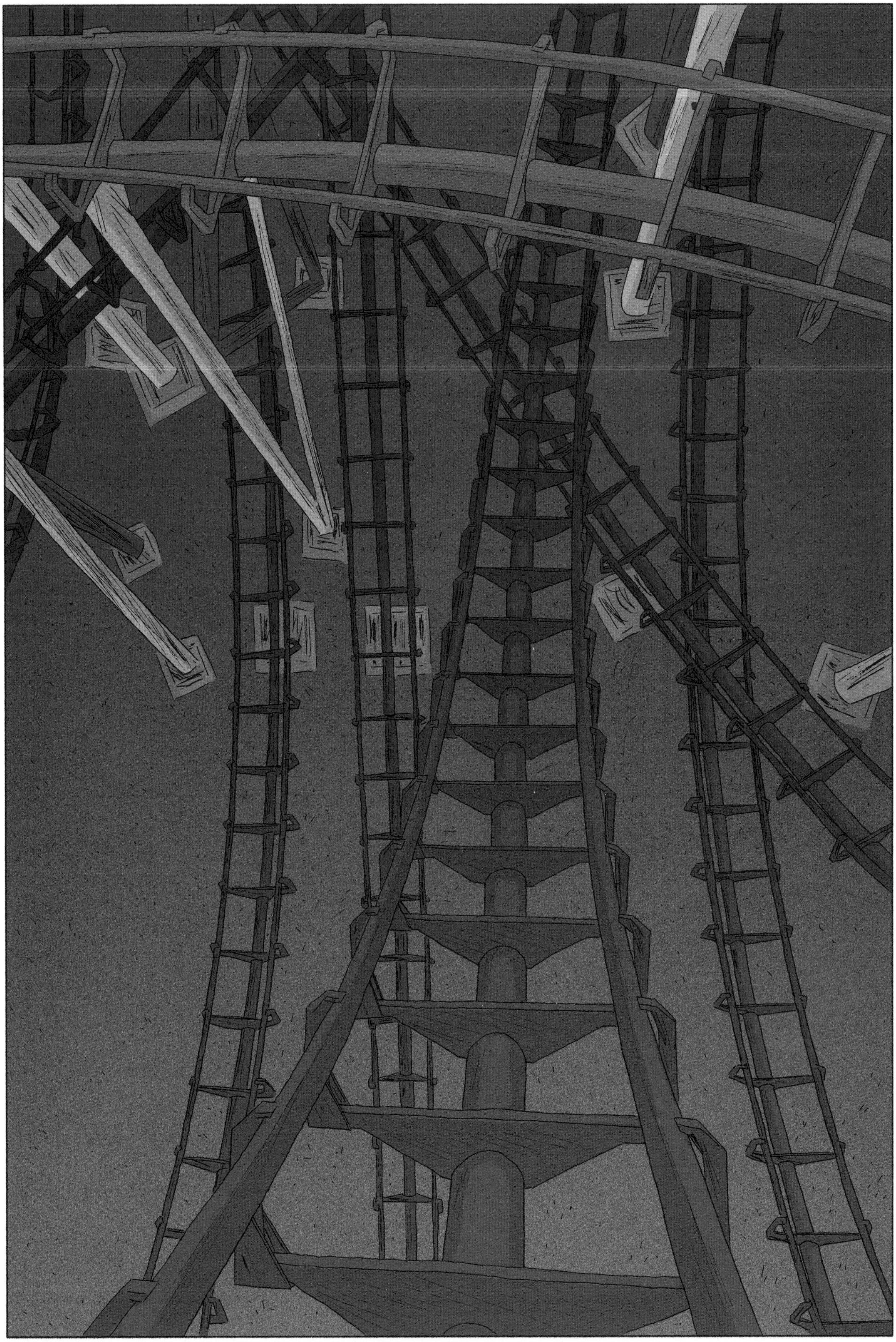

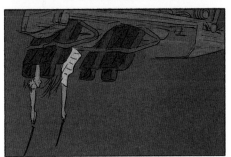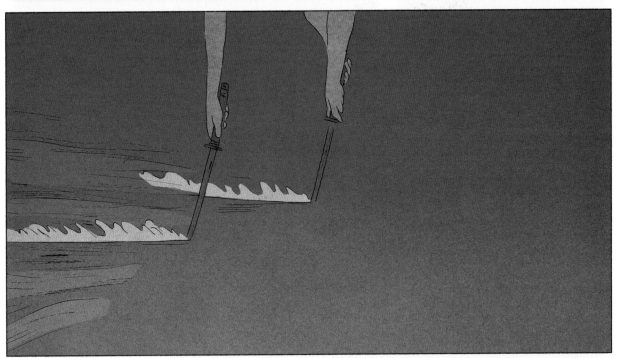

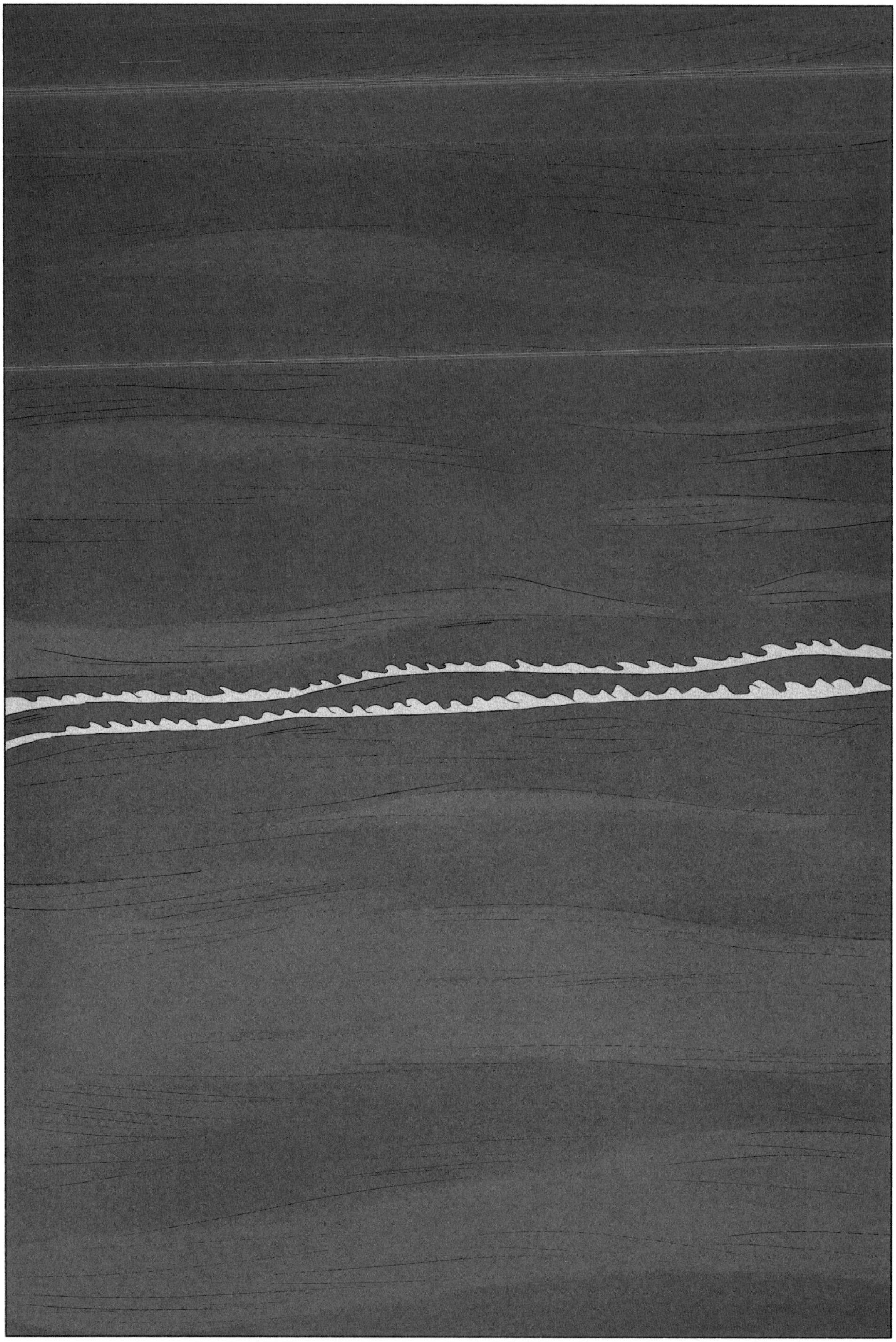

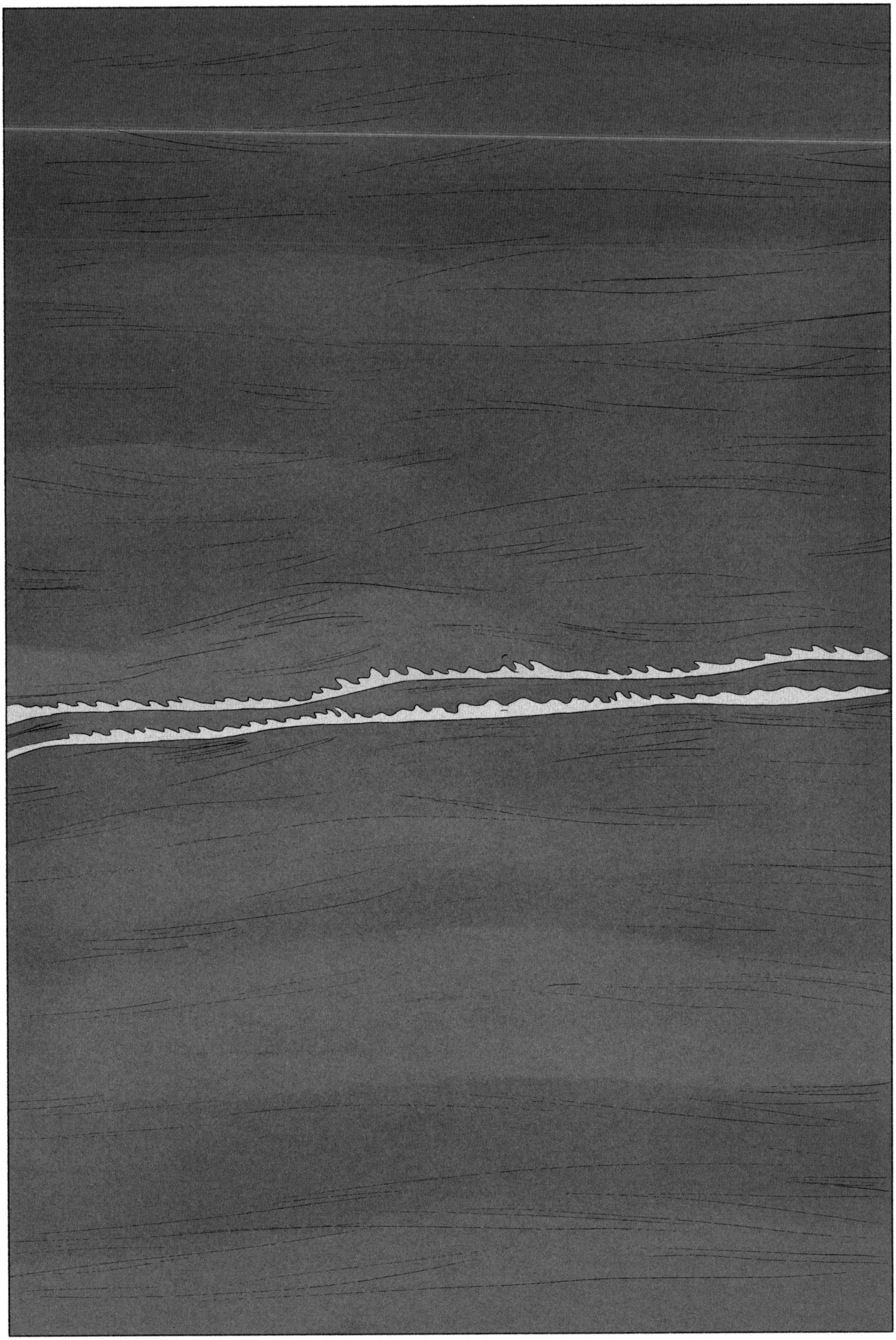

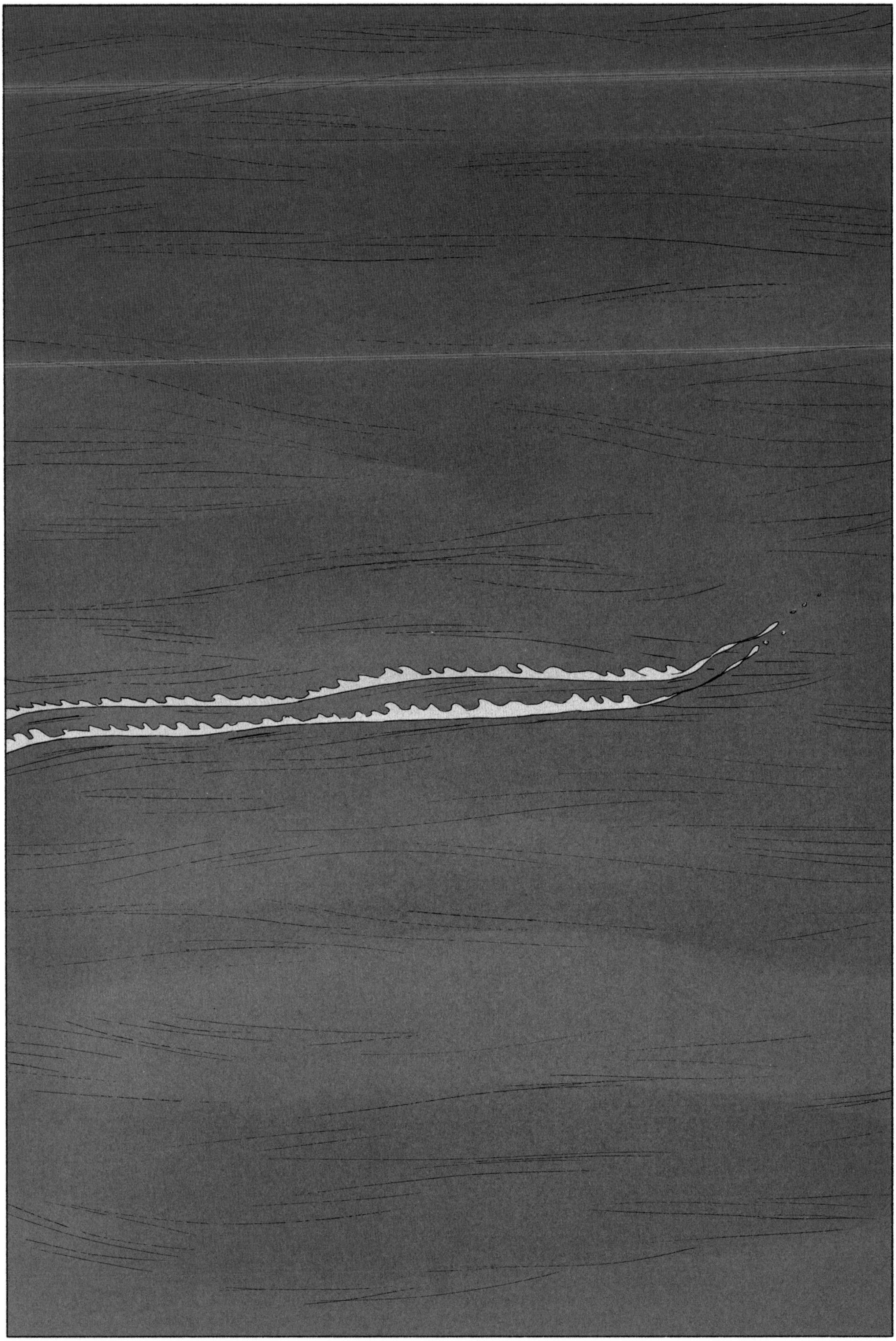

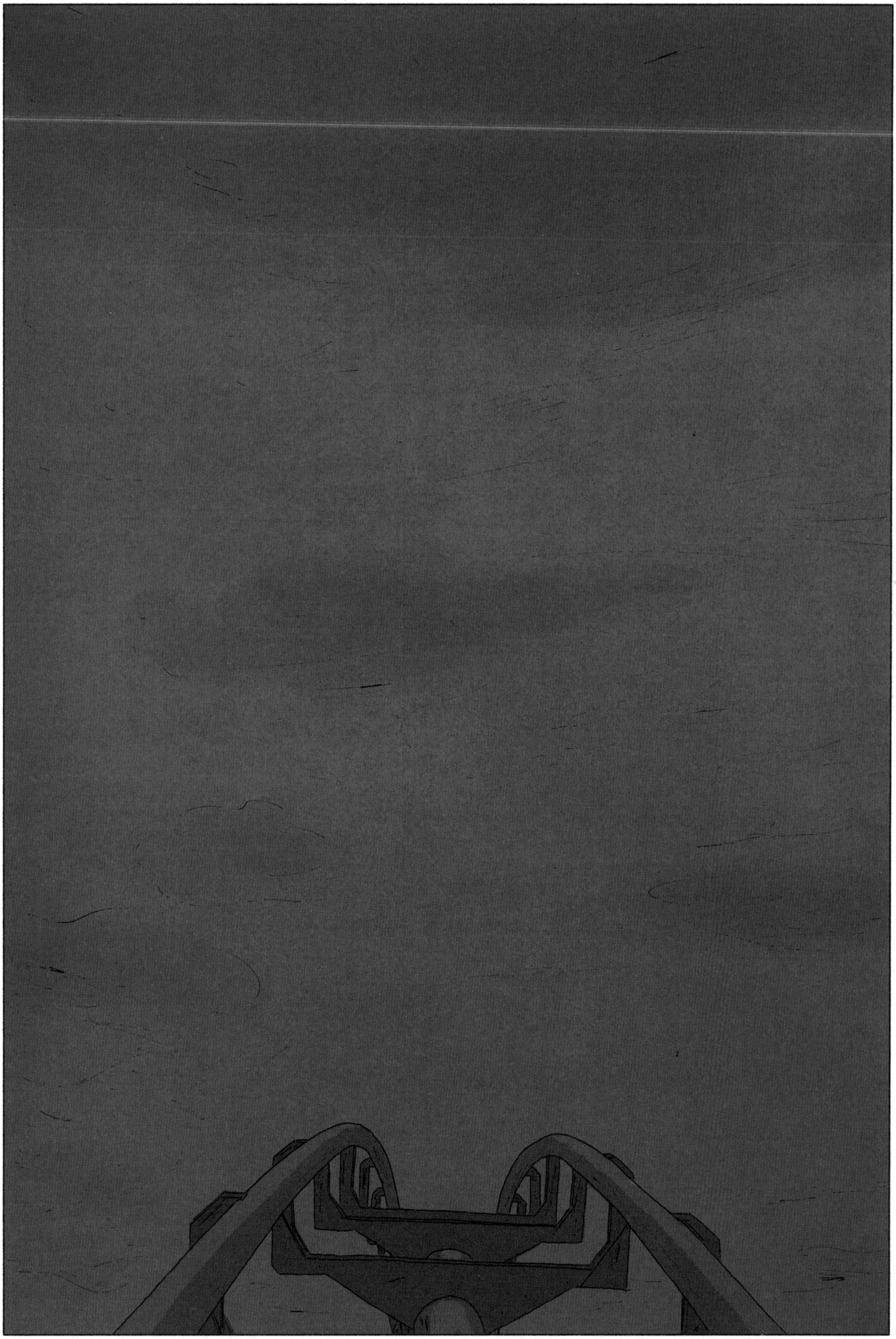

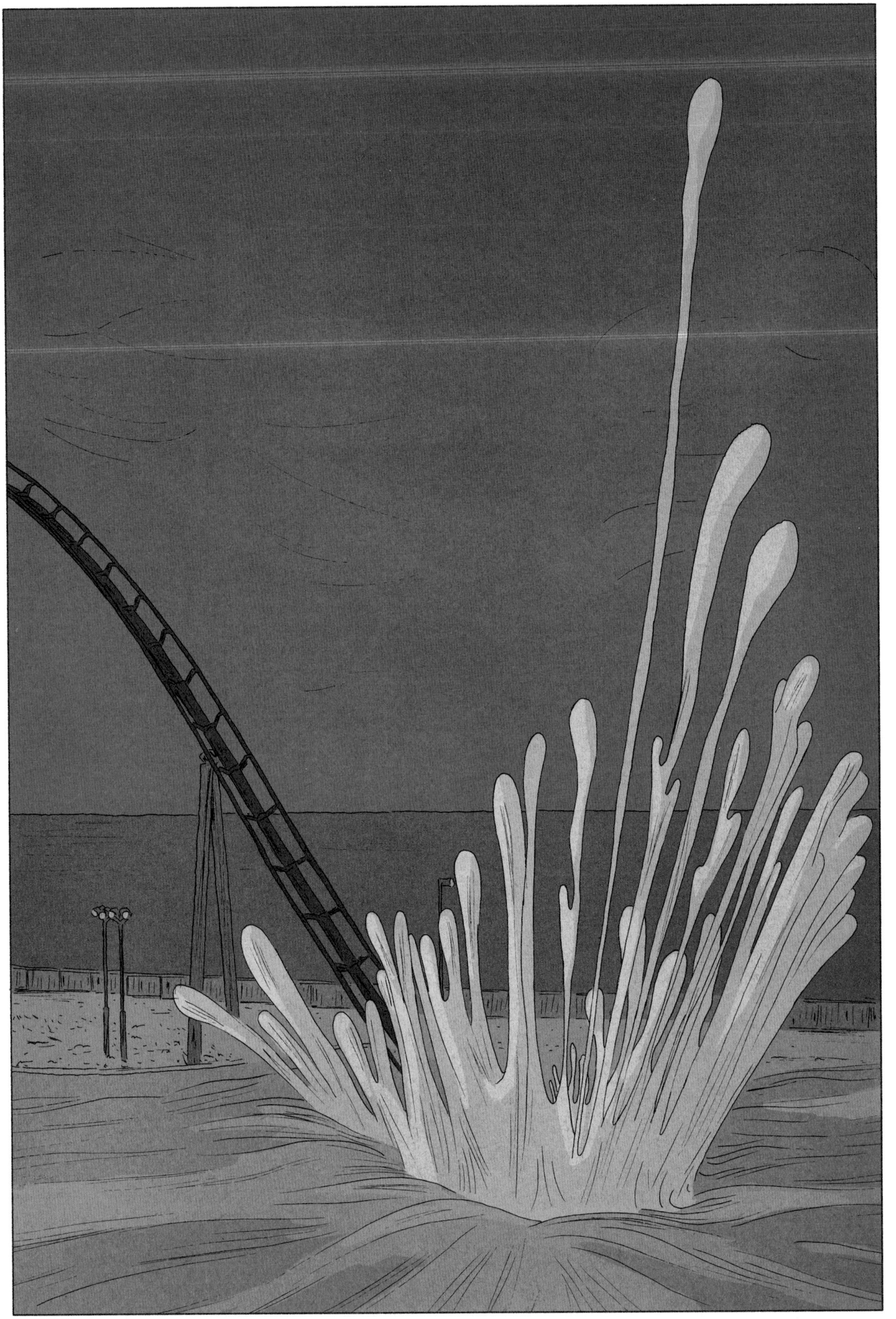

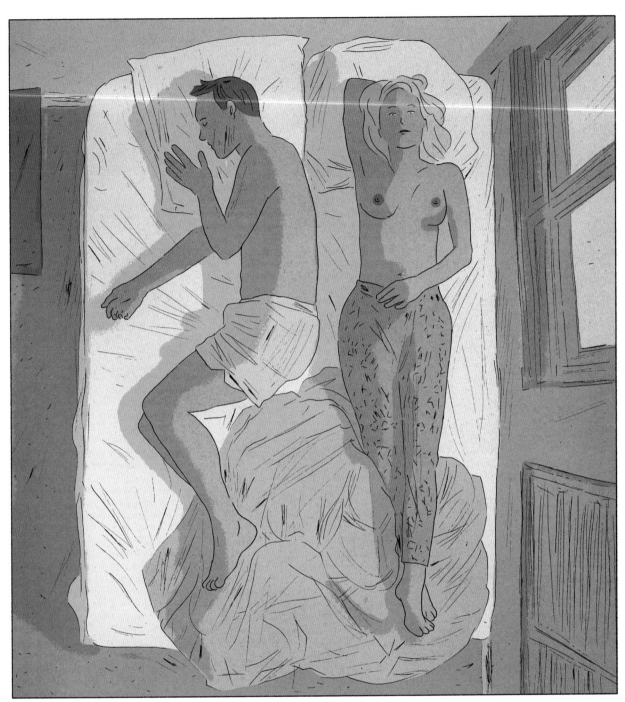

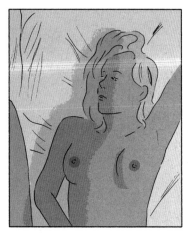

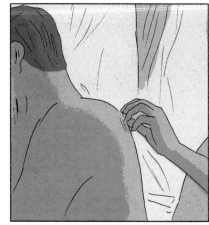

ARE YOU ASLEEP?

JH, DURING YOUR FOUR MONTHS OF ABSTINENCE I WASN'T IN LAS VEGAS

I WAS IN PARIS

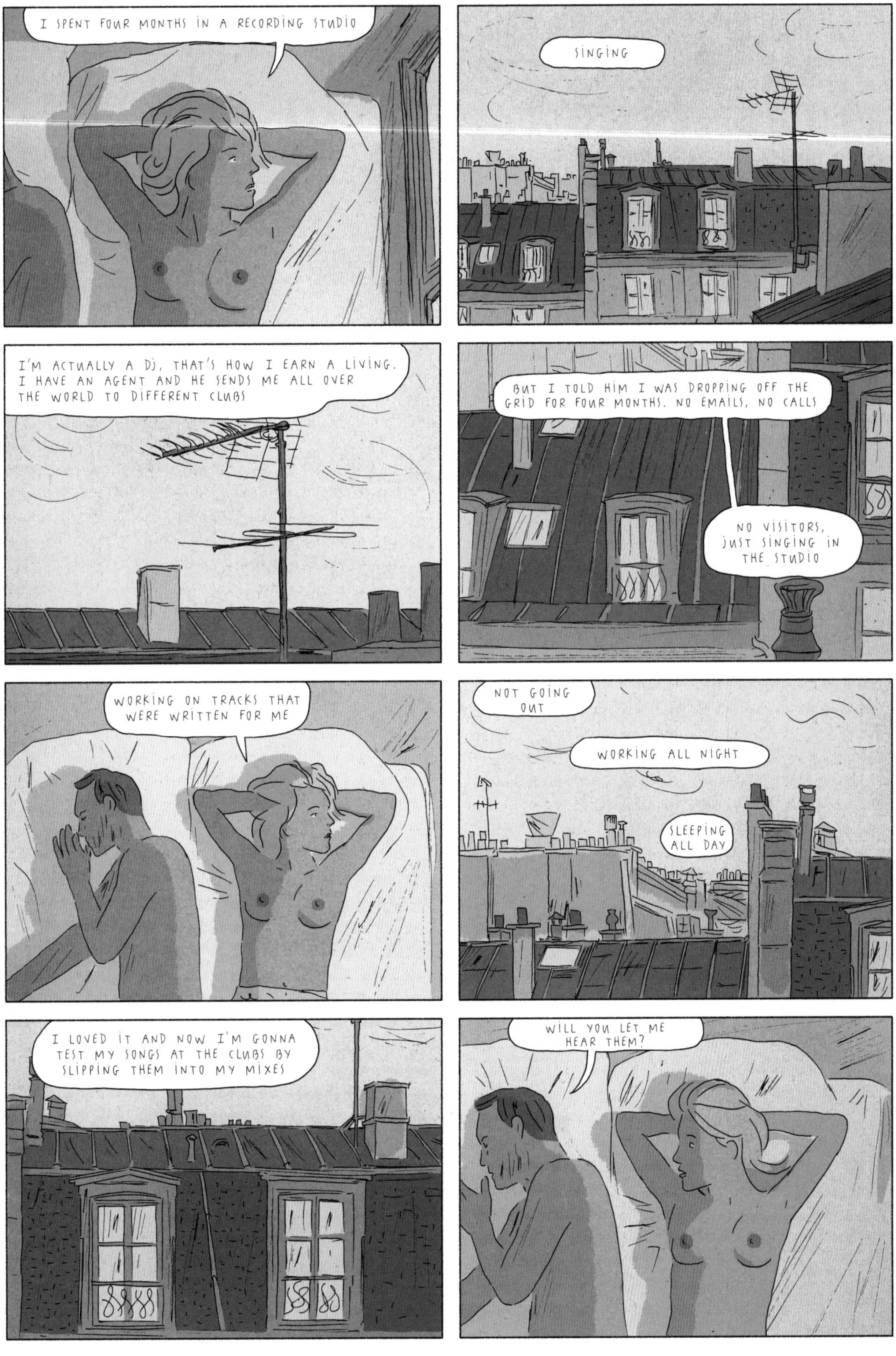
I SPENT FOUR MONTHS IN A RECORDING STUDIO
SINGING
I'M ACTUALLY A DJ, THAT'S HOW I EARN A LIVING. I HAVE AN AGENT AND HE SENDS ME ALL OVER THE WORLD TO DIFFERENT CLUBS
BUT I TOLD HIM I WAS DROPPING OFF THE GRID FOR FOUR MONTHS. NO EMAILS, NO CALLS
NO VISITORS, JUST SINGING IN THE STUDIO
WORKING ON TRACKS THAT WERE WRITTEN FOR ME
NOT GOING OUT
WORKING ALL NIGHT
SLEEPING ALL DAY
I LOVED IT AND NOW I'M GONNA TEST MY SONGS AT THE CLUBS BY SLIPPING THEM INTO MY MIXES
WILL YOU LET ME HEAR THEM?

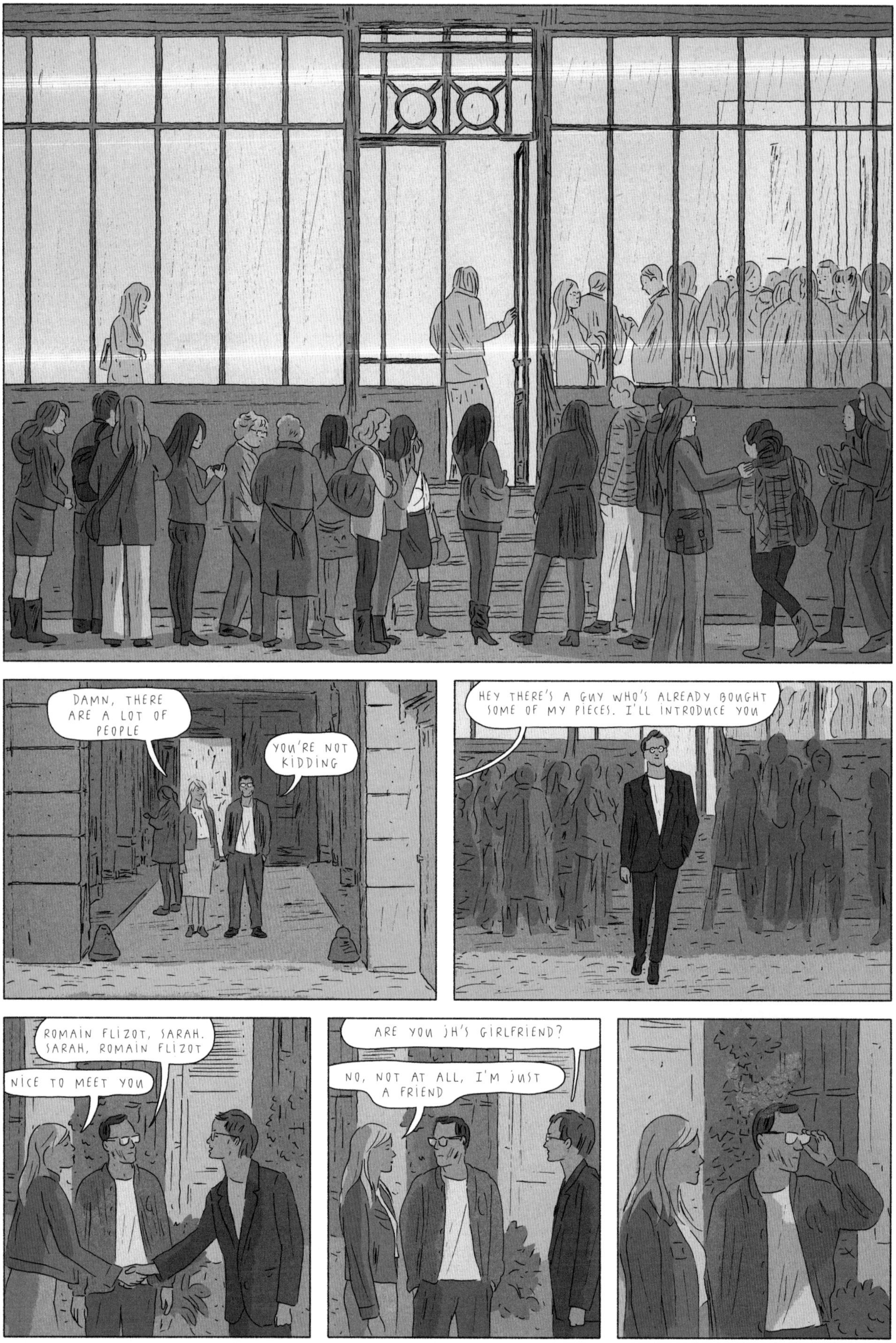
DAMN, THERE ARE A LOT OF PEOPLE
YOU'RE NOT KIDDING
HEY THERE'S A GUY WHO'S ALREADY BOUGHT SOME OF MY PIECES. I'LL INTRODUCE YOU
ROMAIN FLIZOT, SARAH. SARAH, ROMAIN FLIZOT
NICE TO MEET YOU
ARE YOU JH'S GIRLFRIEND?
NO, NOT AT ALL, I'M JUST A FRIEND

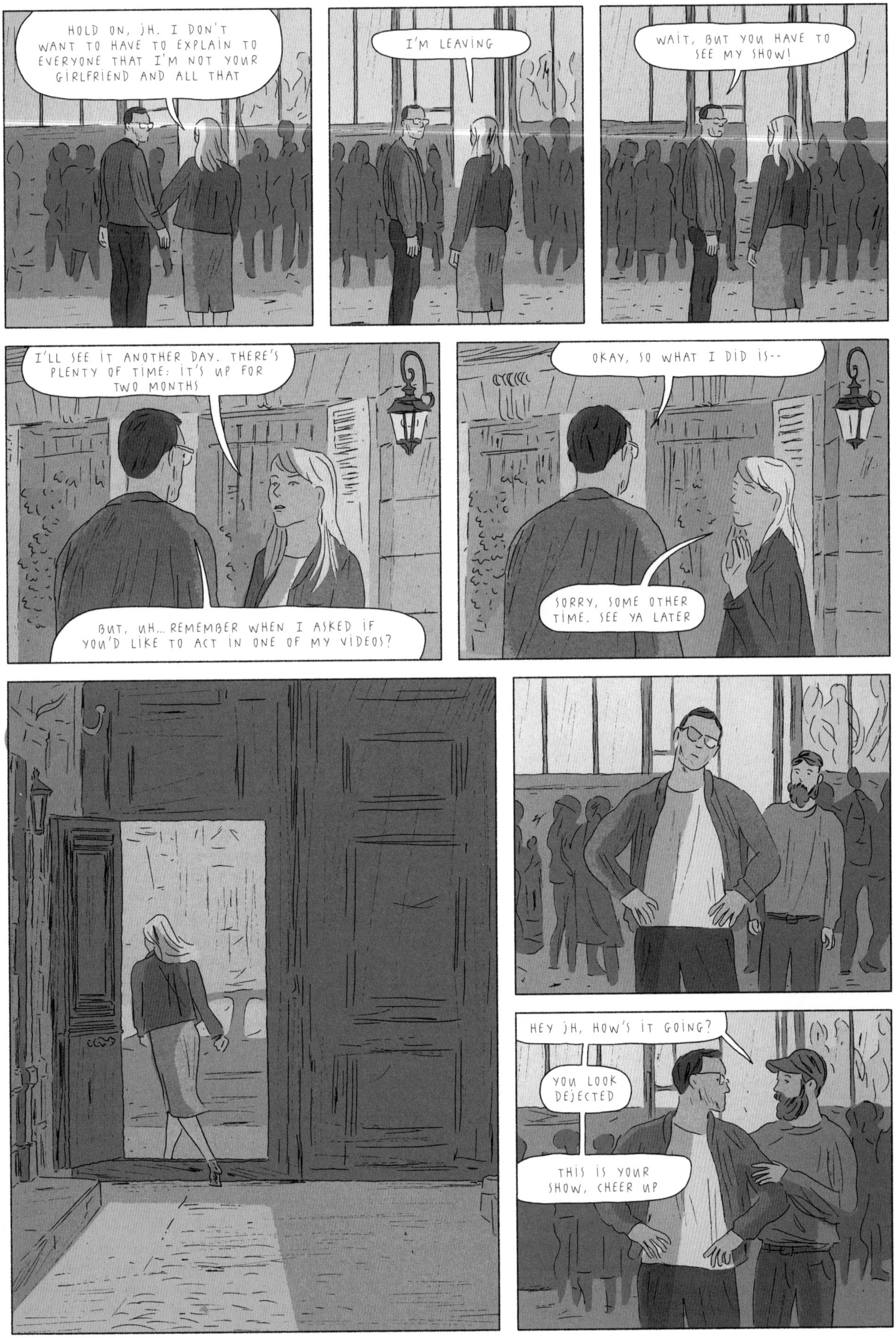
HOLD ON, JH. I DON'T WANT TO HAVE TO EXPLAIN TO EVERYONE THAT I'M NOT YOUR GIRLFRIEND AND ALL THAT
I'M LEAVING
WAIT, BUT YOU HAVE TO SEE MY SHOW!
I'LL SEE IT ANOTHER DAY. THERE'S PLENTY OF TIME: IT'S UP FOR TWO MONTHS
BUT, UH... REMEMBER WHEN I ASKED IF YOU'D LIKE TO ACT IN ONE OF MY VIDEOS?
OKAY, SO WHAT I DID IS--
SORRY, SOME OTHER TIME. SEE YA LATER
HEY JH, HOW'S IT GOING?
YOU LOOK DEJECTED
THIS IS YOUR SHOW, CHEER UP

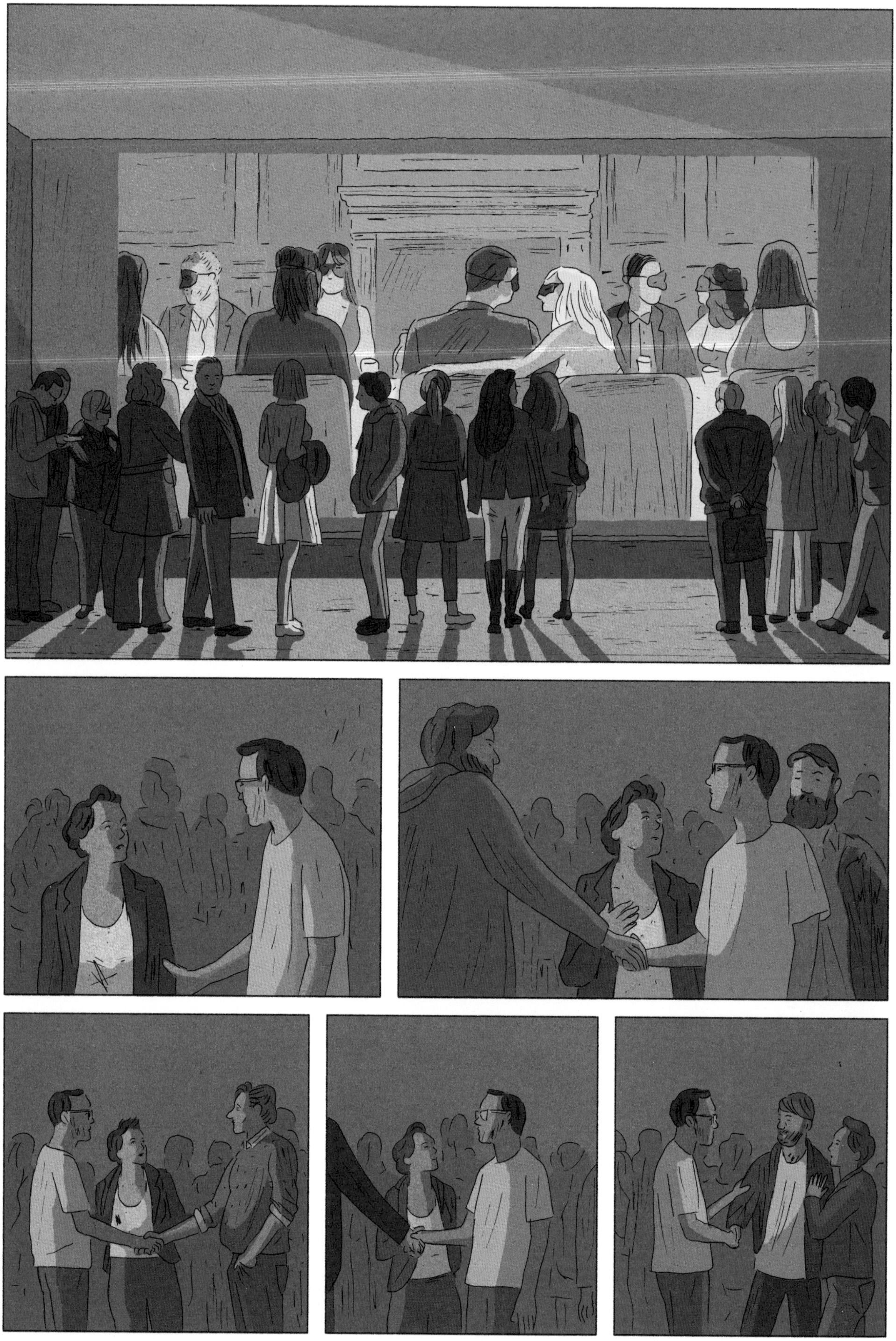

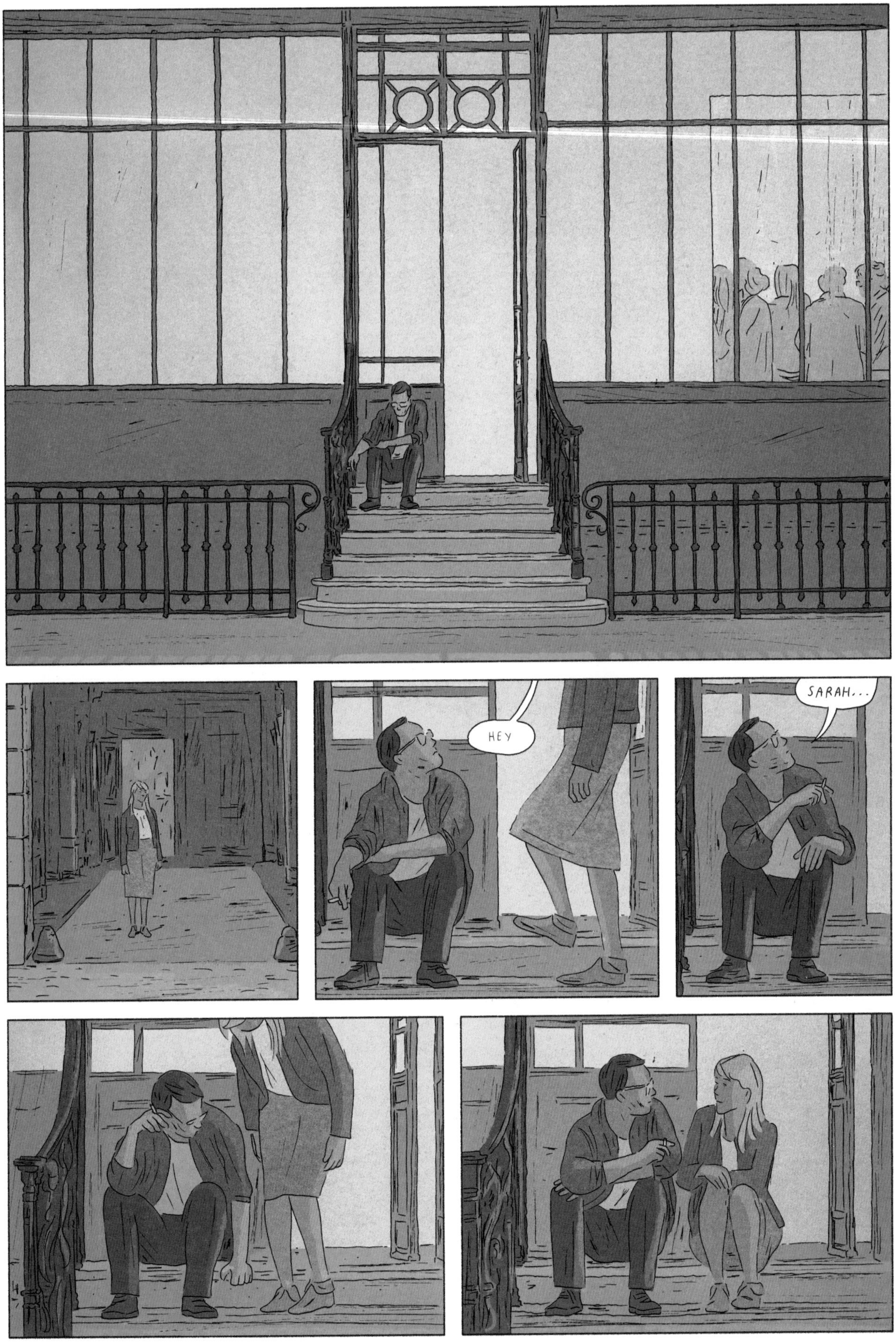
HEY
SARAH...

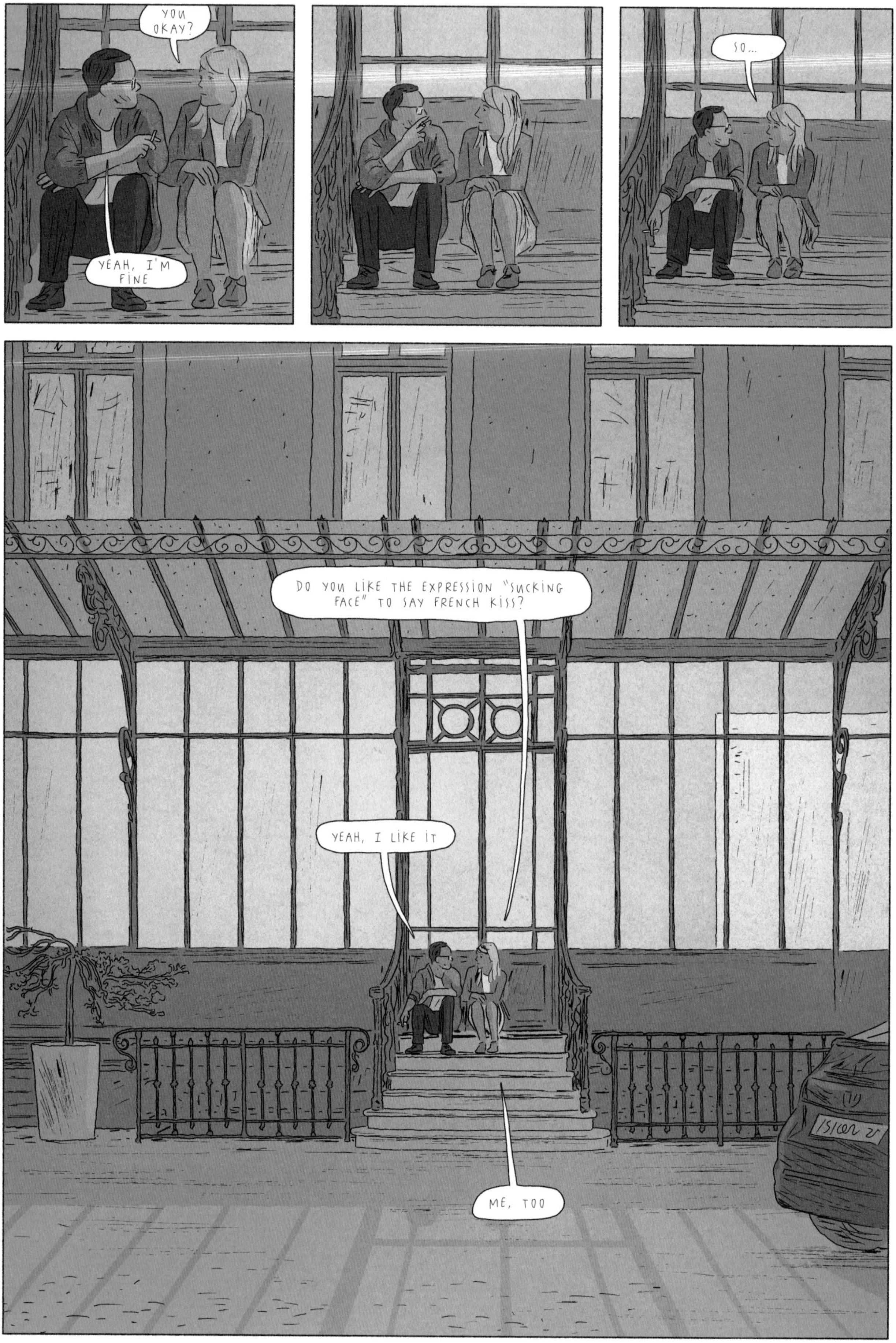
YOU OKAY?
YEAH, I'M FINE
SO...
DO YOU LIKE THE EXPRESSION "SUCKING FACE" TO SAY FRENCH KISS?
YEAH, I LIKE IT
ME, TOO

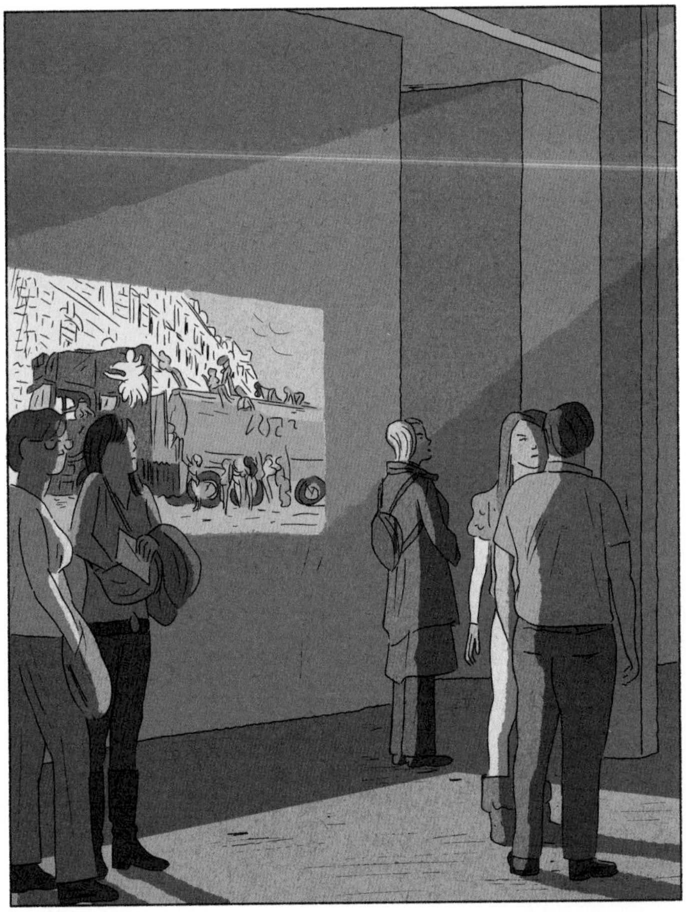

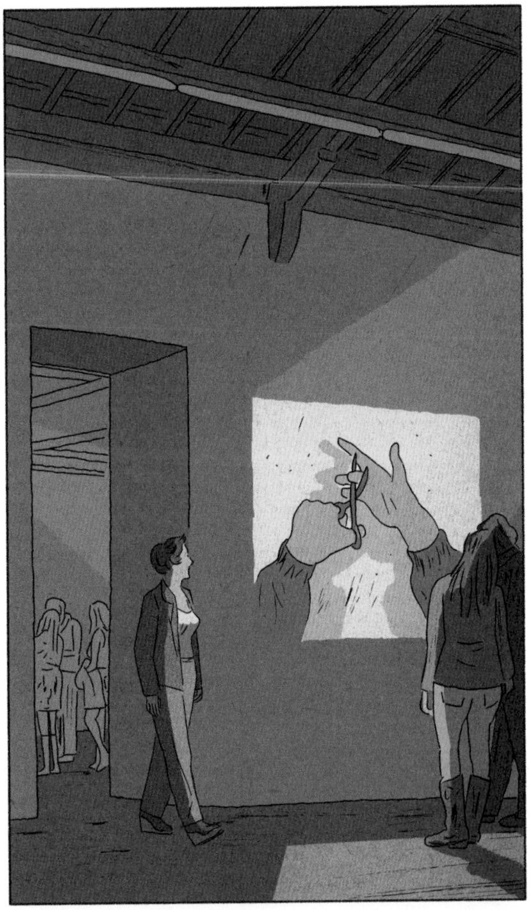

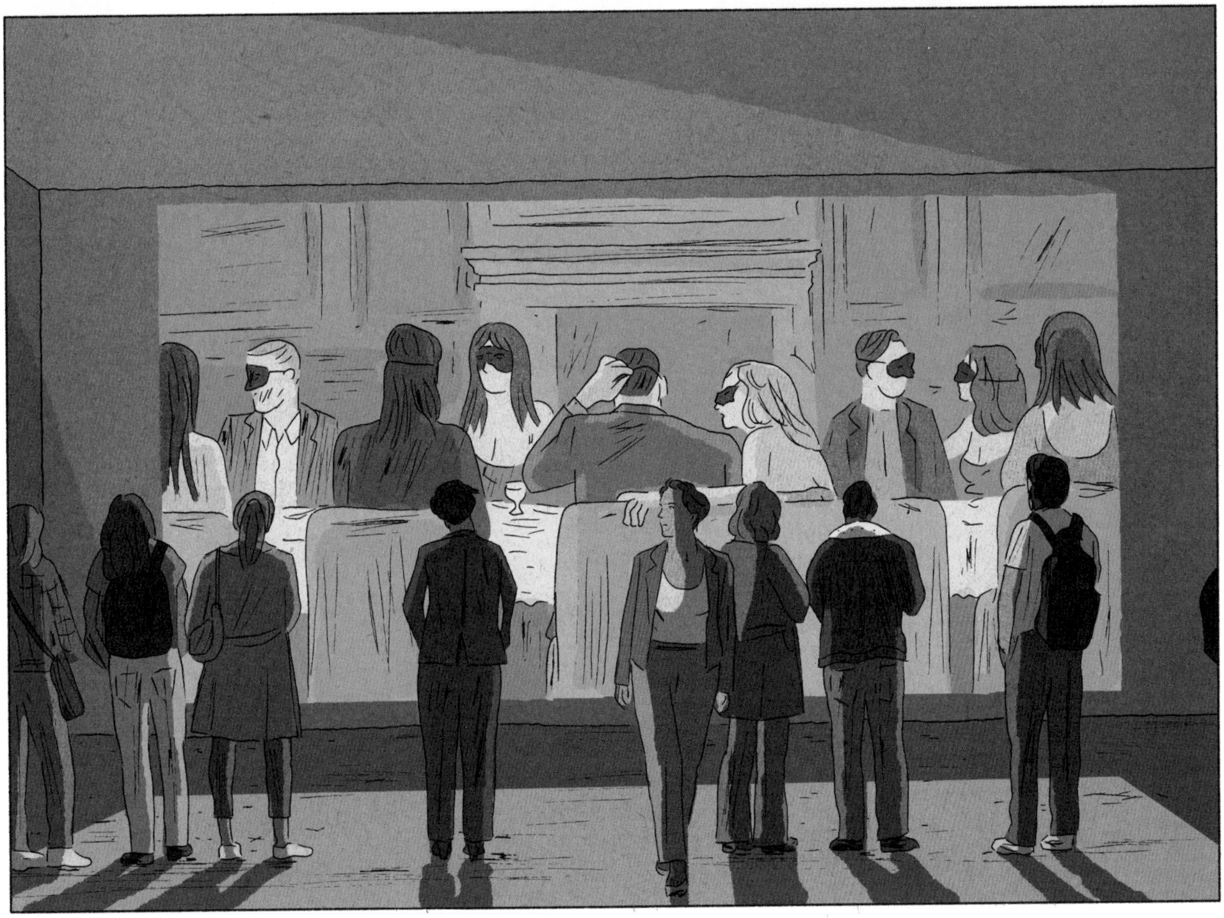

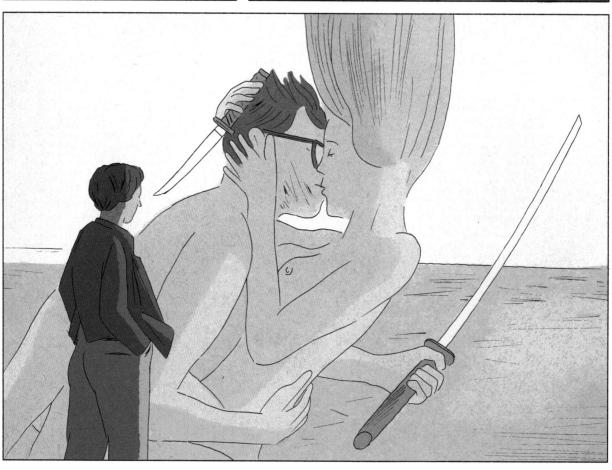

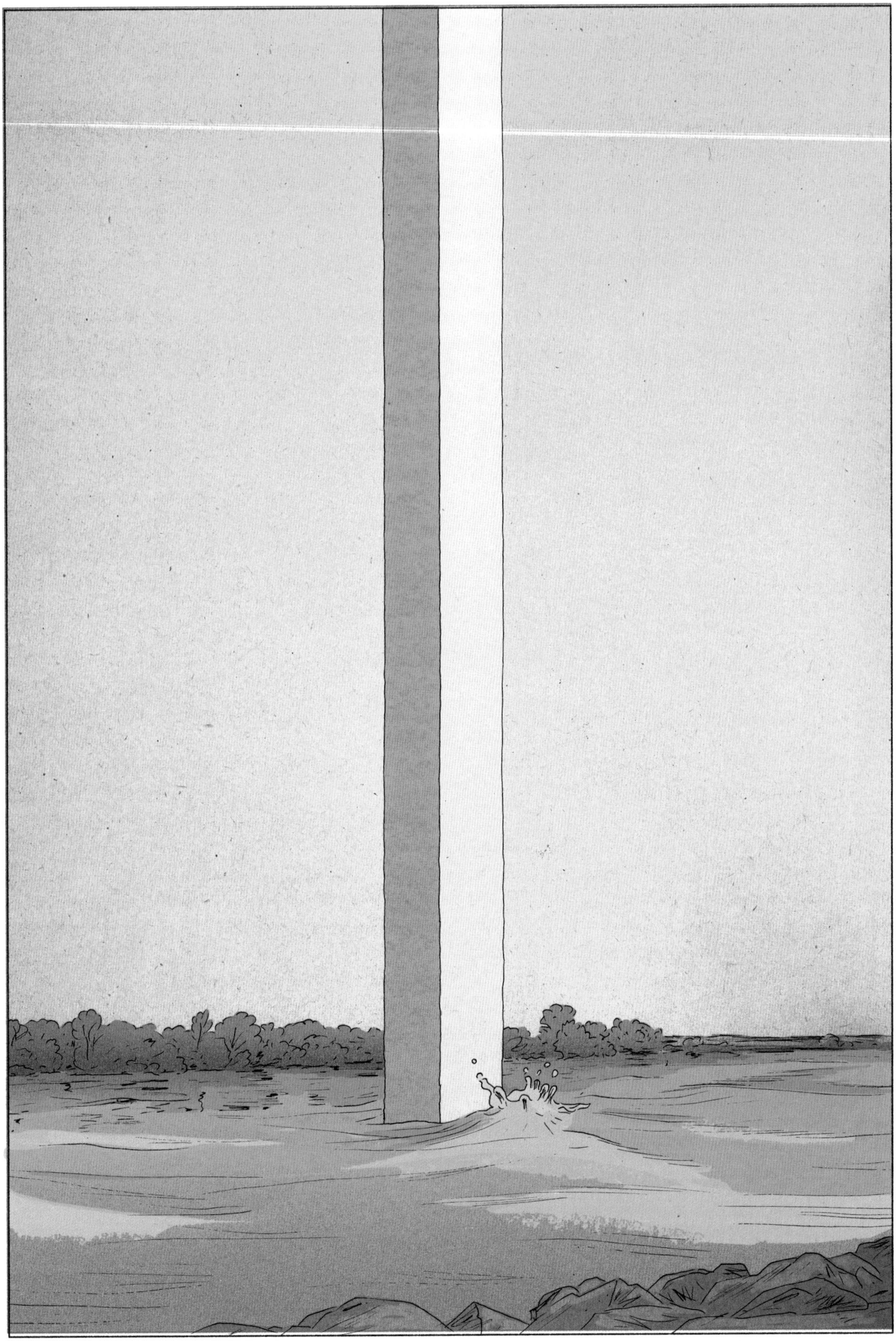